Nobber

Oisín Fagan

JM ORIGINALS

First published in Great Britain in 2019 by JM Originals
An Imprint of John Murray (Publishers)
An Hachette UK company

1

Copyright © Oisín Fagan 2019

The right of Oisín Fagan to be identified as the Author of the Work has been
asserted by him in accordance with the Copyright, Designs and Patents Act 1988.

Nobber receives financial assistance from the Arts Council

A CIP catalogue record for this title is available from the British Library

Trade Paperback ISBN 9781529389098
eBook ISBN 9781529389104

Typeset in Sabon MT by Palimpsest Book Production Ltd,
Falkirk, Stirlingshire

Printed and bound in Great Britain by Clays Ltd, Elcograf S.p.A.

John Murray policy is to use papers that are natural, renewable and recyclable
products and made from wood grown in sustainable forests. The logging and
manufacturing processes are expected to conform to the environmental
regulations of the country of origin.

John Murray (Publishers)
Carmelite House
50 Victoria Embankment
London EC4Y 0DZ

www.johnmurray.co.uk

For Yanina and Santiago

Osprey de Flunkl, who wants everything he sees and whom you will call Sir, in a retinue of four, moves through a valley at a tired pace that all his men have conspired with him to make appear leisurely. De Flunkl, a young man in his late teens who leads the procession, is singing la la la la la tunelessly. Due to the yawning dimensions of the valley that contains him, these superfluous noises are, in a lessened form, returned to him in lagging echoes. Behind him, his serving man, Harold Tuite, carries his gear for him in a brown sack, across his back. This man is all crooked and bent over with the heavy sack, which, he feels, is weighted down with the sins they all filled it with in Trim. The sin is that oldest one, that of property, and de Flunkl has made off with much of it, abetted by his serving men and the advantage of the deepest sickness.

They have been travelling for three days. Yesterday, they were in Trim. Now they are moving towards Nobber in an attempt to accrue some more sins, but please, see them as though from above.

A young fox follows them, darting behind tall clumps of grass at a distance. Bluebells, nettles, strange strains of French hollyhocks, clearly imported, but how they came upon a place so remote is only to be wondered at. A thrush lands on a foxglove, tipping it over with its weight. It opens its beak to them, and chirrups, insanely, its little black eyes vacant. An ocean of nettles ripples in the wind. They smell sweet and dusty. What they have left behind them is the dark blue of the Wicklow Mountains, the outline imprinted against scant, dreamish clouds, giving them definition and shaping them. There is a hardwood forest on their left that creeps upwards with the valley at a gentle slope. This throws total shade on them. Underneath the nettles that occasionally, as though they are making love, form complex symbiotic knots to catch their legs, hidden, are middle-aged trees' dead stumps, fresh and raw, still bleeding sap from recent hacked amputations, and for this the procession has had to dismount so as not to break the two horses' legs and, now, the last man in line, William of Roscrea, leads the bridle of the first, and the other follows of its own will, occasionally dragging its sensitive, black nose through the tall grass.

De Flunkl sweats under his cloth tunic and daubs himself with a dock leaf, cupping the sweat in the fold of the leaf, and then licks it away to maintain the equilibrium of his internal humours. On the right, above them on the other side of the valley, the quadrants of fields have broken down into one another. Heifers, heavy sows and ewes, their lambs at their teat, laze along the way. The fields above them are untilled and unmanned in a quiet confusion. Pleasantly low-key chaos, idyllic almost, is everywhere.

All these animals, but especially the sheep, whose wool is particularly receptive to nature's adhesives, like the entrapping filaments of spiders' webs, are lightly dusted with pollen, turning them into a dull yellow parade of faded, tired beasts. The pollen-coating on their fur, skins and wool makes them appear very slightly further away, and more dead, than they actually are.

These broken fields are awash with June's buttercups, glowing and bright in the sun. The whole upper side of the valley is a fractal legion of golden faces, a yellow multitude only occasionally punctured by tall clumps of thistles that look menacing and dark amongst so much golden shining.

Cattle, having broken down walls and burst through hedges, now freely mingle with squawking geese, going where they will. It is all very friendly, though earlier in the day the retinue had been overtaken by two escaped warring bulls that bucked and kicked and stampeded down the path in sideways bursts and kicks, stumbling and hurtling their horns against one another. They had met one of the bulls later in the morning on its side, along the path, a gash in its haunches, bawling sadly, its eyes raised towards them, baleful and confused, but it was toppled over by colic, not the horn that slashed it, its sides heaving and bursting with too much plenitude of rich grass, dark like the shade they are in, encompassed.

'Noah's vessel must have been a vehicle for great incestuous confusions and fornications,' de Flunkl says to himself, almost happily, gazing at all the loose congregations of animals, and William of Roscrea gives, out of habit, his nodding assent.

Out of the forest, like another deeper echo or some auditory mirror, comes the tuneless humming la la la la, the perfect mimic to de Flunkl's previous annoying humming.

Harold groans, beads of sweat blinding him, creating shards of light in his eyes like rainbows seen through a prism of crystal.

'This,' Harold says, 'is no echo.'

'Is this a bird?' de Flunkl asks.

William of Roscrea is also blinded by a well of hot light from a gap between the heavy summer foliage, this absence made by a branch hanging solely from its sheath of bark that was, at some former point, struck by lightning. He blinks the glaring shine away and sees that four Gaels have run out of the woods, though maybe not, as they seem to always have been there from the steadfastness of their stance, the steadiness of their breaths. They hold the way ahead, which is also the higher ground.

Harold doesn't know when this happened, nobody does. He drops his sack, and the procession comes to a halt.

An abrupt meeting – a gift from nature. The fox, far behind them, darts into the woods, the clatter of metal from inside the sack scaring it off, quelling its curiosity and alighting its self-preservation.

'We wouldn't have been warned if they wanted to take us,' Harold says.

'I know that,' de Flunkl says. 'Get the banner.'

The Gaels are all male, all bearded, all armed with spears. Their faces are sunburnt above their braided beards rounded off with beads. The front halves of their heads are shaved to the scalp and the hair behind grows long, beyond the shoulders. They have spirals painted onto their foreheads. Round their necks, hanging over their multi-coloured robes, are thin bronze chains that carry rudely carved wooden figurines, about the length of a hand, of circular women with no hair on their heads. Big-clitted women smiling little mysterious smiles out at the world, dragging the walls of their pussies apart, delighted with themselves. These little figurines are alien and puzzling,

4

their facial features strangely sexless and vaguely surreal though non-threatening; their expansive vaginas twice as large as their already-oversized heads. That which lies beneath their heads, and above their gaping vulvas, is a minuscule torso; and de Flunkl is disgusted to see that not only are these little, wooden extra-terrestrial whores pulling their massive sexes apart, but that their long, apelike arms pass under their stretched legs at the knee to do so.

'Ready yourselves,' he remarks to Harold, who cocks his head absently, slanting his eyes so his nose becomes visible to himself, and wondering if these necklaces, merely, are literal representations of Gael women's anatomy.

The Gaels, like their tokens, are also delighted with themselves. Untouched by the ravages of the sickness, they have become even more wandersome over the last three apocalyptic months, and their raiding, like their mourning and their weddings, is always strangely good-humoured. It is unsettling, their ways – good-humoured in times of strain and difficulty, ferocious in times of calm and mournful during feasts and while listening to musical refrains.

Saint John of Barrow, the fourth, the youngest and the least of the retinue, hitherto unmentioned, a quiet child with two missing front teeth and shocking green eyes, waves the black cloth over his head, back and forth, to signify that they are infected and to approach no closer and the four Gaels start calling to them in at least two different languages: Manx and Gaelic, and possibly there are smattered smidgeons of Catalan amongst their confusion of words.

'They will not be diverted. They can see we aren't infected,' William says.

'What are they saying?' de Flunkl asks.

'The one on the right is questioning the legitimacy of our eldest sons.'

'Tell them to go back to their mountains, and to take their skinny sheep and phlegmatic wives with them,' de Flunkl says.

'My Lord, they have the higher ground.'

'Translate, miscegenist,' de Flunkl says and William does so, and one of the Gaels, the eldest, whose vermillion cape is folded in on itself and squirming as though it is alive, talks back in that queer guttural language de Flunkl knows to be mountain Gaelic. It sounds like the sheep the Gaels and peasants live in such close proximity with, and he speculates whether some foul Gaelic crossbreeding accounts for the choking sound of their r's.

'He says they have presents for us.'

'Tell them,' de Flunkl says, 'these heathen sons of bitches that marry their own slaves and who, without papal recommendation, propagate with their own nieces, and who have never seen a looking glass save the ones made by the pools of blood their women leave when they menstruate shamelessly in public. Tell these hairy sodomites that give their mothers and sisters control over them with their barbaric courts they can only hold in shanty huts. Tell them that they will have to kill us if they are exacting a toll because this is not their highway, this is not their path, this is not their country, this is not their valley. It is the king's land, guarded by much deeds, held by esteemed Christian men with mighty forces and many grateful dependents.'

William, looking at his master out of the corner of his eye, translates perhaps eight words from his statement. It seems much too short a translation for de Flunkl's liking, but nevertheless the man with the crawling, bustling, demonic cape answers.

'He says they are Christians, and that he was just talking to the king yesterday and that he said it is most definitely their land.'

'Dubious claimants, I'd say,' de Flunkl says, looking like he is adding some large figure in his head.

'I think they have their own ones.'

'Oh, I see. Tell them if they are Christians they shall render unto Caesar, but also tell them that they're not. And also say they'll forfeit their tongues for questioning orders with such speechifying.'

After another bout of the Gaelic tongue, which de Flunkl now is suspicious of because it all seems very amicable, William says, 'He tells me that they definitely are Christians and that's why they're all alive, and that we're not proper Christians and that's why all our society is being destroyed.'

'Ask them what those things are round their necks,' Harold calls out, from behind, as he lets one of the horses nuzzle his open palm. 'They're very strange.'

'That is a good question,' de Flunkl concurs. 'What are those slight bitches round the neck?'

'I want to know, too,' Saint John says, speaking for the first time since dawn, munching on a fistful of grass to remove the mank dust that has whistled and drifted through the gap in his teeth and accumulated in his mouth from letting his jaw hang slack while breathing so heavily along the trek.

Harold looks at the sky during a lengthy conversation in which two of the Gaels talk over one another, while William's lips move silently in delayed comprehension. A batch of swallows disrupt the trees at head height, bursting out of it all at once like sweat from pores, and they are above their heads, warbling, arcing high over the valley like the curve of the world, and then they are gone.

'Well,' William of Roscrea says finally, the sweat on his back turning cold from inaction, his tunic sticking to him, 'he says because we, he means you and I, or our people, are engaged in eliminating the family, which I suppose does mean his tribe, maybe, and do place youth as an attribute to be eternally guarded and envious of – I suppose when he speaks of he, he means his tribe, or the McMurroughs, or all of them, I'm not certain at all – and because we do not claim our children as our own if they are out of the strictest bonds of wedlock, but yet engage in much licentious freedoms with infected, unpropertied French whores, often infamous for their pestilential barrenness and knotty wombs, our mode of attraction has become warped, and that which we find attractive has become some non-fertile thing, because our women are applauded for their lack of fertility and dying in birth, for that does free up much bonds and property, and the applause does stretch to their unvirile lack of voracity regarding marital duties that they, our women, can only regard with trauma and revulsion. Therefore the women we find attractive are non-fertile, thin, childish and white, amorphous androgynes, strange weakling beasts who die of minor fevers or get caught in drizzly showers and then tremble to death in the autumns and dark solstices from the dampness within their clothes; women who cannot compose poetry or turn backwards calves in the womb or participate in any land disputes, or even cross

8

rivers or small hills without pausing to take breath or to die, and because our women cannot give birth without dying themselves, they claim that these unlively properties do stretch to our menfolk and that, of course, it is impossible for us, with such a sickly culture as we do possess, to appreciate such a fine and beautiful passage as the woman round his neck does display, which has been carved for him by his own lively wife, so why bother explaining their healing properties when a beautiful woman in an eternal prime, which is the age of all women if their souls be strong, could only scare our kind?

'The other, the younger,' William says, his throat parched and his voice quavering from the length of his spiel, 'seems to disagree somewhat and says that these enormous lower regions, stretched wide as the valley we are currently shaded by, do not ward off evil or sickness, but welcome it, embracing and holding it inside themselves, smilingly, and that women do not eat the evil of the world by their mouths, but digest it by the healthy internal fluids of their hidden regions that they can call forth at will, that attract evil diseases, and, but only incidentally, weak Norman men from Dublin and Kilkenny both, with their promising smells, but then that once inside they are eaten by the goodness of their women, held there until unleashed through the incarnation of the weak children they bear who will die without our – yours and mine – unnatural and interfering surgeries that give life to those who should die.'

'I suppose,' de Flunkl says, 'it is rare to converse with such leisure and with no busyness in such an indiscriminate manner with such people, and in such a place. Though the surmise was confusedly told, I feel, momentarily, almost relieved from my ambitions and fears, but ask the eldest, I presume him the eldest, if he does truly believe those bald sluts round his neck have protected him from the sickness that does not even respect merchantry, or the king's cousins, or God's appointed clergymen?'

William of Roscrea sighs, his mouth dry from his long, complicated, but artful interpretation, and looks behind himself.

Harold is leaning sleepily off his horse, unafraid of death from these Gaels after this last spring, feeling it would be a good, pleasant way to go, by a spear or a sword, rather than what he witnessed in his own household, his wife and his young daughter now in a mass grave, sewn up in sacks and hurled down without prayer or service, though he did say a-one, even if he didn't know which two sacks in the pile below him he was directing his praying towards.

'I have heard,' Harold says softly to Saint John so as to distract himself, 'a Gael has a way about himself of soliloquying so much, with such an incessant flatness in the voice, that the listener is provoked into falling asleep on the very spot he stands, and that the Gael does do this so as to make his murdering all the easier.'

Saint John of Barrow does not answer. The stupid child is on his hunkers hungrily eating an entire troop of mushrooms indiscriminately off the path, not listening to the translations. Harold Tuite wants to warn the childish boy away from the ugly fungi, but a wave of tiredness and sadness overcomes him and, besides, the Gaels have begun to speak again.

Once the Gael, in turn, is finished speaking, William of Roscrea is silent for a while.

'Well?' de Flunkl asks.

William sees that his master's hands are trembling, and have been for some time, the scant muscles in his light-haired forearms every now and again spasming in large uncontrollable flickers that remind him of the sudden leaps of a fire.

'He says he is a Christian and that God is good,' William says, 'as is shown by the highly discriminate depletion of our populace, but that he is still a Christian so he does not believe in it, or in the magical properties of any tokens that do not relate to the blood of Christ, but that it functions all the same, and until its operations have been disproven, which they have not yet been, he shall continue to wear it, out of not only respect for his women, but also out of the shrewd prac-ticality so famously belonging to his people that he ventures even we would not deny – his practicality, that is – if we have ever had the great fortune to trade with a Gael.'

De Flunkl looks at the Gael's cape, which is now bulging and becoming more hectic and bustling, twisting and animated in movement, so much so that Harold momentarily believes he sees a demon's features pressed up against the material, trying to escape.

'This is a strangely rational madman,' de Flunkl remarks, 'a hybrid hermaphrodite of wantonness perhaps, but one in sound control of his faculties. Tell them we shall readily spare them, and receive their gifts.'

William of Roscrea and the Gaels sally back and forth. Eyebrows creased, William of Roscrea says, 'I am told that I have a wonderful facility for the earth's native language and for that reason I am to stand behind a tree.'

'Well, do it, so,' de Flunkl says, and William of Roscrea

strides over to an ash tree and leans his face against its coolness.

The Gael with the tumultuous cape drops one of his arms into its folds, grunts and withdraws his hand with a young rat hanging off his thumb, Gael's blood seeping down its black eyes. It thrashes its body and long tail around, as though kicking from a noose. The Gael rips it off with his other hand, sucking at the torn skin, and hurls the rat at the procession. It whistles by with a squeak, landing in the grass behind them, where it rights itself and scurries off into the woods.

'What is this?' de Flunkl asks.

The other Gaels are in a circle around the caped Gael, lifting fistfuls of rats out of the folds and throwing them down at them. One large rat sails by de Flunkl's shoulder and hits Saint John in the face. He holds his cheek and keeps chewing mushrooms. Another slaps Harold in the leg, rustling his breeches. It lands on its back, scrambles away.

'What power do they believe these creatures possess over us?' Harold asks, watching the rats fly through the air.

'As projectiles, their use is, I would venture, limited,' de Flunkl says.

'There is much squeaking,' Harold Tuite says. 'Should we shoot back?'

The Gaels are now spitting on the rats, or licking their backs, before they throw them down.

'Not yet,' de Flunkl says.

'Maybe they're considered to be bad luck,' William of Roscrea suggests from behind the tree, his head peeking out.

The youngest Gael has a rat attached to his nose and he

starts screaming, slapping it away, and the other Gaels are chuckling, along with Saint John, who drools mushroomy spit out the gap in his teeth and down his chin. He leans his head back in mirth and yells with laughter.

'Maybe,' Harold says, shrugging, 'they are good luck.'

And then, three or four rats later, it is over. One of the Gaels shouts something at William. Then they run, laughing like children, back into the woods, and they are gone.

'I am informed that they will see us again,' William says.

'They will not catch us unprepared next time,' de Flunkl says.

'Why wouldn't they?' Harold says. 'We will be as alone then as we are now.'

Possibly seventeen rats were catapulted down at them, most pups, or fat, pregnant dams; only two or three making direct hits on the retinue. One pup is dead on the ground, accidentally squashed under Saint John of Barrow's clumsy boot, its guts squeezed out of its sides. He bends over, scoops it into his cap, says a brief prayer over it and tosses it into the thick darkness of the woods.

'This is why I am not worried about the McMurroughs' incursions into our lands,' de Flunkl says, shaking his head. 'Their brains cannot produce the aim necessary to penetrate a mere woman, never mind a town.'

'Should we, albeit, be wary of continuing?' William says.

'No, let us go on into Nobber. I want to be there by midday.'

De Flunkl begins walking, and has taken a few steps before he realises the others are not following him.

'What is this?' he asks, looking back, wiping fresh sweat

off his forehead. 'The glimmerings of mutiny? Or the summit of cowardice?'

'We are not on a worthy venture,' Harold Tuite says. 'The worthiness of our venture has not been expounded, and has yet to be. Those rats were divinely sent to remind us that we are not on a good path, and have very recently become sinners. This is the road to hell.'

Harold points at the clumps of grass at his feet.

'This is not a road and Gaels cannot send divine emissaries,' de Flunkl laughs, leaning off a cherry blossom tree that shakes its soft petals down on him. 'You are a sinner for even giving voice to that thought.'

'We should go back to Trim,' Harold says. 'We should recognise the strangeness of these signs, even if they are unchristian, and make reparations to the people of Trim. A spray of rats doesn't mean nothing. It cannot. This is the foreshadowing of hell. Nobber is hell. I can see it clearly. I have fleeting recollections of the future, as though I remember it faintly. Harm will come to us, deserved harm.'

'We cannot go back there. We will not be humoured, or our lives guaranteed, there after what happened,' William of Roscrea remarks. 'But soon you shall be dead or rich and, if it is the latter, then you can buy back your soul with an indulgence in any monastery by the wayside. I heard tell there was a-one in Nobber. You can buy back any soul you want.'

'We are venturing marauders, pirates almost,' Harold Tuite says, glancing down at Saint John, who is sitting on his hunkers, examining a blade of grass.

'You are not,' de Flunkl says. 'You carry my things, the objects I either find necessitous or desirous. I am the adventurer.

It pains me to think, as a noble, I must carry things in my hands, but circumstances have beleaguered me and I find myself ill served by braggarts who I protect with the strength of my vision and the sturdiness of my direction. You will not disobey me. But you will follow me, for, as luck would have it, in its strange ways, I have no time for you to do otherwise.'

Harold points at the sack. 'In this sack,' he says, 'I have the papers for the most of Trim, the half of Summerhill and a part of Moynalvey. I have Fanagh, Doolinstown, Agher, Kiltale, Ardenew and where else I don't know. On my back I have carried most of the land we have travelled through, and it is like all its earth is weighing down upon me, and it gotten at such desperate prices and in the midst of such suffering that it has breached the walls of my soul. I feel I have become some mere talking ghost that moves about the place, buttressing half a world on me. Have you not enough?'

De Flunkl shakes his head. 'I do not understand,' he says.

And William of Roscrea sees de Flunkl does not. This young man who he serves, skinny in the shanks, with down on his upper lip that resembles the paltry remnants of a flayed rabbit's fur, grows more ridiculous by the hour; more childish and stupid and greedy; his feats of language becoming more laughable, more heightened, as the bizarreness of life stacks itself up in extenuation against them on this vaguest of quests. It is as though this Osprey fool believes that by the steadfastness and formality of his flighty language and by the endlessness of his ambition he could somehow shift matter and counterbalance the panoramic breakdown that engulfs them. William of Roscrea can also feel Harold Tuite's hatred of the young man, and though Harold is the gentlest of men, he feels this hatred will soon explode into violence with the hot pressure of the endless sin they are all building together.

This William, who is thinking this way, is tall, slender and pale, with sunken cheeks of a sallow colour. He has looked ill his whole life, but now the rest of the population have normalised his odd hue. He has a long, crooked nose that was broken in a tavern's brawl not of his own making. Everything in his life that is broken was not broken by him, but he always let it happen without protest if it seemed judicious at the time. He was once lively, now he is just alive, and this, he feels, is a great achievement, one worth maintaining.

'We are almost there,' William suggests, wondering if this alone could diffuse the tension gathering about their persons. He wants to cool wounds that are being made, but does not want to exert great effort, or take sides, in doing so.

'Much strangeness is on the world,' Harold Tuite says. 'Much strangeness has always been on the world, but now the world is growing tired. That is the difference between now and the famines and wars and floods of the last twenty harvests. Now we are being expelled from the earth. And I want to know why. Why are the Gaels so strong? What milk are they reared on? What magic comes through the animally large, dark teat of their wives? What have I done? Not to be alive, but to not be dead. What distinction is there to draw between me and the dead? Regarding merit, health, humours, character, loyalty, am I not worse than so many perished?'

'You are not responsible for the humongous death that stalks and empties the towns, if that is what you are asking,' William says. 'That is obvious. It is nature, and nature is being most natural at present.'

De Flunkl yawns and stretches demonstratively, brushing cherry blossom petals off his cap and his shoulders.

'And,' de Flunkl adds, 'you may still get your chance to die.'

'We are all sinners, I suppose,' Harold muses, 'even my daughters and wife were, though it is hard to fathom that they weren't in life some light-handed preparation of angels, a shaped, fleshy mould through which beautiful spirits would solidify and burst free, on earthly death. Butterflyish creatures, they both were.'

He coughs with tears, and covers his mouth, turning away, so the men will not see him cry.

'You will not,' William of Roscrea says, wondering if out of the corner of his eye he sees de Flunkl stifling a giggle, 'fathom your way out of this.'

'There has been much disconnection in these last few days,' de Flunkl says, his hands still raised in the air, taking great strain to exert his scant properties of leadership, 'and in the recent events of this morning, and even in the last few days, but once we attain our goal, like a loom nearing the final weave, everything will come into vision at once, layer upon layer fitting into a sensible tapestry. Everything will make sense that preceded this, and God will thank us for soothing and fostering an emergent order on our own little, modest terrain, amidst so much disarray. We are replicating the very patterns God himself would nurture were he in an intervening mood.'

'I deny that self-serving interpretation,' Harold says into his sleeve, still pretending he is not crying. 'It is nonsense. Is this infection not a more overt interventionist humour of the Lord's? Or perhaps his temporary absence is the infection, though I do not wish to stumble into any sentiments that are not of a popish nature.'

'My, you bore me. Even nothing is less boring than you are,' de Flunkl says, ending the conversation. 'We move now.'

He starts walking and, seemingly without alternatives, the others follow him, slowly. Harold comes last, picking up the sack that burdens him.

Raghnailt's flicker of dreams have, since the recrudescence of the sickness, become so perpetual that she awakes each morning in such exhaustion and emotional disarray that she fears the fatigue and heaviness of these dreams will surely kill her. Ceaselessly her father haunts her, speaking to her with the sounds of lapping water. She is never certain if he is addressing her, or if he is speaking eternally, somewhere else, to himself, and she is only happening upon him whenever weariness seals her eyes and nestling sleep makes its little death within her brain.

She is dreaming of her father again, but, in lieu of his head, atop his neck is the enormous black eye. He sits with Colca, her son, on his knee, whose head is also an eye, but Colca's body is that of a grown man's, and he is naked and sprawling, careless in his movements. They are sitting on a chair by an open door, so she knows the world of her dream is set somewhere in the past, for they no longer have any chairs in this house.

Her father, Balffe, eighteen years ago, after the Boyne flooded and the harvest was ruined, was called down to Dublin to deliver specialised horseshoes to an eccentric chevalier who had found himself in possession of a stallion with two cloven hooves. Gone for two Sundays, on the third he stood in the doorway, blocking its light with his form, holding with both hands a small, foul-smelling item all wrapped up. He laid it on the table and called his family together to see it. They gathered around and he unwrapped the bundle, exposing an enormous black eye.

It was like shone glass imbedded in a perfect circle of grey flesh, seemingly melded together by some master smith, and it was the size of two fists. Disembodied, the eye seemed to stare out at them all in calm contemplation, its lower half still bundled amongst its cloths like a swaddled baby.

'The famine has been averted,' her father declared. 'Sea monsters, about five hundred of them, though I only hazard, for no lonely creation can count that many at a single go, caught themselves along the banks of that river they call the Liffey, and the Dubliners, a skinny people, had them within the day parcelled into thousands of small portions. Each monster was like the length of Nobber, and mountainous as well, but they were swarmed over by Dubliners like ants, because that is how city folk move about their own streets, in great numbers, with great hurry, but also in great uniformity.

'There was so much blood that a red mist arose over the whole town, through which none could see the other. That same night there was a fine drizzle, and I left my lodgings to drink ale as I was lonely without my family about me. I was with a lamp to see about me, but there fell on me many great salty liquids. My lamp grew so dim I went back into my lodgings. I was blind and very greatly saturated about the skin, even under my eyelids, and once inside, I saw that my lamp had been covered in great streaks of blood, as had I, and I realised that the night time sky had rained blood.

'I knew none of you would believe me, and would think

me a loose-tongued scallywag of the Kells variety, therefore the moment I saw so many creatures of such enormousness I weaved towards the beasts, through this unruly crowd of Dubliners, a breed who are so savage at the sight of food, despite being so listless in the face of work, and I took an eye. I would have taken the tongue, but it was too long, big as a bed and twice as soft. It was still breathing out its top when I did it, for they do breathe out the back of their necks like Catalans, and I saw it seeing me, but I took it for my children and grandchildren to have them believe me.'

Her family was silent, afraid to avert their gaze from the eye, but little Colca, perched on her knee, had said, 'So it is monster's eye, and then monster is a real thing?'

'Yes,' Balffe said, 'but they do call them whales by the coast and when there are many of them they are called a gam of whales. Call in the neighbours and distribute the meats I brought back with me.'

The little town packed in for two days to see the eye, and many took whale flesh from her father's cart. Amidst a slew of unruly visitors who crowded in uninvited at all hours, her family watched the eye on the table, until the priest, the then-young and headstrong Father Unction, ordered them to consume its remnants or to bury it, because he had heard the Prestons had begun praying to it. So Raghnailt boiled the eye and sliced it into delicate, thin slivers, but her father would only let the men eat it.

While her two brothers, Colca and her father enjoyed it she watched them eating, jealous, and said, 'I have never eaten the issue of the sea, only the issue of the lake. It does make sense that the eyes in the sea would be proportionate to its size, as I hear it is a very large thing, but Moynagh lake is very small, so it does only have small eyes in it. You know as well as I, Father, that I have always remarked that pinkeens' eyes are too small to look out of, especially as water is very dirty and cloudier even than cider. If Dublin fish are bigger than Meath fish, are Dubliners also larger than Meath men, and are their eyes proportionate to their largeness?'

Her father folded a slice of eye in half, let it melt in his mouth, and then spoke. 'Their sense of their selves is very big I will say, but still they are a very small, undernourished people,' he reflected. 'I did see a very big Dubliner, but he told me he was from Antwerp, a vicinity of Dublin I do not know, and he spoke strangely, like a touched child. They are a very rank people, as well, though one would think they would be better preserved than us on account of the salt air. On the whole, they are littler and scruffier than we are, but more violent, though they have fewer Gaels on their lands so they have fewer justifications for it.

'But I know by your hinting manner, daughter, that you are curious to taste this strange morsel, but it would not be proper to bequeath such an eye as this on a young mother like you. Your melancholic disposition is too great to allow it. The eye might spill out in the milk of your breasts in strange concoctions once it has sifted its way through your imbalanced humours. You would poison your son with such a sup. You have always been sad, Raghnailt; you were a sad girl and you are a sadder mother, and this whale, whose eye I plucked out, was the saddest creature I ever did come across.

'Around me, that day, hundreds of sea monsters were in terror, but I alone stood before a very accepting creature.

I felt it did know me when I saw it, and it flapped its enormous tail in a very despondent fashion. I wish I could show you how it felt but I have no tail with which to express the particularity of its emotion, but believe me, I never saw such a desolate beast, and it would be wrong to pass this melancholia on to you for it might purify those tendencies that have already been too strong within you from birth.'

Balffe's prohibition saved her, for he and his two sons were dead of dysentery within two days, and though they all had terribly flatulent deaths, the knowledge of their own approaching demise was so apparent and drawn-out that it allowed for many poignant moments of reconciliation to be passed amongst visiting relatives. Some cousins even came from Kells to make their farewells, and Father Unction had ample time to deliver unusually luxuriant death rites.

This poignancy was tempered, though, by eight other deaths in Nobber, and her father was blamed. The meat he had generously dispersed had been two weeks old. The family's good name was gone.

The only one who had eaten of the monster and remained without complaint was Colca, but even he had been changed by his supper with the eye. Though only a child of five years, he developed strange peculiarities. His face displayed a perpetually vacant look, except for when he regarded animals, and then he betrayed so much confused emotion that the animals, no matter how domesticated, would flee. The boy forgot all the language he had previously known, and he no longer responded to his mother's calls, or played with other children.

Raghnailt recognised intimately the change in her son. He had become selfish, fawning, a nervous dog in his movements.

Society did not concern him. For a family as proud and respected as hers had once been, having Colca as its only and final representative was a burden that daily broke her heart. In her mind, he had ingested the properties of an unworldly creation and, in return for his life, had bartered away the better parts of his human traits. To her at least, he had never recovered.

'Now,' her father says to her, nodding his eye. 'Now.'

The man storms in through the door, pulling at it so hard he upsets its worn hinges, and awakens her from her troubled sleep.

He stands where her own father once stood eighteen years ago when he returned from his journey, and for a moment she thinks it is him, but this man before her is formed very differently to her father, in both body and spirit. Rudely awoken, she grips onto Alannah in fear, who lies next to her, but Alannah pushes her away, turning on her side, still asleep.

'Now,' the man says.

It is patent to Raghnailt that he is already drunk. He sways slightly, surveilling the room with lunatic eyes until his gaze alights on Mary, where she lies curled up on her bed of straw. He moves towards her, knocking over one of the jugs of ground meal that are in his way, and lays himself on top of her, his wattles of fat almost suffocating the girl's breathing.

The house, of late, has become very crowded, though not as Raghnailt had once hoped it would be, with the clamour of happy, drooling grandchildren, but rather with this one-man invasion of evil that rode into town on the back of the sickness and took it over, bringing his spouse in tow quick after him.

Colca had immediately taken up with this new arrival, this brute of a man who changes his name every other day, and one of his duties is to guard the young woman who the man claims is his wife, this lunatic child called Mary, whose insanity and violence are so great that she is kept in chains. Raghnailt does not believe the man is wed; though Mary is used as his wife whenever the fancy is taken.

Mary screams, but once the shock of the man's weight has worn off, she becomes pliant and produces noises that seem to come from some far-off place rather than from herself. They are making love, Raghnailt realises with horror.

'Stop this,' Raghnailt says. 'It is too much.'

The man lets out a howl, and thrashes around in the manner of a hooked fish, and Mary, annoyed at him for yelling so close to her ear, slaps his face. Raghnailt looks away, staring up at the ceiling, enshrouded in its dipping, inverted mountain range of cobwebs.

This habitation was always a frightful, decaying thing, but since Colca reached manhood he has accelerated its decline. The floor is a carpet of soft mud covered in footprints, and on this uneven floor there are, discounting the one now overturned, two jugs full of a substance whose origins and properties Colca has never disclosed to her.

She has asked him many times what they contain, but he only says they are ground meal that fetches a good price in the mountains, and she has often examined the fine, yellow substance, never understanding it.

The walls that enclose her life, even in the depths of this hot summer, drip with dark condensed water. Two bolts run through the wall, off which Mary's chains hang. The furniture is old, broken and sparse, some tools piled in the corner, and two beds, stuffed to thickness with human hair and wool, on which three sheepskins apiece are employed for bedding. To complement the softness of the earth, a halo of meagre hay has been scattered on the floor for Mary to sleep on.

'We used to be a proud house before you two came into it,' Raghnailt says to the lovemaking couple.

This is a lie, but Raghnailt feels someone must say some words to this effect.

The man is gasping, his eyes upturned in his head showing only their whites. Mary recovers her senses sooner than her lover, and wraps a span of her chain round his neck and jerks at it, strangling him.

'No, my love,' he says, coughing. 'It is I, Big Cat.'

The man, choking, tries to pry her fingers loose, and when this doesn't work he begins scratching her face until her grip loosens. He unwraps the chain from his neck and gulps in air, and crawls away out of her reach. Thwarted, Mary screams and thrashes around in her hay.

'I hope she kills you,' Raghnailt says.

The man looks at her out of the side of his eyes, rubbing his throat; an uneven swelling already rising around his neck.

'She is my wife,' he says, 'and she has her duty.'

'You speak of her you as though she were something other than a child,' Raghnailt says.

'She is just mad, and madness has no age,' the man replies. 'Besides, she is a woman. Look at her body.'

He pulls down his own robes, covering his dripping modesty.

'I do love her,' he says. 'She is my woman.'

'You fill this little place so full of bodies,' Raghnailt says, 'and you may put words on it, but she is just another body to you.'

'You think I am responsible for all these bodies?' the man says. 'You think too much of me. We are a mere stopping place for those corpses which de Fonteroy brings through and, once or twice, I won't deny I have been happy to give him certain troublesome ones.'

The man walks to the open door, looks out at the morning.

'This town is my purse. It is mine and I have had it like I would have any whore spread on her back for me. You are too ungrateful. You were starving until I arrived and gave your son function in the world. Who would do business with him, but me? Who will do any business any more in such times as these, but me?'

'Where is he?' Raghnailt says. 'Give him back to me, you corrupter.'

The man turns to her, and she is disgusted to see he almost feels pity for her. He shakes his head. 'I did not turn your son into what he is,' he says. 'You did that.'

He leaves and Raghnailt stares at the open door, imagines her father walking through it, taking her on his knee and telling her that everything will be fine. Alannah, Raghnailt's daughter-in-law, is stirring in bed, silently mouthing unrecognisable words in her sleep. After a while Raghnailt hobbles up and pours Mary a tall jug of cider. The young woman cups portions of it in her joined hands and slurps it up, rattling her chains with the quickness of her movements.

'Well, who do you think you are today, child?' Raghnailt asks her.

Sometimes, when Raghnailt wakes, people seem very ugly

to her, full of evil and bad intentions. Sometimes there seems to be nothing left, and she doesn't even have the strength to be disappointed. Today is a day like that.

'More cider,' Mary says.

The retinue moves along the valley, past the forest, and, once out of the shade, a blast of sunlight makes Saint John dizzy, and for a moment his vision is unnaturally clear and he can see billions of pollen particles swirling around his head, almost imperceptible from the shine of the sun. Rings of light begin radiating within his green irises, making circle in his sight, and even within these the light seems to bend in murderous ways. Birds are chirping so loudly he believes he will become deaf, like he is in some confusing, bustling heaven. Sun-drenched and light-kissed, his head feels airy and vacant, as though all his senses are being assaulted by some natural onslaught.

Finally, after an hour or so, when the sun is almost directly above their heads, they pass a peasants' hamlet, sign that they are coming upon Nobber. In the first excuse of a dwelling, the entryway has been loaded with mounds of shale, as have been the small glassless windows, and a charcoal X marks the wall. Whoever lives inside has been ineffectively walled in. The other hovels are empty, their bare, straw-strewn insides visible as they have no doors. Outside the first, an enormous, sleeping pig suns itself, a crow sitting on its belly that rises and falls with the pig's thick breathing, like an anchored ship bobbing on the sea. A cockerel struts out of the dark entryway, and stands small and proud, its chest out, eyeing them out of the side of its head.

The procession leaves the hamlet at a wide berth and Harold starts singing a sad ditty. The path becomes more trodden and worn. Saint John is going slower now, the mushroom juice drying in yellowish crusts across his chin. He staggers somewhat, tripping over nothing, breathing heavily. And then a mewling moves through the air, picking up in volume until it is accusatory, desultory almost.

'Do you hear that?' Harold asks.

He turns his head and sees, in front of the hamlet they have passed, a small child is standing out in the sun, yelling in an unbroken scream, its limbs swinging madly in a tantrum. It is at that young age where its features are so small that they are sexless and ill-defined. That pain, that madness, as Harold knows well, swells the energy for a quarter of a day before weakness and shivering disable the infected permanently and the armpits swell to the size of autumn apples.

They watch the child.

'If it approaches, shoot on it,' de Flunkl says.

'It is just scared,' Harold Tuite says.

'I can hear your voice, serving-man. You do not even believe your own words,' de Flunkl says. 'This child will not recognise the banner. Fire, all of you, on it in warning.'

'Are you mad?' Harold Tuite says.

'The child is already dead,' William of Roscrea remarks. 'What is at stake is how many of us are dead along with it, but I think it would be a kindness to kill this child.'

The child, she or he, is still screaming, and has been, without taking a breath, for a long time. Harold thinks of that young age where the lungs are still at the control of the will and not the instinct. He recalls his own eldest daughter,

Fllavie, a tempestuous young girl, now dead a month, contrary and fierce like his own father had been, who, up until the age of seven, if she became angry, would hold her breath to punish her parents whenever they had the gall to refuse her a favour.

She would stand before them demonstratively, take a big breath to blow up her cheeks and her skin would turn from pink to purple, until she passed out and fell to the ground. After the first few times he found he could replenish her lungs by slapping her across the back, though one day last summer, after an exceptionally mismanaged harvest, she was so angry with hunger that no amount of beatings could induce an inhalation, so he had dunked her upside down, holding her by the ankles, into a cold pail of water, and when he lifted her head out from the pail, she hung upside down, water wringing out of her ears and hair, and had giggled.

This child, this little and curly-haired creature, within a madness of pain, does not look like his daughter, but Harold wants to imagine the child does. He wants to believe that traces of her small face are still alive out there in the world.

'I have no want to kill a sick child,' he says.

'Though it is much kindness?' William of Roscrea asks, seeming genuinely curious.

'It is the greatest of sins,' Harold replies.

The child is still screaming.

'Indefatigable, these peasants' infants,' de Flunkl says.

The child, almost imperceptibly and never stopping its screaming, makes a small smiling arc across the hamlet, fists and baby-fat arms waving up and down, through long, rustling grass. It makes its way back to the sunburnt, fat sow and lies down on it, hugging it, and stops screaming with a shocking abruptness. The crow that was resting on the sow flies away.

'Oh,' Saint John says.

'I am very saddened,' Harold Tuite says.

'Though,' de Flunkl declares, 'my eardrums have been rattled, and though we have been waylaid and assailed by sodomitic Gaels with murine missiles and infectious infants, we have been saved yet again, not through timely intervention or loyalty or even preparedness, but through luck. We have been blessed, and so has our ensuing venture in Nobber, I believe. Let's leave with promptitude and take advantage of the blessings the Lord rains, in a deserving and ceaseless manner, down upon me.'

'That sow would eat that child if it weren't so hot,' William says. 'Hopefully, it will wait until it's dead.'

'Or until the sun turns and the beast is invigorated by cool shade,' de Flunkl says.

'You sicken me,' Harold says, spitting on the earth, 'the both of you.'

'Shut your mouth,' de Flunkl says. 'Your sadness is lies. Why are you still here? You don't even know what it is that you want, therefore you cannot be content, and your womanly toing and froing riles me.'

No one answers and they begin, almost awkwardly, walking again. Harold Tuite now leads Saint John by the shoulders.

The young man has become completely retarded in the last while, but no one but Harold Tuite minds or even notices as he does not display the marks of infection. The boy is wide-eyed, shocked by everything, and has lost his cap. Harold Tuite, a big bear of a man, gruff, bearded, lumbering, is a natural father, and soon he takes Saint John's hand and drags him on, promising him rest soon.

Harold glances back once, expecting to see the child running after them, but only catches a peek of a young fox trotting through tall grass, darting its slender face between reeds, its focussed green eyes beautiful amongst the danker green of the grass.

Fat, swollen robins flutter out of their path or hop to safety in their threes and fours. Several butterflies are resting, wings folded, on blades of grass, and they do not allow themselves to be disturbed by the retinue's procession. Bees seem to pray around the flowers of furze before fornicating with the stamens nestled amidst the petals. The heady smells are strong in their throats and their heads as the men gulp in air with the strain of their exertions. The horses are shaking their heads too much, flecking slavers of clear saliva across their faces. Saint John seems to grow more confused, slow and limping with every step.

'I wonder if the Gaels are coming for us. I would welcome their assault as I would release, and I would not even raise a finger against them,' Harold says, becoming more hot-tempered as the day's heat rises.

He has been dragging Saint John and the sack for a long time and his hands are clammy and his arms are becoming sore.

'You are unbearable,' de Flunkl shouts, turning his head back. 'I hate you and I rue the day I took you on. It was only four days ago, but it feels like you have plagued me for all eternity. If you speak again I will cut out your tongue.'

'Do what you will,' Harold shouts to him. 'I defy you. You

are a lost lad with more pounds in his purse than in his own weight. Your skin never stops shivering. You are like some demon. Your flesh is like that heaving cape of rats we were welcomed with. There is so much fear in your soul that it escapes through your skin, because you know you would be dead without us to carry your things, to set your fires and tuck you in at night. Saint John has been attacked by a strange sickness of the soul, and if you relieve me you lose him, too. And then you only have William, and he is no lover of yours.'

De Flunkl looks back at William, challenging him to defend him. William sighs and decides to settle on a more formal tone.

'I follow my wages, so long as they are sensibly gotten,' he says, stroking one of the horses' manes. 'But it would do well not to have antagonisms amongst ourselves when there are so many at play in a world that is set against us. Harold, you are an honourable man, but you have become foolish, as though you put no care upon yourself or your travelling companions. In all likelihood, we will be set upon by Gaels before we reach Nobber and I ask you to desist and remain wary, for my sake, at least. Those rats were a promise of something beyond themselves. Of what, I do not know, but I am afraid of their meaning. I value my life, and you would do well to value yours. Saint John needs caring and we must have unity if we are attacked.'

'Nobber will be our last stop,' Harold says. 'I hear the devil calling me. He has loose lips and talks like a Christian gentleman. He feigns politeness, and he wears the signage of Nobber round his throat. He says that I will come to him, on a leash, led by a man-child with undropped balls called Osprey.'

34

'Be quiet,' de Flunkl yells, pulling at his own hair, and knocking his cap crooked. 'Be quiet, you madman. I am a sir, and you will refer to me thusly and respect me.'

'Please, Harold,' William says, appealing to him with his eyes.

Harold pats Saint John on the back and nods.

A momentary peace has been broached, but William doubts he would broach a second one. He doubts he would want to or have the strength to. He is not sure which.

'Whether Nobber is hell or no,' he says, 'at least it is not far.'

As they begin to walk a pink butterfly lands on William's cheek, and this seems like such a gift that he wants to stand still so as to allow it to perch there as long as it would, but there is too much danger in staying still, and, besides, it is ridiculous. I grow stupid with heat, he thinks. The butterfly hovers away, following a scattered path upwards, where it gets lost amidst the foliage of an oak tree. William sees it disappear out of the corner of his eye, and tries to forget it.

Harold begins humming, and William joins in with him.

The babe will not feed. Dervorgilla cradles her hand behind its head, rubs her nipple into its mouth, but it will not latch onto her, it will not suck. It does not love her, she feels, it does not want to become a part of her. She teases the nipple around the inside of its lips, yet when she lets go of it, the breast, disappointed, slumps down. Frustrated, she pushes the nipple back into it once more, feels a dull resistance, and then a stinging impresses itself on her aureole. The babe is almost smothered by the cushioned force of her breath, and, still, it will not suckle. She turns to Long Tedbalt, stretched out across the bed.

'She won't drink,' she says. 'I cannot any more. What am I to do? I cannot.'

Lazy, and smelling like a charnel house, he does not respond, and she grows even more exasperated. She looks down at the child, at the soft fontanelle pulsing like a heart on its crown, and shivers. Ever since the child has been born, she has imagined her fingernails piercing through that soft spot. Unprotected by bone, her nails would slide so easily through the spongy skin, stirring out the brains. She kisses it on its cheek, and then, out of fear that her trembling will upset the strength in her arms, and the child will spill to the floor and break, she places it down in the gap between Tedbalt's rangy legs.

This shivering in her limbs is something uncontrollable and

recent that has been coming over her with increasing frequency, but it is something other than pain; it is almost ecstatic. I was only ever a little nervous, she thinks, but motherhood has intensified whatever unsure tendencies I had in me. I have become an uncaring thing, and I have been shaking for a long time. She pushes her dress down over her shoulders and exposes both her breasts to herself, begins kneading them, rolling them around as if she were testing dough, and then she pinches at her left tit so hard that she grits her teeth, but, still, no milk is produced. She tries the other.

'I am a failure,' she says.

A great sadness was produced in her when Jacotte was born. Dervorgilla had passed out at the first sight of her own child, and when she awoke it was as though she had given birth to both her own sadness and the babe, and if she were to compare them, she thinks, sadness would be the larger, and it would not stop feeding on her.

The midwife, who was called Segnat, was infamous for she had, as though she were a cat, delivered herself of four of her own children, and they were all, save Álmaith, still alive. She told Dervorgilla that she had bled too much, and that they had all thought she would die.

'You have been pale for a long time,' Segnat had said, 'your warm moistures fled. You are weak, and your sanguine temperament, if you did have any on you, may not return until the child leaves the house. Not all are made for motherhood.'

Though she hated Segnat for saying it, Dervorgilla had woken up full of a hate that had never left, but she still felt that it was Segnat's saying of it that had made it true, and she hated her for it, too.

A constant headache buzzes behind her eyes and shortens her temper; everyone looks ugly and cruel to her. Whenever people go by the house, she hears them snigger or guffaw, and, though she knows it is insane, she feels they are all laughing at her. She feels excluded from grace and calm. Nothing gives her pleasure any more, and she wonders why she cannot love such a beautiful, pudgy child, soft like butter and good-smelling. She does not love food or music any more, and she had always loved those things.

What makes it worse is that three of the other girls in Nobber had also had their firstborns that summer, and they are all so full of quiet joy and motherly arrogance that Dervorgilla thinks she would choke on her own hatred if she sees them again, but she sees no one now.

Before the curfew the young mothers would spend their days, weather allowing, sitting on the edge of the fountain, chatting to each other. They would compare their children, the particular qualities of their own motherhood, the trans-formations, like welcome slippages, in their bodies. They would speak about their own lives, how they would rear their coming infants; they would talk about the rush of feelings that would come upon them, unpredictable, expansive and sudden. They shared their secret knowledge, their voices always easy and gentle, but Dervorgilla shared none of these emotions. They were so happy in their stillness, so firm in their postures, that Ambrosio, a travelling hawker who passed through once a year selling and repairing wind vanes and unctuous oils for scabs and the repelling of fleas and lice, had joked that these mothers were the best sundials the town had ever had. Once he had said this, Dervorgilla had examined their hunched forms and shadows they threw, and she found that even the shadows crawled obsequiously around the mothers' bodies. Even the shadows respected them, just like the town did. Dervorgilla, looking at her own shadow, just saw a misshapen darkness that could not be read. She felt hounded, but at the same time felt that no one paid her any attention. She believed that somehow, when the women looked at her, with some intuition completely foreign to her, they knew she was a terrible mother, and she could not stand it. She had known these girls, suddenly women, their whole lives, and still she could not ingratiate herself amongst them. After birthing, they were like new, better people, and she was still lost. They were as tired as her, but their tiredness had a kind of sense to it. Theirs was a soothing tiredness, an enveloping calm. Hers was an edgy fatigue, as though she was constantly hungover. When she spoke to them, she found her own words awkward and forced. She felt their stares become spooked, or offended, when they regarded her, and she would blush and turn away. They found her bizarre; she felt herself a fat pig amongst them, glandular, lunar, crazy. She was the youngest of them; they did not respect her, and she prayed for the rainy days that kept them all inside.

'I know they are talking about me,' she had said to Tedbalt, her husband, one evening after she had spent the whole afternoon fretting about the room.

'Who cares as much as you about anything as you care about everything?' Tedbalt had replied. 'People don't think about themselves as much as you think about them. And what are they to us? Their opinions are nothing. We know them, and we will know them our whole lives, so why worry?'

Behind Tedbalt's quietness, he was articulate and astute, but how could anyone know the range of emotions that passed over her in a moment, confusing her and leaving her in a heap of jagged nerves? I never used to be like this, she had thought.

'You are become too sensitive,' he had said, 'like a frayed rope that has been tautened, you will snap if there's no give in you. Stop mithering the world for something no one can recognise, or understand, and that you can't even name. It does not exist. You are only thinking of yourself, but through the guise of others.'

'I am a new thing,' she says aloud.

Unlike the other mothers, she had not named her babe. Yes, the babe was called Jacotte, but she had not been named properly, because the priest had no time for peasants' or trades-people's baptisms any more, having been called to the larger towns to bless great swathes of nobles who, once the sickness broke out, suffered a great, communal and immediate fear over the state of their souls.

'The priests make a fortune,' Tedbalt had said. 'And Father Unction will abandon his flock because we are not the paying sorts now that the great leaching of the tithes has impoverished us. Nobles, sent into a religious fervour by the scent of a commoner's death if it is of the spreading sort, put a heavy demand on the church, and it is fattened, enriched. I said as much to the worm-faced bastard, and would be perhaps excommunicated if he did not have so many other affairs on his mind.'

Father Unction, shortly after Tedbalt had told her this, took the town horse and did not return, and after several weeks, the lack of him made Nobber go mad.

Unblessed bodies were dying. Widows could be seen trekking out to the woods in penitence, crying that the church had abandoned them, that deserving men, deprived of their death rites and communion, were being locked out of heaven for unknown quantities of eternity. Even from the woods, through the great oceanic noise of the wind passing through leaves, at times a keening would sound, and in the town a head would turn; a door slam shut for the final time.

Then the Preston family, wild boys every last one of them, lost their mother to the sickness, and, full of grief's insanity, they began setting fires in public places. The mayor responded with threats too vague to be effective, and the Preston boys whipped up all the locals into dissent. One evening they all approached the mayor collectively. They demanded a priest from him; a sermon that dissolved them of all their hitherto accumulated sins, and that pardoned their recent dead. They refused to die any more in such an unholy and undignified manner. They swore that they would refuse death until they achieved grace from a priest, any priest, it did not matter who, but one must be produced.

The young mothers had been sitting at the fountain when it had happened, relaxing in the late-evening light of this never-ending summer, their shadows stretched out long and thin across the walls of the houses across the street. Believing that new motherhood filled them with concoctions that bred immunity to the sickness, they had remained in public even after it had been announced, and, now, they watched the crowd gathering outside the mayor's lodgings.

Grim faces sparkled and bounced light above arms full of burning torches and scythes. The crowd stirred, swaying slightly, and in the light of the sunset it was as though they themselves in their collective grief were a greater, more intensely orange sunset, a little sunset amidst the greater one. They had converged like some holy procession; it felt like a final moment, and above them was a new man no one could ever remember seeing before. The stranger sat on a fine, big horse of unusually high quality. His face was so flaccid it was inexpressive, and his eyes and bearing revealed nothing of his station or his intent. Though he never said anything, Dervorgilla felt he had somehow involved himself in some plot greater than the simple and profound pain of her neighbours, whose most expressive organ was the mob in which they found themselves.

Long Tedbalt, full of the peasant's intelligence for unspoken things, could feel the violence coming, and he yelled at his wife to get back in the house, immediately. She could see him, head and shoulders above the other townsmen, only smaller than the stranger on the horse. The light was bleeding out of the town, turning them all grey, dissolving the starkness of the shadows. She obeyed her husband.

He came back a few hours later, lay down on the bed and said, with a great sigh tagged onto the end of it, 'We, and the whole town, are now under a curfew.'

'What happened?'

'It is not women's talk, but that pervert child of Raghnailt's has told us that if an outsider does inquire we are to say we did it to ourselves, and it is to stop the intermingling of infected sweats, and that is all we are to say.'

'This is ridiculous.'

'What is not?'

He turned away on his side. His face had been blackened with soot; the eyebrows had been scorched off somehow. Pale white lines, like worms stretched on muck, marked their absence.

That had been six days ago, and now the sack of grain in the corner was nearly empty. She stirs the cup in the bottom of it, but it picks up nothing. The grain is too shallow along the bottom. Thousands of tiny and brilliantly white needles grow on what remains, a fine film of evanescent, almost glowing fungus. She covers her mouth with the back of her hand so as not to inhale any of it. The water basin beside it is covered in specks of dust that float above the membrane. Stirring her finger in it, she breaks a thin yellow film on its surface, releasing a stagnant smell that sets her coughing, and she realises the water had not been covered by dust, but by many sleeping midges. Unsettled, they rise up all at once in a hazy cloud and disperse around the room. She blinks, and looks at the door, almost able to feel the heat it lets through.

'I cannot,' she says. 'The child will die. I am not milking. Even the animals of the field can feed their young.'

Light seeps through a wide crack in the rotting door, and motes of energetic dust stir through it, but the rest of the house is unlit, full of a green darkness. The candles are long spent, and the firewood that remains is not dry, though everything is hot. She paces about, casting glances at her family laid out on the bed.

She goes to the door, presses her eye against the crack, but the light is too thin, and it is too bright. A sharp pain enters through her head and a second tiny headache blossoms like a flower behind her left eye. She cannot make out anything any more.

'I care not for their curfews or the stupidity of their prohibitions,' she says. 'They all think me useless and ineffective, but I am good, and I shall prove my worth to those who would pass judgement on my rearing. Jacotte will be fat with food, undamaged and safe, and they will say, Oh, there goes Dervorgilla, a fine mother, and her child's is as fine as any's.'

She is convincing herself that she loves her child, but she is still not sure. The light is a finger gesturing towards her. If she leaves the house, she does not know what she will do other than beg something off the Prestons or the Toqvilles. Perhaps they will think I am dying, she thinks, or have been abused, because of my shaking, but I am just energetic with love for my family. I will come across little Conn, sooner or later. He will give me something. He would give me a mob of lambs if I asked it of him. He would even give me his life if I asked him to lay it down for me.

Conn's visits, she reflects, are what she has missed most in the town's imprisonment; his visits, and his flowers.

She pulls up her dress, opens the door and a flood of light engulfs her.

It is a long time before she can open her eyes, and when she does they are in a squint, her whole face looking like pinched skin. There is no one about, and a nauseous dizziness comes upon her. She is unused to light. All the houses have been closed up. Already, from so brief an exposure, her head is itchy, prickling with heat. This is a dead town, sealed and rotting. The dogs fled a month ago, or were cooked in communal fires. Her headache grows larger and a new kind of pain is coming upon her. She has felt it once before, but does not remember where. A horse neighs down the street, and she jumps with fright at it, and her foot comes into contact with something slippery. At her feet are a dishevelled bunch of rotting sweet peas, may blossoms and lupins, disarranged and entangled like hair in the mornings. Their vibrant purples and pinks have bled out, and now they are brown and grey, a weak mimic of the town in which they have been placed. The petals are dry and crumbling like spent ash, but the stalks are wet and decomposing, sticky amidst her hands. Everything goes flat and horrible in death, she thinks, as she gags at their rank smell, kicking them away. Conn must have left them for her at some point after the curfew, but near enough its beginning.

'Is that long enough ago to kill flowers?' she asks.

Conn, four years her junior, is truly a boy. He must be thirteen by now, she thinks, and he was born in the summer. He has spent his life wandering between Kilmainhamwood and Nobber, minding the bishop's sheep. She has known him since before he could speak. He loves her, but he was too young, and she had always been promised to Tedbalt by her father.

She had been married at midnight near the woods, by torchlight, as was the local custom. She remembers that night seeing Conn hidden outside the ceremony, concealed behind head-high ivy that entangled an oak tree. His sobbing marred the whispers of their vows; a pigeon cooed above his head, she remembers. But it was a gentle love Conn had for her, and even Tedbalt himself allowed the boy to leave his wife tokens outside the door: arrays of hollyhocks he had gathered, buttercups, diced nettles for soup, strange stones from Newgrange, proving, Tedbalt had said, that long ago Gaels had known how to read. Conn came into town only on Sundays to go to Mass. Sometimes he slept at Widow Gertrude's, and she would feed him, but every time he set out again, before dawn, he would pass her door and leave her something.

He is wandering the plains now, she imagines, seeking shade in some thicket, perhaps beside some lake or gurgling river near here, perhaps the Boyne, or Moynagh lake, his eyes lazily surveilling trotting lambs, free from the madness of towns, the decimation of the sickness, the violence of men.

'You slavering whore.'

She looks to the right and sees a blackened and naked devil sprinting towards her. It is Colca, his feet bare and covered in dust, but she cannot see them they are in such a flurry of speed. He is tall and demonic; he gallops towards her like a horse.

'Get back into your house,' he yells.

She scrambles back into the darkness, and shuts the door, leaning against it with her back. His footsteps are close, and then the door is rattling. Colca, outside, is hailing down furious blows on the wood.

'You infectious and sweating whore, I'll slash your throat into seven parts if I see you again. I'll rip your slut's face open. You will kill us all. Are you mad?'

The man is so enraged his yelling soon becomes wordless. His blows reverberate through the wood, rattling her back and jarring her teeth. Suddenly, the door stops rattling.

'It is only for your own good,' Colca says, his voice now soft and whispering. 'The sickness is a spreading thing, and we must hide away from it, my dear. I only scare you to be good to you. Stay, like the good child you are, stay.'

Then a padding sound retreats; he is gone. She wants to call after him that they are dying, that they need food, that they need light, but instead she feels ashamed; ashamed that she has broken the curfew, ashamed that her sally outside has been cut short; that she fails at everything she attempts. She slides to her knees, and knocks her head backwards off the door. It is a gentle knock; tears are brimming in her throat. She feels their upwards gurgle.

Her beautiful baby is asleep, as is her kind husband. All easy sleepers, she is the family exception. She envies them for the ease with which they lie there, the dreamish escape they have inbuilt into their lives, the salve that their peaceful sleeps give them. Since Jacotte was born, she hasn't had one good night's rest, and it has driven her to lunacy. She is even afraid of her reflection in water now lest she see the black impressions sleeplessness has given to her eyes.

'I am sorry,' she proclaims.

They are not listening. They never listen, and so she can speak freely.

'My nervousness has stopped kindness flowing. I only think of how to manage my being needed, rather than the need itself, but none of this would matter if I could provide, and I cannot. I am too weak. I apologise. I apologise for my failure.'

She gasps, and throws her hand over her mouth. Near the end of her speaking she overheard her own voice and realised she had not been speaking words, but instead formless groans. Half sentences and half words, indecipherable and without meaning, have been pouring out of her mouth in an unbroken stream, though that which she had intended to speak was perfect in her mind.

An ocean of sudden sweat, in one holistic sheet, bursts through her skin. She has never felt its like; even her toes are moist. She is damp, covered in a glowing sheen and her breathing is ragged. A summer rain came from within her, and left. The sweat turns cold; she is shuddering, and even her vision vibrates.

'You will all love me,' she says, but she is babbling again, saying nothing.

In a frenzy, she pulls her dress down again, and she is squeezing at her left breast with both of her hands, grunting with the effort. Her movements are violent. She screams in pain, but her struggle produces nothing. She lets go of her breast, and leans her head back, awaiting the shooting and raw pain that will soon overcome her breast before numbness eclipses it, and then, she sees a movement and feels a quick release. She glances down at herself. Out of her left nipple, gleaming and dark, leaks a single drop of blood.

The man leaves Raghnailt's house, and, around him, the street is empty and all the doors are closed. These few houses are squat, crooked, their ugliness exposed by the full light of summer. The town's only movement comes from his horse flicking its tail to remove a fly from itself, and then, for a moment, everything is still. He stops to take it all in, his dominance of this place, his total victory over it, but everything is so ragged and fractured that it feels like no achievement at all; it almost feels like a defeat. Such a scraggly place, he thinks. There are bodies by the monastery and bodies by the forge, and there were bodies where he slept this morning, too. The whole town is overflowing with death.

'This is sloppily done,' he says.

Putting his fingers to his throat, he feels the rawness the chain left upon it. That, too, he thinks, was sloppily done. This is happening because he is drunk. De Fonteroy had warned him about alcohol; and if he remembers correctly, he had told him those very words in a tavern.

'There is a kind of awareness necessary to stay alive that is blunted by the sweetness of alcohol,' de Fonteroy had said. 'One must perceive what is, but when drunk one feels like everything is possible, and that is never true. Is everything wrong, or is just one thing wrong? You must be able to tell, or any whore can cut your face open and steal your purse.

Everything feels like doom, and, of course, everything is, but the problem is if you do not mind it. You must be the one who creates the littler and more immediate doom about people, and then weave the consequent sense out of it; that is the only doom worth a damn. And I do not work with drinking men.'

De Fonteroy had taught him everything over the course of that one night, and by dawn they had gone into business together. At first, they had made a fortune taking bodies from towns abandoned by the sheriffs and the nobility, and within three weeks, almost by accident, they had slipped into managing the towns themselves, selling them off part by part, or claiming them for themselves using different names. In some of the towns, no one was left who could read, and they had made off with all its properties and lands in less than an hour by showing some few survivors a faded vellum that detailed how one made a salve from honey and lavender, claiming it was a writ from the king.

But de Fonteroy had been gone for some days now, and it is so hard to maintain sanity on your own. Colca was worse than no company, and just a little alcohol made it all feel so easy, made the violence around him seem much more necessary and natural.

To wake up sweating, there is nothing like it; you can be certain the world is against you already, and he had awoken so early that he had felt like he was losing his mind. Six nights since he had slept properly, and a sound of sawing near him had opened his eyes. He had woken up thinking that someone was cutting off his head with rusted teeth and when he looked around for the noise he found it was an ocean of flies buzzing over the dead family, a noise that, though it had been constant for days, all of a sudden seemed grating. He had begun drinking cider in order to get back to sleep, and that just made him crave Mary.

This town is unravelling me, he thinks, and I will slide into death with such carelessness.

He came by this place too easily, and he knows it has made him arrogant and stupid. It is bringing me down to its level, and he doubts he even has the will to stop drinking any more. It was a mistake to take Nobber. De Fonteroy had thought they needed some secluded place out of which to work, but he was wrong. It has only created more problems, robbed him of that spontaneous looseness so necessary for this kind of undertaking.

It still surprises him how little work it all took; a few suggestions and the violence poured out of the people. It is always inside them; one just needs to know the words that release it, the words that direct it. Stopping it again is always the hardest part because that can't be done with language alone, but he had been prepared for that. Eoin Preston was the man to break before the rest would follow. At first he had thought it would be Joseph Toqville, but that man had already been broken by something else, and Eoin Preston broke in four or five movements.

'What happened to your neck?'

Colca is standing naked in the doorway of the registrar's office. The man remembers how the moment Eoin Preston was down, Colca had placed his foot on Preston's neck, threatened to take his life, meaning every word of it.

'I was just thinking of you.'

'Your neck, though—'

Since he took over the town, Colca has remained naked. His face and arms are black from the forge he worked over for several years, but now his feet and legs are covered in streaks of pollen from the fields of buttercups he treks through every night; his belly all covered in rashes from the woods he has crawled in.

The man looks at the degenerate he has cast his lot with, and, for a brief moment, considers killing him. Colca is a part of the sloppiness overtaking the town, but then again, he thinks, so am I.

'Mary,' the man says.

'Why do you keep her?' Colca asks.

'I love her; she is mine.'

'She is mad.'

'We are all allowed one vice, no? You, of all people, know that.'

'But she has a demon in her.'

'She is just a woman,' the man replies.

'If a mare kicks you break it, get it pregnant, or acquire a new one,' Colca says, 'else you are a dead man.'

'You only think of horses.'

Colca laughs at this, and the man feels annoyed by the coughing sound of it, as though Colca had never learned how to laugh.

'This should be a welcoming town,' the man says, pointing at the forge, and then at the abandoned monastery. 'Remove these bodies from sight, and prepare that little family for transportation. They must be enshrouded. Even in this depopulated land their faces are famous. Their deaths, even in this charnel house, would be too revelatory.'

'It would be far easier for me to scratch out their faces,' Colca says. 'It is hard to recognise a face without its eyes.'

'No,' the man says. 'There is too much blood already, and theirs is old and fetid. The stains are hard to hide, and there are already too many flies. I can hardly sleep with the noise.'

'Will you let me play with Emota first?' Colca asks. 'Then I will work till nightfall for your leisure.'

The man shakes his head. 'Is Emota the only reason you have sided with me against your own town?'

'You do not know what it is to be hated,' Colca says. 'And, besides, who is to say enforcing a curfew won't separate the sickness within itself and kill it off. It has as much sense to it as anything else the people do. I do not do too bad a thing, and am a little freer for the doing of it.'

'I am not using Emota today, but first drag the bodies from the forge. The day is sweltering, and we must begin. When de Fonteroy arrives everything must be ready; that man is not the waiting sort.'

Colca tramps towards the monastery and the man stands on the wall of the fountain for his morning address. From his higher vantage point he can see some large black thing at the midpoint between the town and the woods. He knows he should care about this new thing, but he does not. It is too hot, and he can still feel Mary's chain round his throat.

Making his voice high so it will project, as per his religious training, he calls out to the town: 'Nobberians, to those of you who remain I say you have done well, and you must do well some more. To those of you who have suffered, I say you have suffered well and you have suffered so your fellow may live; and you must suffer some more. The curfew will go another day at least, so bed yourselves in a little deeper and continue praying. What God asks of you is hard and that is why he asks it of you, for it is the depth of your hardship that is the measure of your soul's worth, and what is that puny thing measured against eternity? I would be surprised if any town on this island were as . . .'

He pauses, struck by one of those unwanted insights that are gifted so suddenly to the drunken, and realises that in all likelihood no one can hear him; perhaps they never could. He has addressed the town every morning since he arrived and there has never been any reply, and if there ever were one he would silence it. I compose soliloquies over a silent crowd, he thinks, pour monologues into a void, recount sermons to the dead. This is all a waste of time. There were perhaps over a hundred people here when he arrived, now there may be no more than sixty. They are dwindling, he thinks, and my faculties are dwindling with them, as though our strengths were all connected.

'If you have a loom in your house you should be working,' he calls. 'If you have clay in your house you should be building, forming. Work goes on beyond the man who works it. It is the legacy we leave to our—'

About to say children, he catches himself; their children are probably dead, and he should not have them thinking too much about a coming generation that will not arrive; it is a bad line of arguing. He scrambles around in his mind to find a new way to start.

Peasants, de Fonteroy had said, are impossible to persuade, but easy to manipulate for the same reason; while the rich are even easier to break because they believe in flattery, but there are no rich here left to flatter. Fear, then, the man decides, is what the sensible sort would impose.

'There are only two things,' he calls, raising two fingers to the empty street. 'There is the sickness and there are the Gaels; both are here, invisible amongst us, waiting for us to weaken. They reek of the death they will bring us. I can smell them now. Do you not feel that burning in your nostrils? That is the Gael, that is the sickness; that is the devil on the edge of town, storming the boundaries of our lives, overcoming us. And yet every town has that. What town is not doomed? Every mother cries. Every good man falls. Every child starves, but you have a third and a fourth thing that these other do not.'

He raises four fingers to the sky.

'You have me, and you have the curfew I gave you,' he yells. 'I will stop the Gaels and the curfew will stop the sickness, but it takes a little time. I know you crave justice now, for ye are just, but this is the seventh day, and on the seventh day God rested, and who oversaw his dominion on that day? On that day did the devil reign supreme? No, I tell ye, the care-taker did. I am that caretaker. I am your caretaker; that is all I am. You have no priest, no mayor. The sheriff fled; the king himself crumbles under the weight of his own fecklessness, avarice and lust, but you have me. I am here for you. I am yours.'

Behind him, he can hear Colca dragging bodies from where they lay at the forge. The heavy, dull sound of it makes him lose the thread of his thought again. He blinks for a moment, feeling thirsty, sways slightly. I feel like I am disintegrating, he thinks. Perhaps I, myself, have become full of fear. I must be careful not to fall back into the fountain. If I could only sleep the better part of this drunkenness would fall away.

'All the other towns die because they leave their doors open, they let their sins pile up and they become dead,' he says. 'I have heard that but two days ago in Mullingar the people left their doors open and those who didn't die by nightfall were swallowed into the earth when it cracked open, because if God is away, the devil is not. Only two women survived and as they came to give me the news a band of Gaels took them, tried to plant Gaelic children in them, but the Gaels were so drunk that the women were only sodomised. Thankfully, the two women were in the early stages of infection so did not have to suffer this disgrace upon their honour for too long a time. If only they had listened to me!'

He is rambling now, his inventions becoming too ridiculous and sporadic, and he doesn't remember what the women were supposed to have listened to even if they had really existed. I am forgetting myself, but it doesn't matter. No one can hear me.

'The curfew will go on another day,' he calls. 'Adieu.'

Colca lets go a body he is dragging and rewards him a few claps, before picking it up again by the ankles. The man scowls at him and then steps down and washes his face in the fountain.

'When you are done,' the man says, 'go out the town and see what that black structure is. I have work to do before de Fonteroy arrives.'

Colca nods, picks up the feet he had let drop. The man watches him leave and then goes into the shade of his room. In truth, he is disgusted at how easy all this is; how stupid these people are. He could continue making mistakes for years and they would not stir forth from their houses. They are like animals, and he hates them. So much better if he had taken a town like Drogheda, he thinks, but that place would be too big, and he knows he would be just as unhappy there. He has gone many places and spoken with many people and Mary is the only person he has met who doesn't disgust him; the only one who gives him any joy.

He sits by a table, scratching entries into a codex with a squat nib, but he cannot concentrate; the noise of flies is too much. Pushing his inkpots and ledgers to the side, he takes his wooden rosary from round his neck and begins to pray, his head down and his eyes closed, counting off the beads between his fingers.

This is not for God, he believes in him, but he is versed enough in scripture to know that any man who makes a fortune has already been consigned to hell; he does this for the awareness that comes from the isolation of a revolution of the rosary. Usually the repetitions soothe him back to a deeper sense of reality and its consequences, but after the second decade he gives up.

'There is nothing behind my eyes when I close them,' he says.

The flies are too loud in his ears, his breathing is a flurried mess, his neck swelling, and he is still drunk.

'Big Cat,' he says, opening his eyes.

He looks at the dead family in a pile in the corner for a while, and then begins drinking again.

The retinue soon comes upon the Dee. In an opening in the growth and weeds, they see more freed cattle watering themselves lazily on its banks. Some calves are playing there, breaking occasionally into exuberant trots, straddling each other's skinny backs with their young haunches.

They skirt around Moynagh Lake, engulfed in oak trees. Glimmering water glimpsed through the thickness and shade of the summer trees. A black-haired woman with a large blemish on her face stands on the edge of a crannóg, stepping onto the bridge that sprouts from it, a large axe slung over her shoulder. Behind her is a mud hut. She waves at them. Tools line the bridge, hanging down, slung off leather hoops, wind whipping the water beneath, shivering them in ghostly swingings. William of Roscrea waves back and then she begins heaving the axe down on the bridge.

'It would seem she's destroying it,' William says, 'so as to more happily isolate herself from the cares and ravages of this diseased land, or so it would appear on casual observance.'

'I did not think those dwellings were still habitated,' de Flunkl says.

'Humans enter available space, regardless of fashion, tradition or superstition,' William says. 'And often they invade unavailable space,' he continues, glancing at de Flunkl.

'I too would enjoy a little fairy island on which to ruminate,'

Harold Tuite says. 'A few sacks of grain my only company, a gentle blanket of grass beneath my weary bones. Still water lapping around me, rocking me to sleep. Magnificent clouds above me sailing by, multi-formed shapes dazzling and awakening my imagination, heaving me in turns with their vengeance of tumultuous dreams every night. Birdsong lullabies and windy trees like soft-edged chimes with many hands the only noise external to the body in which my bruised heart does rock gently within me, measuring out the space of my heartbreak until I join my beloveds in heaven.'

'You will eventually join your family, but you may yet get your more immediate wish,' William says. 'Property is vacant, more than we could have ever imagined when we began this quest, and a claimant may lodge his suit with the only remaining sovereign power, which is, on all appearances, and in many cases, the unprotesting dead.'

'You best hope that's not the truth,' de Flunkl remarks, throwing an evil glance at William. 'You best hope that's not true, for our sakes, mine as well as yours. You best hope that chaos respects the limits of property.'

Harold rubs a shivering Saint John on the back and shrugs on William's behalf.

'She may be infected,' William says, referring to the woman on the bridge. 'Though she seems too invigoratingly vibrant and vital with her manly axe swings to be yet stricken. I hope I too have the courage to isolate myself if I am taken by the precipitous trembling and weakness that foreshadows, or rather foreswears, the sickness, with its promise of imminent and painful death. I hope to do it somewhere as beautiful as this earthy fortification, the fruits of an earlier, stronger and more nimble people.'

'I wish I knew her name,' Harold says, dragging Saint John after him by the arm. 'She seems to be a fine woman.'

'That deformed hag a fine woman?' de Flunkl says. 'Only one who was a woman themselves would prattle such idiocies, but maybe that is what you are degenerating into with your big, soft tears that even a beaten bitch would be ashamed to have shed so plentifully as you have done today.'

'There are plenty of fine women,' Harold says. 'The world is happily thick with them. They are blessings, the true companions of the earth. They are born, live and die every day, but it takes a man to see them, not a boy. The eyes of a man are soothed by the sight of any woman who does carry the burden of her life well and with generosity, whereas the eyes of a boy are always half-closed, and when they are open they do not understand what they see, unless it is their own thwarted pleasure, and I will thwart the pleasure that is the breath in your lungs if you question me on my manliness once more, you littlest of boys.'

'I insist on quiet,' William says. 'I will not intervene if you two play at insults. I will ride on and leave you behind, and you may navigate this treacherous land without the skills I bring to bear on this group.'

They walk on, having to pass into thick undergrowth, the little chorus of evenly spaced axe blows on wood trailing behind them, growing dim, complementing the breeze that sets the trees' branches in musical contact. They find themselves beating their way through a thicket, its diverse life and dimensions that of a forest, but its size too shy and enclosed to classify it as anything but a glorified grove. The heat is close and dirty, a heavy thing that is alive.

And then the noise of the woman's axe stops, and for some reason this is deeply unsettling to William of Roscrea, far more unsettling than when the infected child stopped, with cut suddenness, screaming. A noisy silence surrounds him. A weariness beyond physicality envelops him. Birds rattle, screech and warble; insects gurgle and crunch under his boots, but all this noise is just inhuman silence.

He was not frightened by the Gaels, nor by the infected child, nor by the depleted landscape, nor by the free animals unresponsive and forgetting of their manly masters. He was not scared by the uneasy frisson in the glimmering eyes of the skinny peasants in Trim. He is not afraid of their insane quest. None of this has frightened him. But now he is afraid because the woman stopped swinging her axe, and though he hopes she will begin destroying the bridge again, he realises that the only thing that scares him is the death of industriousness, the death of work; whether it be destructive or creative, it is all of a piece to him.

He thinks of the Gaels with their insanity and their strangeness and their mysterious rats and admires them, secretly, the secret even secret to himself. They have been here for a long time and still their industry is invisible, but sociable, everywhere complementary of the landscape, temporary and fluid, but it is there, undoubtedly, and so it is harder to break than the hammer and smash of his people's industry with their mills and their looms and their stony, towering structures that fall into neglect and nothingness at the shadow of adversity, whereas the Gaels only add to nature's existing edifices to harden nature's instruments, and so it is more difficult to erase. They complicate nature with a softness that is unimaginable to him.

The problem with the Gaels is that they are too free, and this freedom, he realises, is their only reaction to the devastating losses they have sustained for almost two centuries, but all these displays of wild freedom are flailing attempts to hide an enormous and smothering anxiety; and anxiety, he believes, is the root of all manmade things.

But everything is green here, nothing is manmade, and, still, I too am becoming anxious amongst all this naturalness, he thinks, noticing his breath has grown quick.

The horse he is leading accidentally clops away a portion of stripped bark, capsizing it, and hundreds of woodlice squabble and clamber over one another in fear of the light. They are as he is. They too are the expression of his wordless anxiety, a centreless hurrying and scrambling, confusion the only unifier amongst them.

He is sick of everything being so dark and green, his eyes rejecting the uniformity of the untameable world. He longs for a bright bird, or a pink butterfly, or a red rose, something to break the browns and greens, but nothing ever comes.

There are so few humans in the world. The earth is an unconquered thing, leafy and overgrown, uncaring. A monotonous thing with no edges that swallows up lonely travellers. It is terrifying to behold. It is terrifying to be so small within it.

And then William's internal eternity ends. He looks up and sees the markers of civilisation, Nobber, the dregs and remnants of this old place, the point that divides the fine ports of Drogheda from the more ragged wildernesses of the midlands.

They have finally come upon it, but between them and the town stands an enormous man, blacker than night, in a posture of greeting, his arms outstretched.

Harold salutes, and then halloos the man, but receives no response.

'This, too, is strange,' Harold says. 'Perhaps he has been crucified into that posture, burnt into that colour. His body is ill-shaped, as though his spine has been broken and, many times, rearranged.'

De Flunkl squints at the figure in the distance, making a fan of his hands over his eyes to enhance his vision.

'It is a blackened devil, mayhaps a Gael standing atop another Gael,' de Flunkl says. 'Ready yourselves for conflict.'

They approach cautiously, and the closer they get the more deformed and bloated seems the unmoving figure that guards the town.

An ash is growing in the house; in its middle, and it has become a point of some marital discord between Glynis and Aethelburga. She probably expects him to take care of it; I know by where she leaves her silences, he thinks, sipping his jug of ale, looking out the window. Was there an argument, though? He does not remember, and she is still playing with the children on the other side of the room, ignoring him.

'Who is the goose, and who is the gander?' Aethelburga sings, a child on her lap, the other giggling and burying itself beneath the hay, thinking it is hidden. He is sick of them all.

Their house is one-roomed, like all in the town with the exception of the mayor's, and is the only one that has a window. When Glynis used to come in from the fields he would every day see his wife's little face peeking out at him, framed greyly in the shade from which it stocked up the town's incessant and merciless gossip. Now the window has been boarded up with a plank of wood, but still Glynis stares at it though nothing can be seen. He sits on his stool, his feet planted off the wall, drooling ale through loose lips. Perhaps it would be better if she died, he thinks. I would be a little freer then, and have more time to think the thoughts that do come upon me.

'And where oh where will little Lady Goose wander?' his wife sings.

'Quiet,' Glynis says.

He glances at the ash seedling in the middle of the room, not remembering when it sprang up, wondering if it is a little bigger now than the last time he noticed it. His scythe hangs in the corner, streaked pale with the sticky fluid of a thousand cut stems, dried now into stains, its blade dotted with pollen like the night's stars.

'Will you hush?' he says, squinting at the wood that covers the window, and leaning into it, demonstrating that he is busy with watching. 'The Gaels will hear us.'

Aethelburga falls silent; the children too, but for some reason she is the only one he can see; the children are a blur in his vision.

'They are about,' he slurs. 'Creeping about; the little fools. I did see them slink through the street early this morning, before even the birds awoke. How am I to protect you with such noise? You draw them to us, and they are coming.'

He looks about himself, forgetting what he was to be about; and then sees the scythe again. He goes to raise himself from his stool, but the heaviness in his legs is a paralysis somewhere beyond drunkenness, and he slouches back, staring up at the scythe. He reaches to grab it, but it is much too far away. The seedling may live a few moments yet, he thinks.

The last time he used the scythe was twenty days ago, perhaps longer, he doesn't know. Everything is dark in this house, and any natural division between the days has dissolved.

He had been out by Moynagh lake with the men, stripped down to the waist, trying to salvage what was already unsalvageable. The heat was enormous, in its tenth day, unseasonable for any May. Glynis's hands were covered in blood, his cuts laced with sweat. The grass beneath him was crisp and foul-smelling, and it crackled when stepped upon. It hadn't rained for a month. The hedged field in which they worked opened onto a forest, and from above, it would be as though one of its ends was infected by an incursion of hardwoods; that is where he scythed, on his own, on the outer edge of the other gatherers, anticipating the shade that would swing towards him in a few hours.

All the men of Nobber, about forty or so, were out cutting and gathering grain, the vast majority of which was for the bishop. All were hurried and full of fluster, and still the work was slower than usual. They seemed sullen that day. There was no singing; no one had raised a head since dawn.

Around midday, as the heat became heavy, a low humming sound came up out of the ground, and Glynis looked around himself. The townsmen were far apart from him, slowly moving away, bent over beneath the sun as though in some mobile and communal worship. To the other side was the forest, from which, like shadows hardening in light, four men appeared, all naked, all with sheep skulls tied to their heads, walking towards him. They were not walking together, but seemed to be appearing from different sides of the forest, pulled together by some attracting force, all about to converge on Nobber.

The skulls they wore were greenish with age, some partly covered in moss and more likely reclaimed from nature than slaughter. Even the skinny men themselves had a greenish hue from the light that bore down through the foliage, the green light doubly reflected off the forest floor through which they waded. The skulls were set crookedly upon their heads, missing the lower jaws; packed rows of square teeth, each the length of half a finger, clamped tightly downwards, as though the dead sheep were eating the men's foreheads – and the two sharp ends of the skull, all that remains once the nose cartilage disintegrates, were pointing towards Glynis, and he wondered how such a soft and idiotic animal could have so much sharpness hidden within it and how such enormous black holes could contain such little eyes. Glynis lowered his scythe; kept it loose in his hands, and watched them for another moment to see if he could foretell their intentions. They were humming, chanting something unknown and dissonant.

As they came closer he saw that all of them were dripping. Each new step would loosen drops that would splatter on the ferns below them; small, accidental sounds against softness. At first he thought they were all pissing as they walked, and then he noticed the man nearest him bore a thin switch, which he used every few steps to flick his own balls. The man's crotch was a mess of flayed pulp, raw and dripping blood, like poorly cut meat hanging off a slaughtered beast. The misshapen genitals had swollen to almost tumescent proportions, and seemed to be only dangling from his body by a thin sliver of purple flesh. They were not humming, Glynis realised, they were moaning.

'Stand back,' he said.

The four men stopped, the only sound amongst them all the intermittent dripping of blood. The man who was closest to Glynis, whose skull he saw was upside down on his head, looked at him for a moment, and then, as though in protest, flicked the switch against his own testicles again. A hiss escaped from the man's lips.

'No,' Glynis said. 'I have many men with me.'

The man turned round silently, and retreated back into the darkness of the woods, the others following after.

When they had disappeared, Glynis stared at all his neighbours still working in the devastated beauty of the day, waiting for his breathing to calm. Beyond them was the sparkling of the lake's water, dancing white. A swallow darted by him at elbow height, and he saw in the field four or five more swallows flying low over the wheat, weaving amongst the workers faster than the eye could follow as though they were all playing together. A calf lowed, edging towards the water, its front hooves sinking in mud, its eyes wide in fear. It plunged into the lake with an enormous splash, and someone cheered. Glynis put his scythe on his shoulder and began to walk home.

A little along the way, as he was climbing over a stile, someone touched his shoulder; he turned round and saw Joseph Toqville.

'You do not feel well?' Joseph asked him.

Joseph was daubing his own forehead with a dock leaf, his bare chest glimmering with salt. Glynis squinted up at him. It was just like Joseph, he thought, to supply him with the most generous excuse to save him from his own disgrace.

'I do not.'

'You know it will not be well thought of for you to leave so early,' Joseph said.

Behind Joseph, all the men Glynis had known his whole life were working, and from this distance, they seemed inconsequential, already dead.

'I will tell them that the sun has laid low your head,' Joseph said. 'Your hair is thin, so there will be no shame in it.'

'I do not care what you tell those toiling corpses,' he replied.

'You may tell them the sickness has returned, if it serves any purpose to know such a thing.'

He went home, ignored his wife's cries of outrage at his laziness and sat on the stool. He said nothing to anyone; spent his days looking out the window, drinking from his jug of warm ale.

Several days after that, still at the window, he saw, or rather made out, because he was almost blind with drink by then, two of the infected stumbling into town. They had come all the way from Kells. Within moments all doors had been closed and the infected, two tradesmen, wandered alone about the street, screaming for food.

'I cannot stand that noise,' Aethelburga had said. 'Throw them something.'

Glynis placed his finger over his lips, and looked back out the window. After almost an hour of this terrible noise, Eoin Preston emerged from his house holding a long oak limb. He ran over and hit the nearest one on the back of the head with it, and then, just as quickly, he ran back to the far side of the street, pressing himself against the wall of a house. The infected he had hit, an elderly man wearing a mason's apron, had fallen forward onto his hands and begun gurgling, and the other infected, seeing his fellow go down, limped hurriedly out of town, not looking back.

After some time, the old man sat up on his knees and Glynis saw that one of his eyes had come out of its socket and was hanging over his cheek bone. Glynis burst into loud laughter at the sight of this and the old man turned his head in a blind confusion to see where the noise was coming from.

'What is it?' Aethelburga had asked.

'Hush now, I tell thee,' Glynis said.

The old man began crawling to the fountain to wash his face, or to take a drink perhaps, but he collapsed on his front, and soon there was just the sound of his wordless moaning. Eoin Preston, terrified, still hadn't moved from where he stood pressed against the wall of a house.

Another door opened across the street and Joseph appeared, striding not towards the infected man, but towards Eoin Preston.

'You may finish killing a thing begun,' Joseph shouted at him.

The two youths faced each other, Joseph the taller; and they stared each other down for a moment.

'I have done a service,' Eoin said.

'This is your service?' Joseph said.

'We must stop the sickness.'

The old man was moving towards the fountain again, only using one leg and one arm to drag himself forward. Eoin hesitated for a moment, looked around, but did not let his gaze settle on the crawling man.

'The water,' Eoin had said. 'It will be infected.'

'You are a dog of a man,' Joseph eventually said, seeing his inaction.

He took the oak limb from Eoin's hands, and spat on the ground. Then the infected man, his arm having somehow come in contact with his own eye as he crawled, let out a high-pitched peal of panicked screaming. This renewed Glynis's laughter, and he laughed so hard he spilled his jug of ale over his lap. When he looked up from his lap, he saw Joseph, the gentlest creature the town had ever produced, bringing down the end of the oak limb on the infected man's head. There was a brief clicking sound, the man's feet trembled, and then all movement stopped. Glynis laughed again, drooling ale from his lips.

'What is happening?' Aethelburga said, holding their two children under her arms.

'The Gaels are coming,' Glynis said, teasing her.

After that the people began to die and others set fires around the street, but Glynis no longer remembered anything; still, he felt fine. One night there was a ruckus, and much yelling, and everyone was out of their houses except for him; and then the next day, Glynis was looking out his window and saw a man with a black face looking back at him, grinning widely, and he noticed the man had been speaking for some time.

'It will keep the sickness segmented,' the man had said.

'Colca?' Glynis asked.

'I am Colca,' the man said.

'And how are you keeping in this warm weather?' Glynis said.

'It is for your own health,' Colca continued. 'We must keep to our houses.'

'I remember when your skin was white,' Glynis laughed, 'and you, this tall.'

He put his hand out to demonstrate Colca's former height, and nearly fell off his stool, which set him laughing again.

'We are under curfew,' Colca said, placing a nail behind his ear and lifting a plank of wood over the window. 'Do not come out that door, or I will do what I must. There is no choice.'

The house then turned dark, and there was the sound of nails being driven into the frames. Everything shook and Glynis sneezed at all the dust that had been loosed.

'Fine by me,' Glynis had said.

And it was, because by then he could hardly see anything so having the window boarded made no difference, and he is still staring out of where it used to give onto the town. He has some ale left in the barrel, but his wife Aethelburga annoys him. She refuses to acknowledge the sickness; says it does not exist, that Colca made it up to control them so he could give free rein to his perversions.

'Your brain cannot take all the reality pouring into it,' he says, looking at her. 'You prefer it in a more diluted form.'

'What?' Aethelburga asks.

She is standing above him now, and he sees her face is like rotten fruit.

'Have you been listening to me?' she asks.

He thought it the shade, but half of her face is pulped with a green bruise. It has closed over one of her eyes, plumping up the eyelid.

'What happened to your face?'

She doesn't say anything.

'This ale tastes awful,' he says.

'You mistook the barrel for the pan yesterday and pissed in it,' she says, 'and yet you haven't stopped drinking for a moment. You have grown worse than the animals. You must stop this.'

Glynis laughs at this, and then she is speaking again, but everything is dark and her speaking is so soft it is lulling him to sleep.

'I said Eilís is sick.'

He thinks for a moment, but nothing comes to him.

'Who is Eilís?' he says.

And then his wife has run to the other side of the room. She is holding the children, hiding them from him, and he wonders how women can always be this way, so incessant and afraid. Perhaps she is still angry at him that he hasn't cut down that ash seedling, and then he remembers.

'Eilís is my eldest daughter,' he says.

He chuckles a little, and leans his head against the cool wall; it was just a momentary lapse of forgetting. It is funny because his greatest fear was always losing his memory like his mother had. In the end she couldn't recognise her own family, and now it is happening to him and it is not so bad. I have even forgotten my fear of forgetting, he thinks. What strange blessings drink gives you, and women cry all the time. I have not done too bad a thing, and, besides, it was brought on by the ale. He remembers that he had begun drinking not only so he could feel lighter and more amused, but so he would not have to continue, while at the same time becoming impervious to the consequent guilt of not having to continue.

'Why should I have to invent solutions, where there are none?' he calls to Aethelburga. 'Why should I comfort where there is only nonsense? There remains the sickness; and there is no thinking around it or through it. It is either survived, or it is not.'

Whatever insight glided over him has left, and he forgets the gist of what he was trying to say. The house is completely silent, more so than he can ever remember it being; and his vision is not blurred any more, but it is short and narrow, requiring concentration. This is a dark house. He sways slightly.

'Did you ever consider,' he says, 'even for one moment, that there were perhaps no justifications left to not be drunk?'

She does not reply, and he realises that until the ash seedling is cut down nothing will be right between them. He looks up at the scythe, and sees it is covered in dark fluids, blood, a flap of jagged skin and some strands of golden hair, and it comes to him why the house is so quiet. Perhaps, he thinks, it has been days since she told him Eilís was sick.

'Will you not answer me?' he asks.

Someone knocks on the door a few times, and he looks towards the ash seedling. It has definitely grown a little since he last looked at it, and maybe it is too pretty a thing to cut down. It is so funny the things you notice when you are drunk, he thinks, like how the hairs move ever so slightly on the backs of his arms, how the crows were silent this morning; you can even see a tree growing upwards if you concentrate hard enough. He leans against the wall, and lets his weight go so he collapses off his stool, and he begins crawling towards the scythe, but all his movements seem so slow and the ground is too close to his nose.

'A moment,' he calls to the person who is knocking, 'just a moment.'

When he reaches the scythe, he pulls it down from where he is sitting on the floor. He hears his babies crying, and looks around, but his vision is gone again and nausea is rising in his throat, making it difficult to breathe. The blade is not covered in blood. He runs his fingers against it, feeling nothing;

perhaps he imagined it all, but what is sad is that it makes no difference any more.

Even if they are here I am alone; that is the summation of every life. There is nothing behind this alcohol inside me; nothing left of me. Once it evaporates I will disappear. He finds this funny; laughs again, rocking back and forth, the scythe lying ready across his lap.

'Come in,' he shouts to whoever is knocking at the door. 'Come in while I still have something left to give you.'

Raghnailt is resisting the urge to run her fingers through her daughter-in-law's hair; she would not wake her. Alannah, a Gael and a very little person, seems peaceful, her broad face unguarded and delicate in sleep. Raghnailt gets pleasure enough from just looking at her. Having given birth to four stillborn daughters, and having destroyed her own life by allowing herself to feel responsible for each one of their deaths, Raghnailt has always craved the presence and love of a younger woman; and two years ago, at the age of fifty, she finally received it. Alannah's marriage into the family may not have had the intended effect upon Colca, and it has surely been a catastrophe for Alannah, but it has brought love into Raghnailt's life, and that long after she had given up any hope of it.

Mary, the intruder amongst them, is also asleep once more, still holding her jug of cider between her arms. She looks like a child, and Raghnailt hates to see her there. She always faces away from her.

'It is hot already,' Alannah says, later, from the bed. 'Usually, the crows awaken me when the morning is up. They are the earliest risers, but there were no crows at all this morning.'

'Since Concessa ate the cockerel,' Raghnailt says, 'yes, I suppose they are the earliest risers.'

'It must be near midday. It will be hot for some time.'

'We are approaching it, but how did you sleep at all?' Raghnailt asks. 'I am hot all the time. I cannot stand it, but perhaps it is just the age I am at. I cannot breathe any more without an open door.'

'Did Mary attempt a strangulation again?'

'She did.'

'I heard it, but with my eyes still closed my dreams improvised upon the reality of the moment.'

Raghnailt does not want to talk about the morning's events, about the lives the sickness has claimed, about the men who surround them; she only wants to speak with her Alannah, as though they were alone together.

'Tell me of your dream,' she says.

'I dreamt it would be hot forever,' Alannah muses, 'but that is just a sensation of hell and I do not believe in that place.'

'How can you not believe in it?' Raghnailt says.

'Because Father Unction told me hell is just heat, and on asking him to what this heat compared he told me it was like an Andalusian heat, but I am kin to a man who once travelled to that Islamic place, and, on returning, he said heat was a very pleasant sensation when you are near the ocean's breeze. It is only in this part of the world the heat gives you a headache because there is so much wetness in the ground that when the sun comes it turns the air into a stew.'

'There is no ocean breeze in hell.'

'Well, then you would have me believe that there is no ocean there,' Alannah replies, 'and if there is no ocean, then there are no rivers to flow into it, and if there are no rivers you would die of thirst there, and if you die in hell surely you go to some other place.'

'That is too Gaelic a way of thinking for me, so let sit that matter,' Raghnailt says. 'Just continue your dream talking.'

'This sensation of heat was the end of the dream. It came to me after I was killed in childbirth by a bleeding that could not be staunched. The child who came out of me was a blond girl, her neck wrapped in the noose made of its own umbilical cord, and it dangled out of me, scared of the world it had found itself in, and though I could see, I was dead, too, and could not disentangle the child, so it died.'

'What does it mean?'

'It has no meaning,' she replies. 'It is just the expression of any woman's fear. Say me your dream.'

Raghnailt tells her about the eye, and Alannah is silent for a while.

'It means,' she says, eventually, 'that if I bear a child it will have Colca's properties, but you didn't need a dream to tell you that, no?'

Raghnailt is silent, staring at the jugs of powder on the floor, Colca's tools in the corner, and wonders at how so many unwanted secrets have accumulated around her little family.

'Do you suffer?' Alannah asks.

'I did not wake well. The day has already been too much for me, though it has just begun. Another Colca cannot be heaped on the next generation of Nobberians, or the town itself will surely die.'

Alannah, her face still soft with the sleep it has recently abandoned, sits up and stretches out her body. She goes to the door the men have left open behind them, looking out at the day.

Her husband is dragging corpses by the legs from his forge to the abandoned monastery, where he conceals them beneath the thick tangles of ivy the centuries have bequeathed upon the crumbling structure. He resembles some scavenger of carrion with his black face. His wide movements and darting eyes are shy in an animalistic fashion, full of a constant fear that has been bred out of a lifetime's worth of hiding.

'I do know it,' she says.

'When that man took over the town,' Raghnailt says, 'I was almost happy, for I believed his evil was so great it would eclipse our family's disgrace, like brighter stars blotting out lesser ones, but their evils have only complemented one another. He colluded so quickly with the outsider.'

'You shouldn't be afraid,' Alannah says. 'He has not had me since our wedding, and he did not perform well on that night. Your line will die out.'

'That is also sad,' Raghnailt says.

'Your line has done much great hurt to its own town.'

'We were very upstanding once in our community,' Raghnailt says.

'As was I,' Alannah replies.

Raghnailt cannot give answer to this, and Alannah's thoughts are elsewhere. Having finished disposing of the bodies, her husband is now standing tall, caressing Emota in the distance, giving her kisses all along her long neck.

The perpetual curfew on the town has made Colca brazen. There has been much superfluous carnage and reordering, and Colca, always quiet and slinking, has now been unnaturally writ large on the town, and it has allowed him to become more like himself. If he had acted in this manner on the street even a month ago, Alannah thinks, his neighbours would have killed him before they could tie the knot to hang him. Now he is almost Nobber's ruler.

'Do not fret over your dreams,' Alannah says. 'Perhaps superior beings like Gaels have dreams in which the unfolding of the universe is inscribed, but there is no meaning in your dreams. They are just the errata of a life, and life is strewn with symbols that do not chime with anything.'

A dank breeze roams the room behind Alannah, and sets off a small motion near her that catches her attention. She looks to this disturbance, and sees a crow's feather has been stuck to the outside of the door, the breeze making it flicker like candlelight. The feather is at her eye-level, where only one as small as herself would be likely to notice it. She peels it away and holds it between her thumb and finger. It is dishevelled, stuck to the door with saliva.

It could be an accident, she thinks, one of those meaningless things.

And then, outside, Colca begins to trot out of town, across the dirt until he is out on the grass, and he keeps going. Alannah watches him until he is out of sight, then turns back to Raghnailt.

'Let us free Mary now,' she says. 'Your son is temporarily away and I cannot see the other man.'

Raghnailt is quiet for a moment, her head down.

'No? Do you not love her?' Alannah asks. 'You have said many times you wanted her free.'

'I do not love chains on anyone,' Raghnailt says, 'but Mary is dangerous; and after this morning . . .'

She trails off.

'If let go she is as like to cut our throats as to kiss our cheeks.'

'Let us ask her, so,' Alannah says.

'But there is no use in it; you cannot get any truth off such a person.'

Alannah ignores this, touches Mary's shoulder. The girl opens her eyes, but doesn't move.

'More cider,' she says.

'No,' Raghnailt interjects. 'You have had enough to kill a horse.'

Mary pulls herself upright and begins drinking from her jug.

'Would you kill us if I let you go?' Alannah asks the girl.

Mary, her face deep in her jug, does not respond.

'If I was sure you would not, I would free you, but I do not believe you would not,' Alannah says. 'Tell me this, do you love your man, or do you hate him?'

'I hate him,' Mary says. 'He did terrible things to my daughter, used her, and she not of age.'

'Silly woman, you lie so much. You have no children,' Alannah says. 'You love your man, tell the truth. He gives you a sort of pleasure.'

'No, I hate him,' Mary says, shaking her head. 'I will cut his throat till it is a smiling thing.'

'You will indeed have to kill him to be free of your love for him, I feel.'

'Desist,' Raghnailt says. 'I cannot stand the violence of this talk. What are you putting in her head, Alannah? What secret plotting are you at? You fill this room with cruelty when the land is full enough of it already. Free her if you will free her, but do not draw out the act. You are a cat with a sparrow.'

'If I free you would you run?' Alannah asks, ignoring Raghnailt again. 'Or would you sit here, waiting like a bitch for its master?'

'I would run,' Mary says. 'I swear it.'

'You would not make it far before Colca stopped you. He moves so fast,' Alannah says. 'You would have to take Emota. They would be after you quick.'

'Stop this at once,' Raghnailt says. 'If she takes Emota, Colca will hurt her.'

'And if she doesn't, she will be caught again,' Alannah answers.

Raghnailt hears footsteps outside. She takes hurriedly to her bed, throwing the sheepskin over herself and turning on her side. Colca appears in the doorway, blocking out most of its light. He stands there, hunched over with breathlessness, his hands on his knees.

'Well,' he eventually says. 'I heard ye talking. Do not pretend silence with me. Are my own mother and wife so afraid of me that they cannot even look at me?'

None of the women respond; the only sound is Mary's drinking. Colca looks around the room, shakes his head.

'Never mind,' he says, 'there is trouble coming. You must all stay indoors today. It would seem that the Gaels have marked the town. They will come for us. Today is that day.'

'What has happened?' Alannah asks.

'There is something outside the town, some structure, I think. I do not know what it is, for I've never seen its like.'

'What nonsense,' Raghnailt says. 'No matter how much

fear that new man may stir up, and no matter how much rumour is prattled in Kells, it will not undo the matter that the Gaels have not attacked us since Alannah arrived. Even before that we always had good relationships with them. No one at all is in their right minds today. I will not stay a-bed for this foolishness. Not again, it is too much.'

'Things are not how they were, Mother,' Colca says. 'How do you not understand that?'

'Is this structure in the shape of Jesus' death?' Alannah asks, hiding the crow's feather behind her back.

Colca cocks his head at her, regarding her with suspicion.

'No, it is more crooked than that,' he says, 'but how did you guess so closely?'

Alannah shrugs, and Raghnailt is surprised, feels uneasy.

'Do you know something?' Raghnailt asks.

'I have been by your side in this room these last six days,' Alannah protests.

'This is true,' Raghnailt says.

Colca brings himself up to his true height and puts his hands on his hips. 'Stay indoors, I tell thee,' he says. 'And you, Mother, stay in bed.'

Raghnailt throws the sheepskin off and faces him. 'Am I not allowed to move around the place?' she says. 'Must I spend my last years in bed when I should be caring for the sick around me? They are our kin, too, if you have forgotten?'

'You will visit no one and you will do nothing,' Colca says. 'Gaels coming in from the south and an infectious sickness bred off sweat, and my own mother would go about gallivanting. You would have me in a place where I would have to kill my own mother out of mercy to save her the pains of that death. That is not motherly, that is not good. Will you think for even a moment of what you are saying?'

'But I am not the sweating kind,' she says. 'If I have not it yet, I will not have it at all.'

'How many have said that and died?' he says, throwing his arms in the air. 'Do not rise from the bed. I plead you. Do not drag me through that sadness. What I do I do out of love for you.'

Alannah lets out a brief laugh.

'What?' Colca says.

'You stand in the doorway, naked as a spawn,' she says, 'like you are somehow proud of yourself, like you are somehow a man, and so I laugh. What you do you do not do for the love of your mother, and you do not do for the love of me; you do it for the love of a mare.'

Colca hammers the door with his fist once, letting out a shout of anger.

'Why are unreasonable bitches always nagging at me?' he yells. 'I need not listen to this. I have work to do for I am the man of this house, the last man of this town. Do your duty towards me, and stay here, as quiet as is becoming of decent women.'

He leaves, pulling the door closed behind him, and after a moment of silence Alannah says, 'You know he will not change. He cannot love; it is not in him. I was married to a violent brute, and there is no corrective for what already is.'

Alannah watches as Raghnailt's shoulders begin to heave up and down. A great panic has overtaken her chest, and her breathing is all awry. This panic had simmered all morning inside her gut and has now been loosened by the mention of her son's perversions. Perhaps, Raghnailt thinks, Alannah has only done this to taunt me, to impress upon me the sick reality I would rather ignore. She puts her head in her hands.

'Free the girl,' Raghnailt says, and her voice is muffled.

'Are you certain of this?' Alannah asks.

'Once I would not have had the strength to displease my boy,' Raghnailt says, 'but he has grown so violent and self-serving of late, and he indulges his sickness so openly, that I do not care any more.'

'He may use us badly,' Alannah says.

'Just free the girl,' she says. 'I would flee this place too if my legs could take it, but I fear now it is my heart that could not.'

Alannah takes the keys from where they lie in the corner, goes over to Mary, puts the crow's feather between her teeth and unlocks the chains.

'Run,' she says, patting the girl on the shoulder.

Mary gets up, stumbles over to the corner where the tools are, in great disarray, kept. She takes a cleaver and approaches Raghnailt. For a moment, Alannah is still with fear, her breath drawn; certain that this mad woman is about to slaughter her mother-in-law. Instead, Mary curtsies, picks up the cider.

'Thank you for all the drink, Mother Raghnailt.'

The girl leaves, sipping from the jug, the cleaver over her shoulder. The remaining women stare at the open door.

'Perhaps,' Alannah says, 'we have made a mistake.'

A sense of acceptance pours over Raghnailt, but still her breathing is too quick and she can feel her own heart knocking at her throat.

'I do not care any more.'

Mary is staggering down the street now, flailing around. She has nowhere to go, but still she moves forward. The sun, high, throws no shadow below her, and Raghnailt can see that she is moving towards the fountain.

'Things will get better now that woman is gone,' Raghnailt says.

'You do not believe that,' Alannah says, 'even in yourself you do not.'

The room feels empty and peaceful with only two people in it. Raghnailt reaches out to take Alannah's hand, desperate for some comfort, but Alannah does not see it. She leans out the door, her eyes searching the horizon.

'It is coming,' she says. 'It's almost here.'

Maybe it is not menacing, William thinks. Maybe it just is. It looms, though, and not many things can affect such a stance as that. It has not moved a mite since they first saw it. As they draw closer to the figure, Harold says, 'It is so oddly shaped I would believe it to be a drowned man hung out to dry. Drowned men do double their weight, filling like bladders or stomachs, and can sometimes reach unimaginable proportion if they have too long been submerged in liquids.'

'Well, then what of its blackness?' William asks. 'There are no black men in the world.'

'Blackened by pitch,' de Flunkl replies confidently. 'I would say it was a robber, or a man-witch, who was boiled before he was drowned to ensure he had the properties of a human. Skin does crackle and blacken when heat is put on it through water.'

Saint John falls to his knees. Harold goes behind the boy and hauls him up by the arms.

'Or give my prognostications some weight,' Harold says, 'and say it is what it most looks like, which is the state in which most things find themselves.'

The closer they get to the thing, the more apprehensive William becomes. His heart is knocking against his throat, making him feel nauseous.

'What state?' de Flunkl asks, his voice hurried. 'Your words are foolish.'

'The common state of the world is that things are most likely to be what they most look like,' Harold says, dragging the boy forward, 'and this does look like a Nobberian demon that will confiscate our souls on entry to the town, so one could surmise it is most likely to be that very thing.'

De Flunkl pauses his steps.

'You look like a coward,' Harold says behind him, 'and you are one. You see? It is a simple thing. My point, having weight and sense, has been immediately proven.'

'There is no such thing as demons, though some people would have me believe it,' William says, shaking his head. 'Not on this land in any case, though I dare not speak of their applicability to the next world. Let us not lose our good faculties. This is not beyond the realms of normality, and will be explicated summarily on closer inspection, and, to my mind, this ill and twisted shape will most likely be the given form of that result of frequent violence that is proper to man.'

Unawares, William realises that they have all stopped walking, and are standing still looking at the shadowy figure.

'Your certitude is so lofty that I say you should be the man to approach it,' de Flunkl says.

William licks away the dryness of his cracked lips, and stares at the boy for a moment, tired and unmoving.

'No, I will do it,' Harold says, dropping the banner and letting Saint John's hand go.

He strides towards the figure, his hands up in a show of surrender. The sun is in front of him so the form of the sentry does not become apparent until he is very close to it. On seeing it, he motions the other men forward.

'What is it?' de Flunkl calls.

Harold glances at the thing again. 'I cannot say,' he shouts back.

They approach and see Harold is standing below a cruciform of wood, nailed together into the shape of a man, but on it, thickly laid like a skeleton's musculature, are reams of dead crows, and they give the form a certain plumpness and lifelikeness from a distance. The dead crows are strung together with thin sprigs, or nailed into the wood at the outer extremities. Their stony beaks poke out at strange angles like mussels sucking at rocks by the sea. Their eyes are uniformly closed. It is a monstrous, feathery thing, standing two heads taller than a big man. Atop this strange structure, encircling three crows' bodies, sits a peasant's cap.

'Have you ever in all your days seen the likes?' Harold says, his voice full of wonder.

'What could it be?' de Flunkl asks.

The thing is deeply weird, William thinks, and with its mixture of man and animal, should not belong to this crossing between a civilised town and the great monotony of nature. It is an obscuring veil between two different places, he feels, though he knows the thought to be nonsensical. His breath quickens and, in the corner of his eye, he sees a crow arc in the sky above them, into his vision and out of it again.

'Whatever power this crow-man has,' William says, 'though I would maintain it has none, it achieves it through its unknowability and its senselessness. It has been placed here to confuse uncivilised men, I feel, who do spend too much time thinking of ancient taboos and unseen forces. Perhaps a Gael has done it, it is in their style.'

'I do not know what it intends to portray,' Harold says, gazing up at it, 'but whatever it is that it does portray, it portrays it very mightily. It does not fit into anything, though it does at the same time seem to remind me of everything.'

Harold's simple, childlike curiosity gives William confidence, and he begins to set his thoughts in order.

'I am sure it is some confused appellation of the very word scarecrow,' William says. 'Some fool heard the word, and being struck by how it is compounded together believed it was a thing meant to scare, but also a thing of crows and, having too much time, as all fools do, set about fixing it together, and produced this remarkable oddity that he was somehow so proud of he placed it at the entryway of the town where it could not be avoided.'

Harold looks at William, raising his eyebrows. 'There is no peasant on this land,' Harold says, 'who does not know the proper construction of a scarecrow.'

'You do not know that. Some peasants have not travelled,' William protests. 'Most have never even travelled to the towns that are their neighbours. Some have never even gone beyond their masters' own fields for fear of being killed. Besides, I said I think it Gaelic.'

Harold shakes his head. 'You are looking for too much order in the universe,' he says. 'It is a mistake. You are looking to ease your mind by creating fanciful tales that you believe to be less fanciful than what the world has chosen to put blatantly before you. If you were honest, you would recognise your own sensible explanations are just as fanciful.'

The crow that was hovering above them lands on the arm of the structure, staring at the men out of the side of its head.

'I know peasants,' Harold says, 'and a peasant can make a scarecrow with two fingers in less than half a day. Give them three pieces of straw and a twig and they have it done if they want it. This is not that.'

He points at the dark structure, like a heap of twisted nightmares, and sees that the landed crow is pecking at the flesh of one of its dead brothers.

'I said it was not that,' William says.

'I believe we should turn back,' Harold says. 'A crow preying on its own kin is a murderous sign.'

'Ha,' de Flunkl says, pointing at Harold, delighted to have caught him out. 'It is you who is the coward.'

'I am no coward,' Harold says. 'I merely respect what I do not understand, that which is set before me. I will go on if you all go on, but I have told you how I feel.'

There is a ruffle from the chest of the tall crow-man, and then a flurry of unexpected movement like the heart of this thing is about to explode, causing the feasting crow to alight, and all the men, saving Saint John who stares on dumbly, leap backwards in shock.

'It is alive,' de Flunkl shrieks.

A crow is moving a single wing amidst the structure. It does not comprehend it is tied down, and weakly flaps its wing as though it were the structure's arrhythmic heartbeat. This crow opens its eyes, and for some reason, the green glare of its irises is so strange amongst the panoply of tightly packed black feathers that William audibly retches.

'Move on,' de Flunkl is yelling hysterically. 'Into the town. We must go on.'

They begin walking, William leading the horses, Harold dragging Saint John and the sack, the banner left behind, and de Flunkl trotting ahead. Before they have passed the crow-man many more wings begin flapping. Tiny, green eyes open, one after another, in no sensible sequence. They have awoken, and it is as though the structure itself is trying to take lopsided flight. It has become a buzzing, blurred thing. Many crows the retinue believed to be dead were asleep. Tied to their dead brothers, the living crows are in a mutually enforced panic so great that they have created a new being unified not in motion but in fear.

'Run,' de Flunkl shouts, breaking ahead.

'Why?' Harold calls after him. 'There is no rush. As I understand it, once you arrive in hell, you may dally there a while.'

In his scrambling, de Flunkl trips over, but the crows' squawking is so enormous that it drowns out Harold's laughter.

Too many lunatic summers, dull and sluggish, drag the sense out of a hot skull. She looks around, remembering vaguely where she is. This place, Nobber, like any object, has been worn down by too frequent a use. It has lost its ambience, its texture smoothed to nothing. Too much familiarity has made it insensible, drained it of meaning. Every footstep is a sign, but there is no one left around her who makes these marks. Her shadow is another self that walks ahead of her, but sometimes it stalks her, wishes her harm. It is nothing now; the sun is too high, and she is unfamiliar with so much light. Every door is a new history. New rooms are new consciousnesses; thresholds of the self, created in the crossing. Other bodies, multitudinous and full of breath, are portals to keen pain and oceanic pleasure. The world, at every moment, is renewed, and it is shocking, and it is cruel. A vague pressure mounts behind her forehead, making her dissonant and jarred. The sickness is like this pain, not an immediate reckoning, rather a slow attenuation that unravels into a lazy catastrophe. The persistent throbbing emerges from behind her eyes and creates a swirl in the centre of her vision, a little blur whose borders are the clarity of life. She grits her teeth, and to escape the constant pain in her, invents herself. Mary will become a new person, one who does not suffer, and there will be no meaning behind her transformation but the pain it conceals.

'It has never been so bright in my lifetime,' she says aloud. 'I am covered in filth. I have never seen how dirty I was.'

She takes a few steps and some muscle in her knee spasms. She awoke drunk, she thinks, but perhaps I have been drunk for years. She sips at the cider as she moves. Behind her the little Gael is hurrying her on, calling after her. A chestnut mare ahead of her, unsteady on its feet, sidesteps.

'I will ride you to Moynagh lake,' she says to it. 'To any lake, it does not matter. I must wash myself.'

The mare watches her out of the black rectangle embedded within its eyes, shuffling its hooves. Its nostrils quiver like slowly blinking eyes. She wants to lean below its nose and feel its moist breath on the back of her neck, but the horse can smell the drunkenness off this woman; it angles away.

'You will not protect me?' Mary says to it.

Colca comes out of a dark doorway. Naked as he is, it seems as though the house is giving birth to him.

'What are you doing?' he yells. 'How are you free, my God?'

She laughs at this, and drinks more cider. A single, small cloud is above her head, so low she feels like she could touch it if she reached out her fingers to it. The cloud is thin, ragged, like it has been torn apart by the sun's fingers; a mere tendril in her vision, blurred by the blank in her eye.

'Are you in love with this mare?'

She looks to Colca, and he doesn't answer. Over his shoulder, she can see the man's head peering at her, and in her vision it is like Colca has two heads.

'This is a very quiet town,' she remarks. 'You have made this a very quiet town, you two. I will not have it.'

'My love,' the man calls. 'Put down the cleaver.'

Mary takes another drink.

'Once little children played in this street,' she says. 'They threw water from the fountain on one another, and danced amongst the old people who loved them, and you took it all away.'

There is a sucking rush above her head. Pigeons are circling the little cloud, unsure of where to land their unified body.

'I had a daughter once and you took her,' Mary shouts. 'Colca, do you love this horse? Do you love it?'

Colca does not say anything.

'Answer me on my daughter's life,' she says.

'You have no daughter,' the man growing out of Colca shouts. 'You never did. We have discussed this, many times we have discussed this. Would you put down the cleaver now, my love?'

'Do you love her, though?' Mary says. 'You two-headed man. Do you love her like I loved my own daughter?'

'I love her,' Colca says.

Mary puts the jug down and begins stroking Emota's haunches.

'And what of my love?'

She puts both her hands on the cleaver and drives it into the mare's guts below the ribcage. The mare shrieks and kicks, dragging the blade through itself. The motion hurls Mary down and the cleaver falls from her hand. From the mare's cavernous, open belly she feels a wave of clammy heat expelled onto her face, imbued with the thick stench of fresh excrement. The mare, snorting heavily, trots a few steps and a bright sliver of grey intestine emerges from the thin wound. The intestine is thick and glistening, curled in on itself; it has the slippery quality of fresh fish.

Mary crawls backwards out of the horse's way. She glances

to the side and sees the man stepping over Colca's prostrate, slouched form.

The man runs towards her, grabbing up the cleaver from the ground, and approaches the horse cautiously. The mare, in a frenzy, kicks at him, forcing him back. It kicks again, and its exertions force a long loop of intestines out of it, hanging so low they drag off the ground, picking up dust.

The man circles it carefully, cleaver held aloft, and then the horse sidesteps, and in this motion entangles a loop of its own intestines round its front fetlocks. It trips on its side, collapsing, raising a panoply of dust. The man leaps on the toppled beast straight away, hacking at its throat with long swings. The horse's whinnies grow weaker. An artery is severed, and a vermillion spray cascades from its neck, a single spurt whose film is so thin that, for a moment, rainbows flash within it.

The man stands over the dead horse, gulping in air.

'She was the only horse from here to Drogheda,' he says. 'And she was a good-tempered one. There is no way out of this damned town.'

Mary scrambles to her feet.

'If I am trapped here, so are thee,' she says.

She runs to the other side of the fountain, as though hiding from him. He knows he should restrain her, but he would not know what to do with her even if he could catch her.

'What happened to you?' he asks.

Mary looks at a bloomed waterlily in the fountain, and leans over, delicately removing the cloying creeping jenny that tries to strangle it.

'You never give me flowers any more,' she says. 'You never give me any favours. Do I not merit them, lover?'

This sudden softness in her brings quick tears to the man's throat.

She had never used to be this way. Once, when she was fourteen, she had kicked an elderly fruit vendor she thought had tried to cheat her out of some pears until that woman was unconscious, her stall overturned on top of her. He had thought it was just foul-temperedness; but then, a little over a year ago, her thoughts had become scattered. She began forgetting little things, inventing fanciful stories to explain her own lack of memory, but the stories became more absurd until she was trying to convince everybody she came across that he had abused some daughter she had never had.

Still, all this he could have put up with, if it weren't for her violence, and it is becoming more constant; but this is the first time she has been violent twice in one day.

'Where is that girl I fell in love with?' he asks. 'Where is my companion?'

She covers her lips with her forefinger, hushing him. 'Who is that knocking on my door?' she says.

She points to the sky, but the cloud that was previously above her head has crumbled under the heat and her fingers point at nothing.

'I don't understand,' the man says.

Mary looks up. The pigeons above are giving a warning with their patterns, she feels, or etching something impermanent into their wake, but where they wheel and shimmy there is no trace of where they have been, just a ceaseless passage of movement. She takes the jug of cider and sits in the shade of a doorway, her legs still in the light.

'Come in out of the heat,' the man says.

'Why are you not gentle with me?' she says. 'Amn't I only a little thing? Why are you always so mean to me?'

He lays the cleaver down beside the fountain, and moves towards her. There is nothing in him that can remain afraid of her.

'How did this horse come to die in so public a place?' she asks.

He stops. 'You do not remember?'

She shakes her head.

'It was you.'

'You will not put this death on me,' she says. 'I do not even ride.'

The myriad of pigeons has alighted somewhere unseen, as though scared. The whole world is still, the air hot and sticky with some unseen threat, and he turns away from her, unable to even look at her.

He washes his face in the fountain again, this time to cover his tears. The water is fetid; he douses his forehead and under his arms.

Whatever he loved in her, he realises, is gone; it will never be how it was. He should have given her to the nuns the first time she had said she had a daughter, but he had loved her then; had even loved that madness creeping into her. He loves her still, and there is no solution to love.

Once he has stopped crying he sits on the edge of the fountain with his head in his hands.

Perhaps Colca was right – or was it de Fonteroy who said it, he does not remember – but a man is not allowed even one vice. All the violence he has meted out, all the death and confusion he has brought on undeserving souls, and, still, he cannot bring himself to send her away, even to somewhere she would be safer and he could visit her from time to time. She is the mistake I continue to make, he thinks.

He remembers their first days together; she liked to sleep with her head on his belly, to walk her fingers across his legs when she woke; her sudden tantrums would make him laugh; there were long-delayed reconciliations where she would tantalise him with silences until she could no longer stand to go without talking to him. She used to call him Big Cat, lean on his arm when they walked together.

No, it is not urgent, he decides, shaking his head. It will come to a head naturally. There are more pressing matters at hand, and she may still recover some of her sense; even a little of it would be enough. If we both stopped drinking so much she would have more clarity and I would learn better how to manage her. A few more days cannot hurt; a little more time to spend with her; that's all I need, some fresh memories to hold her by once she is gone.

He calls out for Alannah. She soon appears at the end of the street, playing with a crow's feather in her hands, coming towards him. He notices that she does not even look towards the dead horse.

'Have you been crying?' she asks.

The man is speechless for a moment. 'You do not like my domination, do you?' he finally says. 'How easily I run the town; you cannot support it?'

'I do not mind it,' she says, glancing towards her prostrate husband, 'as well you as any other. Is Colca dead?'

The man shakes his head. 'You would make a nonchalant widow.'

'And, so,' Alannah asks, 'what do you want from me?'

'You have endangered my wife.'

'She says she is not your wife, and she is treated by you like a slave and a whore; that I have seen with my own eyes.'

He looks away from her; grips the sides of the fountain until his wish to strike her has subsided. 'You know nothing of us,' he says. 'What outcome do you seek?'

Alannah points behind him. He turns, and in the distance sees five men standing in a semi-circle, two horses behind them. Their outlines are vague, but he can see one man in front is unnaturally tall, like a giant, and he is black.

'These are not your men,' she says.

'On the contrary,' the man says, 'a horse is taken from me, and I receive two more.'

'You believe yourself the match for five Gaels?' Alannah says. 'You are not a match for a-one.'

'Why do you believe they are Gaels?' he asks. 'Is that why you have been making havoc? Gaels do not approach towns out in the open; they slink like rats, concealed. No, these are not Gaels; they even walk too much like men. Today, I shall make some money.'

'What name will you use?'

The man has had many names, and has always been able to discard them at will, moving as he does amongst so many illiterates. None of them have ever made any difference to him, though; never touched at his essence, and he has always felt like names are tricks people play on themselves to obscure their great sameness, a cheating way to distinguish between different nothings. The only name he ever had any fondness for, the only one he wished had stuck a little, was Mary's name for him; Big Cat, but that is a private name that would be muddied by use in anyone else's mouth, and she does not call him that any more. Perhaps she has forgotten it, he thinks.

'Ambrosio,' he says.

Alannah looks up at him, sees his red eyes, his nodding head. 'Whatever skill you had when you took over the town is gone,' she remarks. 'You have been crying like a woman, and are still drunk. There is nothing left in you.'

The retinue, still indistinct, are coming towards the town; the man gazes at them, wishing he could sit alone under some shady tree and drink until he went blind.

'If you saw me work,' the man says, 'you would see my talent; see how I talk around these men until they are so split amongst themselves that they all attend my leisure, each to their—'

He trails off, notices that only four men are running towards the town; they have left the tall dark man behind. He wonders at it.

'What is it?' Alannah says.

'Remove Colca while he is still fainted,' he says. 'Keep him under lock. Use the barrow beyond the monastery. I fear he will harm my woman, and I would not have it. Mary will be set up in my lodgings where I can watch her, and keep that cleaver away out of her reach.'

'And if I do not?'

The man rests his chin on his chest; lets his eyes close for a moment. He is so tired.

'Go against me ever again, Alannah,' he says, 'and I swear to God I'll dispatch you to hell. I swear it.'

Alannah smirks and curtseys, but he does not see it.

Approaching a thicket, Monsieur Hacquelebacq, who has – given certain recent tumultuous upheavals – lost his past in an artful manner, sees high above his head four geese flying in a ragged V. They glide far over his head, only occasionally flapping their wings, and then one, as though struck by an invisible impediment, spirals down in long, sloping spirals, each turn becoming smaller and less graceful. For a brief moment, its fast shadow blocks Hacquelebacq's light, and then it disappears beneath the distant treetops. He cups his ear, but still he does not hear the goose land.

The cool thicket invites him into it, but he fears that the thicket will turn into woods; and to be lost in any woods, no matter how little, is deadly. They are too similar and confused in themselves, the woods, like the stirred contents of a stomach, and they have a way of making you forget yourself. Though he wants to, he will not follow the goose's final trajectory.

He tautens the ropes of the animals he leads, renews his grip on his sack and skirts along the thicket's edge. As he proceeds a knocking sound becomes faintly perceptible and slows down his pace. One of the black-faced lambs behind him bleats noisily at this interruption. He drops his sack and raps the lamb between the eyes with two knuckles. The lamb falls to its front knees, shakes its head.

The knocking sound continues. Glancing at the woods to

his right, he decides that confronting whatever may be ahead is the lesser danger. The badger is gnawing at the knot on its noose. He kicks at it from a distance, not getting too close.

Whenever he stops for a brief rest the badger bites at the rope, and while he travels it drags its legs. It is very strong and wilful, and if it bites him in the night he will have to cut off its head to be free of its jaws. He caught it because he likes to possess things other men have not, but, still, it is more trouble than it is worth.

He has, so far, noosed two lambs, two calves and the badger. One of the calves he caught prancing by a lake this morning, and it is placid enough, easily led, though its eyes are distressed. Having lost its mother, the panic in it increases the further they get from the lake. And the badger, Monsieur Hacquelebacq reflects, is perhaps an addition too much to his little ark.

If animals are jumbled up too greatly in species, and confined too closely, disastrous things happen. Little confused microcosms set themselves up. Beasts, who should emerge into the synechdocal perfection of predator and prey, too closely combined begin to act in an erratic and unpredictable manner. Both of the lambs think one of the calves is its mother. One of the calves thinks Hacquelebacq is its mother, and the badger, who should prey on the lambs, instead wishes to prey on him. Noah's ark, he feels, succeeded through the perfection of separation, whereas he has just a misshapen, blended troupe. He has been too ambitious and coveted too much, but, still, he wishes to travel through these deserted lands accumulating more and more diverse creatures.

He has begun with animals, and he would have humans and money by nightfall. I have enough rope to noose an army, he thinks, and, for the wandering man, these are times of plenty, because there is, like some invisible web cast from the heavens, a reordering at play in this world; or, at the very least, general across this island on which he roams. Intransigent chaos has blurred man into animal, turned law into farce, shifted man into corpse, yoked child into slave, disposed of all previous hierarchies more ruthlessly and indiscriminately than any uprising has ever done, and, why, amidst so much confusion, carnage and distress, should a healthy, resourceful man like himself, who has always had so little of what he has craved, not become a little richer?

Curious, he leads the animals forward until he comes upon the source of the knocking, and is immediately overpowered by the strangeness of what he sees.

A woman, her dress stripped so its upper half hangs down over her waist, is struggling to cut down a dead, leafless ash tree with an axe that is too big for her. Her shoulders, ears and arms are soft pink with the foreshadowing of sunburn. It is as though a gentle dye has been poured on her from above, the pink diluting as it descends into the milky paleness of her lower back. She is shapely, and grunting with her efforts; he sees her only from behind. He watches, for some time, her back rippling, the generous deposits of fat around her hips shuddering with her motion. Her black locks are damp, stuck to her shoulders. Hacquelebacq's peeping is finally interrupted when one of the calves, the lonelier orphan, bawls, and it is a very melancholy sound altogether.

The woman turns round, lowers her axe and leans on it, puts her other arm against the tree. There is an imprint of blood around the axe handle from where her hands, freshly blistered, had gripped it.

'That looks like little Glynis's calf,' she calls.

He wonders which one she is referring to; they look the same to him.

'I assure madame it is not,' he says, wishing he had some still water in which to regard himself as the heat always makes his brilliant orange hair frizz and stick out like tangled brush.

'May I approach?'

'Whose calf is it, then?'

Her voice is hissing, expectorating and messy with each utterance.

'My own,' he says.

'And who are you?'

He licks his palm, and flattens out his mop, feeling a little handsome once he has done so.

'Perhaps its face looks similar to some other calf's,' he says.

'No, their faces are as distinct as humans, and more recognisable from afar, their eyes being more expressive than ours. Who are you, man?'

The pink of her wide nipples is faint amongst the lighter pink of her burn, but her breasts are too developed and heavy; repulsive to him as a ewe's udders.

'I sell hanging ropes, my fine lady,' he says. 'I was coming towards the town of Nobber to see if there are any tradesmen who would like a calf, or some rope perhaps. Some people use it for hanging, but it could also be used as a lever to bring down trees, I suppose. Children can swing out of it for amusement, too, if it is attached to the sturdier boughs, even using the same knot as hangmen use, which is the only knot I know of. The children find these things pleasant.'

The ash tree itself is some way off from the greater body

of the woods, as though, for its twisted deformity, it has been outcast from its brothers. Some of the bark has been flayed off it, but not much deeper damage has been done to it. The woman's axe has barely bitten it.

'Who are you?'

'I am Monsieur Hacquelebacq, and it is a great honour to meet such a comely sparrow, and so unexpectedly.'

'I wouldn't sell Glynis's calf in Nobber,' she says, 'or he'll have your throat test the strength of your ropes.'

Hacquelebacq finds this peasant far too confident; her uncouthness jars him. He looks away, sees the badger gnawing at the rope again. He tugs at it – he will not stay long.

'Is Nobber infected, madame?'

'Infected with the sickness, yes, and something else much more particular to itself as well,' she says, spluttering slightly. 'I am of Nobber, but have not been there for some time. Still, I have heard gossip that it was overcome, subdued by a sheriff or a monk. A mad and powerful man he must be for it is usually a rambunctious place, producing much noise, drunk-ards and ruckus, but has fallen quite quiet this last week. My cousin passed through it three days ago, walked clean down it in a straight line, and said there was no one in its street at all. Will you help me with this tree, man?'

Hacquelebacq steps forward, his animals trailing after him, and on coming closer sees that the woman has a wide cleft lip. He had thought her nose cast a shadow on her face, but it was not a trick of the light; it is her face. There is very little between her lip and her nose, only a gummy darkness. He stops quite suddenly.

'No,' he says. 'I will not.'

'Because it is a faerie tree? Do you know it? I did not think you from Meath. You do not speak after the Meath fashion.'

When this woman opens her mouth, it is as though she has a second smaller mouth hidden inside it. Hacquelebacq runs his tongue over his teeth, feels their firmness.

'A faerie tree?' he says. 'I thought only hawthorn made faerie trees. And this tree is already dead.'

Her face breaks in two, fractures and comes apart, and then it becomes sombre and whole again, except for the cavern in its centre. She was smiling, he realises.

'Ah,' she says. 'It is my face, which you think is unnatural. I would not give you the axe anyway. There is some despairing thing in you, and I have some sense with men. They do seek me out enough.'

Monsieur Hacquelebacq shakes his head at this. 'I must be on my way to Nobber,' he says. 'The day is too hot for dallying. There is no shade under that tree. I would not join you.'

'You do not believe me, do you, that men seek me out?' she says.

As she says this drool rolls down her chin from the crack in her face. She wipes it away with the back of her hand and laughs at her own clumsiness.

'That is unfortunate, but even this is life spilling out of me,' she says.

She lifts her hand up, covered in saliva, for him to see. It glints in the light.

'Look at this stomach, these breasts, these eyes. I am strong and fresh like cool mornings. Sickness does not touch me, because all the particles of the world have been flowing untrammelled into me since birth. My cracked face is the rap on the mouth that God gave me to break me into life, and it rejects nothing. But more important than all my vanity, I emanate luck from my face. It is a famous one. You may have heard of it in your wanderings, and you can tell the people this cracked face you saw belongs to Segnat. They will know it.'

She pauses, chuckles to herself. 'Listen to me. I am foolish,' she continues. 'Like a child, justifying myself to everyone I come across as if this face were a new gift rather than birth's blessing. I do not care what you think of it. I have many diverse pleasures out of the society I keep; my children, the work I do. The world is beautiful and I do not need the approval of a man who poaches starving peasants' livestock.'

'If you believe your hideous deformity to be such good luck,' Hacquelebacq says, 'why would you provoke wrath on yourself by chopping down such a tree?'

'It has ceased to produce,' she says. 'Its magic bled out. This tree is a sore testimonial to what was, and I would not look at it any more. It was one of the last magic things I knew of, and it is dead. The disease came and leached its magic away. It is empty now. Magic is a delicate thing, you see, that disperses or dies when challenged; far weaker than man's labour, or his sicknesses, which it is nowadays set against. Nobody understands its delicacy. They think it some great overpowering thing, but it is more like some small creature of the woods, always scurrying away, broken by attacks of the heart and fear when stirred.

'Besides, it draws Gaels, who fill it full of rats and crows, and removing it, I hope, would remove them, and I will not listen to Concessa on the subject any more. She stoves my head in two with her talk of it. She thinks it is a source of the sickness.'

Hacquelebacq looks at the tree and does see a little hollow, but at the angle he is at, he can see nothing of its insides. It is too shaded, but he will not come closer.

'Why do they put crows and rats in it?' he asks. 'It is just a tree.'

'To scare us, and they believe those animals spread the sickness.'

'Do they?' Hacquelebacq says.

He glances back at the badger; it is pestering its noose again.

'I do not know,' she says. 'Everything carries it, perhaps. The words we speak carry it, if a certain inflection is given to them when pronounced. Perhaps when two minds meet over a shared idea, it spreads its asphyxiation between their lungs. My sister made love to a man with it. She did not like him, and she does not have it, and her unborn child kicks away in her belly, with much vigour, so it does not have it either, but that man is long dead. I can only conclude, then, that it is a disease of the brain, a type of weakness you succumb to if your will is of a certain bent.'

This woman makes him uneasy, she is so sure of herself.

'Do you believe in faeries?' he asks. 'You must not, to be cutting down such a thing.'

She looks at him, leans more heavily on her axe. Her gaze is tired.

'No, they do not exist,' she says. 'Do you have dark designs inside you, Monsieur Hacquelebacq, ones that send you running about from place to place?'

He is stunned. Something in the way she stands makes her look like she is a part of the crooked tree, an offshoot of it, some sapling it planted beside itself before death. He wishes there were some breeze. The heat is making him unfocussed. It is not possible she could know anything of his past.

'I do not like you,' he says. 'I do not like the way you speak, the hole in your face, and I do not like this place. I am a simple man. I have hurt no one.'

'You do not like me,' Segnat nods, taking her axe up with both hands again. 'And I am glad you do not like me, but tell me; will you go to Nobber, even though I have told you it is infected?'

'It is nothing to you, madame, where I go,' he says.

Segnat clicks her tongue; the sound is sloppy, unclean.

'There is a deeper infection in Nobber than the more general one; a more recent one, and it is proliferating its own symbols of madness; setting them about the town, and they are profuse and persuasive. I spoke of a usurping man come about the town; I believe him to be only the outgrowth of some deeper disturbance.'

'A curse?' Hacquelebacq tuts. 'You said you did not grant belief to those sorts of things.'

'It is more a process than a curse,' she replies. 'Whichever it be, this town now breathes with a second breath that does not flow from the lungs of the men who have inhabited it. It must be let run its course; even mischief must have its due respect; that is the only way any remnant of the people will survive.'

'I will not be put off my course,' he says, 'by a teller who does not even believe the very prohibitions she herself tells.'

There is a sound of fluttering in the grass beyond, gentle

as eyelashes against skin. Hacquelebacq glances into the long grass; sees nothing.

'And, sir, I will not allow Nobber, in its current state, to be disturbed by parties who would interfere with it,' she says. 'The town must be contained within itself. Certain boundaries have been set that I cannot surpass; they have overpowered me, but I can maintain my influence outside the town, and remove any vestiges as would be made weapons and turned against it by whatever mischief is at play; weapons such as this tree.'

She taps at it with the hilt of her axe.

'This is all nonsense,' Hacquelebacq says. 'The tree is nothing.'

'I think, perhaps, you are right,' she says. 'I, too, think it is all lies, but, surely, this is too crucial a juncture to go against the received knowledges regarding these matters, so I will honour the customs of my vocation with an ardour befitting of the most bloody flagellant.'

'And what might your vocation be?' he says, turning up his lip in a grin.

'Do not mock me,' she says. 'Take heed of me, rather; the town will crack open and bear something newish, or, as is more usual, perhaps, something malformed and stillborn; it may also die in this other thing's birth; but it must not be interfered with during this time. By all means, Monsieur Hacquelebacq, sell your commerce of hanging ropes – new mayors and fresh sheriffs need them more than any – and buy what victuals you will for your sustenance; but take nothing that is not yours to enjoy. There are things even a bandit does not steal; holy things enriching unholy places, they must not be disturbed. The boundary is marked; cross over if you will, and see if that lively town welcomes you and your hanging ropes. So, go on your way to Nobber, and leave me to my duty. Tell Glynis I was asking after him.'

She turns to the tree and swings at it, grunting. He can see the erratic dark hairs, spiky and wiry under her armpits. He grimaces.

'Your wispy brain is as deformed as your face,' he says.

She swings again, and behind this noise he hears the fluttering once again. It is the tumbled goose, concealed in long grass.

He had thought, mid-flight, the goose's heart had overcome it, burst in two, but he sees one of its wings is broken. Sometimes bodies just break, and there is no reason. It is docile enough, though, as he slips the noose over its neck. It waddles away on its flat feet, still sprightly, as though happy at its newfound circumstances. Hacquelebacq glances one last time at the sun-dappled form of Segnat, the dead branches throwing crucifixes of shade on her back.

He is delighted to leave her behind him. Women, he feels, especially peasant women, are always poised on the precipice of corruption; a little push sufficing to topple them. They are abysses, messy and unclean, and they disturb him. He will not allow them onto his little ark once the flood begins.

When he screams, Segnat hears it come over the trees. His voice is small in the distance. She lowers her axe and runs her raw palm over the scarred wood. Her blisters burst as quickly as they rose; she wipes their serum in streaks over the tree. It is smooth, cool to the touch.

She reaches her hands into the hollow.

Coming up through Nobber's only street, the retinue sees the abandoned monastery beyond the village, dead and quiet, dotted with bluebirds and overgrown with furze and a century's overgrowing.

'I'll get no indulgences from that hovel of a place,' Harold says, but no one responds.

They lead the horses to water them at the still fountain that has not flowed for a long time and is choked with pennywort. A bloomed white waterlily sits upon a frond.

On the other side of the fountain is a young woman, covered in blood from toe to top, washing twenty feet's worth of purple intestines, all thickly folded in on themselves, dunking and splashing them about in the water. Their eyes follow the tautened, then sagging, then tautened again intestines to where they disappear round the corner of an open-doored dwelling.

Harold takes a few steps forward and, at his newer vantage point, sees that the chain of appendages belongs to a dusty chestnut mare, dead on its side, round the side, its black tongue outstretched along the earth, unnaturally long; its blank eyes unreflective.

And then the sun dapples off the disturbed, dark water, and a spangle of light is thrown from a quick moving of water, flashing into Saint John's eyes and he smiles at the beauty of it.

'It is illegal to wash offal in public drinking places,' de Flunkl calls, and Harold shakes his head at the constant stupidity of his youthful master, so wrapped up in such unseemly decorum.

'When the lord of the manor sees it fit to provide a public drinking place that doesn't stain my ears with the yelps of killed little swollen-bellied poisoned children I shall see it fit to acquiesce to his recommendations and laws,' the woman says, wiping her brow with the back of her hand, but in effect only covering her face in smears of diluted blood.

She leans over and takes a tall jug off the edge of the fountain and gulps down large doses of a pulpy liquid that soon covers her face and drips messily down her front. The thick smell of fermented cider tickles de Flunkl's nostrils and makes him sneeze.

'This woman is drunk,' William of Roscrea says, unable to detect her station as her inebriation has caused her to slur her words and discompose her carriage.

She is attractive, he thinks, but that is no marker of anything. Many peasants are comely; it means nothing. The lines on her face are dissolute, signifying a misled life. She is preternaturally aged, but in such a particular manner that she is somewhat alluring, maybe even slightly more so for her premature decrepitude. Her hair may be blond, but sweat and mismanagement have darkened it, frizzing it like spring's young thistles.

'A drunkard,' de Flunkl cries out. 'What pitiable world is this? Men turn their backs a moment and unprestigious, shameless whoredom rises and fornicates not only with mercenaries, but with the very appurtenances of the king's estate. Can a good woman be found?'

Harold sighs at this. 'There is something deeply wrong with you, boy,' he says.

'Maybe we should be courteous so as to gather the necessary informations that inform our venture, my lord,' William suggests.

'Courtliness is a misplaced strategy when dealing with filthy whores who are drowned in so much splattering blood and filled with such ciderous concoctions,' de Flunkl proclaims loudly.

'You have no call to speak to me thusly,' the woman says, 'and you have no pity for a lonely widowed woman. A gentleman, on seeing my distress, so great that I must prepare and eat my dead master's horse, and my loveliness, would offer me marriage and protections, but you only judge me. You are a boy and I hate your boyish face; it fills me with disgust. I will retch momentarily as it would seem I am forced to regard it.'

The woman leans forward, clutching the intestines to her chest, and groans and spits in the water, heaving her chest to produce some few bits of thin vomit, but nothing much comes out her mouth. She leans back and takes another drink, slopping what she does not catch with her loose mouth into the fountain.

'I, Emota of Nobber, was wife of a goodly man, and now this?' she says, pointing at everything, almost knocking herself off balance with all her pointing. 'This? I had a daughter and a big furry cat all to myself that would sleep on my knee in the mornings, before the devil came into this sinning town and took everything away from me, even myself.'

The woman puts a bloody hand to her head, trying to feign

a swoon, but too drunk to accomplish one with any finesse as her arms are too heavily burdened with horse intestines.

'Oh, I was beautiful, but no sultry slut was I at all, though they called me many ungracious names,' she says, her words becoming steadily more high-pitched as she proceeds. 'Not me; though I had fecund opportunities; though I had many stockings would send a soldier riding hard across the country to pass me a ribbon, to whisper things into my ear, to promise me anything, even Flemish truffles once.

'And what is left of all that life, and all that living? Some youth with no ribcage, no chest at all, and no bearing, coming into my town, saying I am no woman. I would do well to unhand you of your own sword, wrap these guts round your neck, string you up off a tree and lynch you, and then I would fill your dead mouth with many blooming yellow flowers so something that was beautiful would issue once from your throat.'

'Madame, good morning,' William says. 'I believe we have made a false beginning. May we inquire of you whereat the mayor dwells?'

'Ripe injustice,' she yells. 'Frivolous interrogations assail me. What sheriff will enforce my law? Nothing but a scuttling fat sheriff who fled on an eighteen-hand horse he filched off a beekeeper the moment he smelled the disease. I cannot proceed in this woe-filled world. I will not. I refuse. There is too much injustice. Who will listen to my tale? Who will believe it?'

'I will, madame, of course,' William says.

'Such gallantry,' de Flunkl says mockingly.

She looks at William, shocked into silence, and tries to speak again, but it is as though she is being choked and she falls to her knees weeping in loud, mannish sobs, burying her face in the warm comfort of fresh intestines.

Harold wipes a thin tear away into his beard.

'Woman, I feel your pain,' he says, his voice husky. 'I too am a spent being who dedicated my life to the preservation of what was not to be preserved.'

De Flunkl regards Harold out of the corner of his eye, raising his eyebrows, and at this point a small man pokes his head out of the open doorway of the dwelling near the fountain and halloos them.

On seeing this little head, suspended in shadows as though floating, Saint John begins moaning lowly, like a deaf mute searching for words.

The man has soft contours, his flesh brimming with an unhealthy, shining looseness. But he is not fat, more like an overgrown baby. He has a wide grin and a blond beard so thin and light it cannot be seen except with proximity. He steps forth, out of the shadows, and appears in flowing robes that might be monastic, possibly capuchin, though they have no hood and he has no tonsure.

'Tired wayfarers, welcome to Nobber,' he smiles, raising his hands in greeting. 'I am Ambrosio of Kilkenny. Mary, are you in good cheer? It is not too hot, no?'

'Who is this woman?' de Flunkl demands.

'Mary, my goodly wife.'

'What nonsense are you speaking?' Harold says.

'Has she offended you? A common occurrence. I apologise.'

'She said that her name was Emota, her husband killed, and she widowed,' Harold says.

'Emota is a horse and Mary is my wife,' Ambrosio replies,

still smiling, 'and has unfortunately become somewhat deranged of late.'

'And her children?' Harold Tuite gasps, throwing a hand across his breast.

'She has none, and is only a child herself; sixteen summers seen.'

They all stare at her lined face, de Flunkl shaking his head. She is still moaning on her knees into the intestines, seeming grief-stricken.

'I have seen one more summer than her and my comportment is slightly more developed and I trade fewer barbs with friendlysome guests,' de Flunkl says.

'Yes, I apologise for her nettlish words. But she is not right in the head: remark on her strained visage,' Ambrosio says, holding his hands together like he is praying, his wide smile seemingly permanently fixed. 'My beloved has been vinegared in strong cider since she was conceived, born to a born renegade, a drunken bitch of unholy proportions. I am some days sure the fetid fluid that suspended my goodly wife in her mother's womb was entirely alcoholic in nature, and I am sure that if the umbilical cord that fattened her growing body had been squeezed it would have produced a veritable shooting fountain of whiskey, and, needless to say, she continued her fermented diet the moment she was born and it has loosened the flesh around her eyes somewhat and given her a peppery, tired look. Though, I may add, the repetitious waves of fierce, gripping pox did not abet matters. As a Christian man, naturally, I took pity on her and married her some three years ago. Her mother had been using her very ill, and I fear to think what would have happened had I not taken her. You see, I protect her. I have always done so, and will always do so.'

He is still smiling, and, somehow, he has smiled the whole way through his monologue, but William can see his eyes are distressed and searching, looking everywhere but his own wife. There is something desperate and hopeless in this man, William feels.

'Very interesting,' de Flunkl says. 'We must discuss that soon at our leisure, but presently, do you know where the mayor is at?'

'As fortune would have it,' he says, 'I am the absent mayor's delegate. My lord is away on business in Dublin, and the Bishop of Armagh who usually oversees this fine village, amongst others, is, likewise, engaged. I believe he is in court in another part of Dublin addressing unpaid tithes and a case of a yeoman who still refuses to pay some nineteen horseshoes in taxes.'

He laughs as though he has made a joke and then looks at Saint John, who is acting strangely, and cocks his head at him. 'Is that boy right in the head?' he asks.

'I believe he has fled sanity, at least internally his humour has gone that flighty way, and I believe he did it to escape this cursed town,' Harold says.

'As has the sanity of the man who presently speaks,' de Flunkl says. 'Do not respect this gruff man's insolence and his insult towards your very fine town, I pray you,' he continues to Ambrosio. 'He is not well in the head, either. Much grief has stricken him into idiocy; at least that is my overly generous opinion of the lowly brute.'

'While it is a very fine thing to have a new madman about

the town,' Ambrosio says, 'for they are very amusing and inventive and closer to holiness than we are, I would not have him interfere with my Mary in his madness. The knowing of another fool would perhaps sharpen her own madness through play, like blades running off one another, and I would not have that.'

'The boy is a good boy,' Harold says. 'He does not interfere with girls, and even in his recent stupidity, his heart remains a generous one. One who is good is good in all things.'

Ambrosio smiles at this and continues to gaze at Saint John, who is looking up at the sky.

The sun is directly over Saint John's head, and it is magical. He feels its sense, its power. He attempts to reach it, but his fingers fall short, though he feels the sky touch him. His shadow is short, squat and compressed below him. He breathes in and can feel the constituent parts of the earth in his nose, each filament of light distinct and beautiful, each mote of dust a swirling universe he wants to suck into his lungs. He has been looking at the sun without closing his eyes for several seconds, his instincts hampered, and he has become blind with its strong glowing and is crying heavily, but he does not heed it; even in his blindness there is something to be marvelled at. He keeps his eyes towards the sun.

'There was a construction at the edge of town,' William is saying, 'like some creeping darkness; a thing of crows. Do you know it?'

'I saw something in the distance,' Ambrosio says, 'but I am a very busy man; and have been all this morning doing some very important work. Lonely widows, truculent peasants, diseased nobles may have done it. I do not know. Brazen Gaels, perhaps. They are encroaching on the towns; drunk on our flailing about, they feel powerful, cocksure. They taunt us, put stupid spells on us that only idiots believe in. They have lost the God we gave them.'

'But do you know what this thing is?' William asks.

'No, I do not know,' Ambrosio says. 'It must be new. I do not leave town any more. My master, de Fonteroy, brings me all I need, and takes away all that does burden me. One day I hope he will take me away.'

This man is rambling in a way that disturbs William. Perhaps he has been infected, he thinks.

'Has this town been stricken?' William asks.

Ambrosio waves his arms around, as though searching for an answer somewhere in his fingertips. He is about to speak when a chaffinch starts to sing and he pauses. When the chaffinch stops, he takes a breath.

'I apologise,' he says. 'That chaffinch's call reminded me of something. Of bells, perhaps. My master, de Fonteroy, wears them on his horse so all can hear his approach, and how we all rejoice when he comes, but perhaps it is something else I am reminded of. What was the question?'

This man, William finally realises, is not infected, he is drunk. 'Has this town been stricken?' he says again.

'With the sickness, you mean?'

Ambrosio begins waving his arms again, biting his lip and humming.

'Answer, man, by God,' Harold says.

There is no breeze any more. Saint John hears its absence. Mary's moaning is a low hum, a deeper layer, below life somehow. She is like an enormous bee, somehow, or perhaps she is a quaking of the earth. Saint John can feel her vibrant, energetic pain coming through the humming in the earth, rising up through his boots. It makes him tremble. I am blind, Saint John yells, but no words issue from his lips; everything is dark to him.

'The sickness is, of course, here,' Ambrosio says, smiling. 'The sickness is everywhere.'

A fly, curious and unsure in its movements, crawls along Raghnailt's face, awakening her, and she is full of fear. She does not remember falling asleep, but where did all this fear come from? It is like an animal in my chest, moving about within me, she thinks, exploring my every vein and organ, taking me over until there is nothing between me and it. Since the sickness closed them off in their houses, all there is left is sleep; it comes and goes at its wont, and even it has become tainted and infected with fear.

The fly on her cheek happens across a viscous fluid and begins feeding on it. She slaps it away; misses it; feels her cheeks with her hands.

'Alannah,' she says. 'I have been crying in my sleep.'

This fear is general, total. Perhaps only parts of it are personal to her; the rest is a communal fear, belonging to everyone, and cannot be stopped. It is the natural state of the world.

She wishes she could wander outside and look up at the trees, any tree; not with her eyes, but with the eyes of the child she once was. Then she could truly see it; notice its different layers, imagine all the universes within it, see its leaves breathing and swelling in the wind, hear its rustling, feel its strength beside her; but this curfew keeps her in this room.

No, she thinks, that is not true. Even before the curfew I

did not visit the woods; even then I was afraid, and kept to myself, and if I saw a tree now I wouldn't even see it, I would only see my fear. This is the fear I have brought to bear on my own life; this is my own sickness, not the communal one. I have hidden from death so much and for so long that I have never lived.

'Alannah?' she calls.

The fly buzzes upwards in a spiral until its ascent is interrupted by the ocean of spider webs hanging from the ceiling, and Raghnailt remembers the man called for Alannah again, a second time. She is on her own with her son.

Her heart had almost stopped when Alannah had brought him back; she had thought him dead, thought that Mary had killed him.

'Wake up, Colca.'

He is sprawled on the floor beside her, his hair all covered in wisps of hay, his breathing in havoc. Alannah left him in chains.

'Wake up, Colca. I must speak with you.'

He does not stir. Above her head she watches the fly's small movements, its veined wings twitching against the web. Hundreds of flies, in different stages of decay, are blackly studded against the silvery ceiling. The more ancient carcasses have so decayed that they are a dull yellow, many having crumbled into dust. Four or five heavy spiders, like musicians plucking stringed instruments, gently move between the different levels of their own creation, with the perfect confidence of those who fully own what they have created.

And then a soft weeping begins beside Raghnailt, and, though it makes her sad, she will not comfort him.

'My son,' she says. 'You have broken the town. You have abused your neighbours in their hour of need with that devilish fellow, harvesting their bodies, and keeping them locked in their houses as though they were not the kin they are. You sin; and I want you gone from this house because I cannot take the sight of you walking into your own death as you are doing.'

She is shocked at herself for speaking in this forthright manner. Perhaps this, too, she thinks, is fear that speaks.

'I am so sad, Mother,' Colca says, turning his red eyes to her.

She turns away; cannot look at him. When she sees his face she can only imagine the child whose back she rubbed when he awoke, screaming, from his nightmares.

'You must stop it all now,' Raghnailt says. 'You must flee this place before the curfew ends.'

'The man will find me,' Colca says. 'I cannot stop it now. It is too late for that, and he is like a demon. He has ways about him that he could find anyone. He can read, you see, and I must continue what I have begun. There is no choice.'

And then he begins wailing, bashing his head off the dirt floor, and Raghnailt feels sick, watching him hurt himself in the stupid depths of his emotions.

'Emota,' he moans, amidst his confused mutterings.

'All the love you have rejected from me,' she says, 'your wife's embraces you have thrown off, the harsh words you have spewed at us, and you have this love in you for a horse? I will never understand this as long as I live.'

'Stop, Mother,' Colca says. 'Not now. I cannot bear it.'

'No,' she says. 'I will speak my heart once in my life. I have carried my duties well enough to merit it, and have suffered enough at your hands for my pain to be heard once. Listen to me: when Alannah brought you in on the barrow, I thought you dead, and I felt relieved that you had died so quickly. Can you imagine that my first emotion towards the death of my only child was relief? Do you see what you have done to us? With your treachery and your vile ways that would make a dog blush, you have made it so your own mother awaits your death. Do you see where we are now? Was I not good enough a mother? Is Alannah not wife enough? What can we do to change this state of affairs?'

Colca's eyes are bleary. He gets to his knees. 'Nothing,' he says. 'It is the way I am.'

There is silence between them for a moment; Raghnailt hears the buzzing of the dying fly above her head.

'Is it my fault?' she asks. 'I could have given you up to the church, but I was afraid they would coerce you too harshly. Did I make a mistake?'

Colca shrugs. 'It would not have made a difference,' he says. 'My desires made me cunning from the start. I have always known I would be damned, and I could never be other-wise, so why not use the advantage of the sickness to have at least a few moments of happiness before my eternity of hell-fire? The man came along and I saw a way; that is all.'

'Reform,' Raghnailt says. 'It is not so hard. I will help you. Please, I beg you, reform. If you do it now the town will learn to forgive you, whatever is left of it.'

He shakes his head. 'Do you not think I didn't spend my whole life trying to, Mother?' he says. 'Do you believe it was easy to have every neigh like a rattling storm jarring my senses?

126

Lambs bleating and frolicking in fields making my brain foggy, do you think it was easy? A blessed existence, perhaps? Young cattle released on fresh grass for summer driving me out of my skin? To nearly lose my mind and my life in stable after stable after stable, as though I were in a brothel with unlimited coin, and a thousand young whores were wagging their unclipped tails at me? To see swirling shapes when a flock of sheep would—'

'Enough,' Raghnailt says, repulsed, waving her hands. 'I am ill with your talk. You set yourself against the great common feeling of humanity, the wisdom of its prohibitions, and the wishes of your mother and your wife. You must try to stop this perversion. You are killing me.'

Colca sinks into himself, like something already dead. He runs a chain through his fingers.

'The body has its needs, no?' he says. 'This lust that lies on its side always sleeping next to a man, attached to him by the hip; that is his stalking shadow; that commands him completely. I could perhaps stop, but I can never stop wanting.'

'You act as though the great common feeling of the masses were created solely to stifle you,' Raghnailt says, 'as though their object was to harm you rather than to form you into a shape that would fit you easier into themselves. You do not see the good sense of the people. Do you hate them so much?'

Colca looks at her, his mouth hanging open, as though he could never imagine her being so stupid. 'Of course I hate them,' he says. 'For one transgression they have thrown me outside of them. My ostracism is too enormous for what I have done. Even when I repent I am still shunned. I confess, and once my confession is done, they accuse me of having done what I have just confessed to. Is that propitious to my sin?'

'The people are clumsy and violent,' Raghnailt says, 'but their reasons are deeper than your needs. They are the undercurrent that ties the generations together; and if you continue in this manner they will tear you apart.'

'It is I who am on the side of the coming generations, not them,' Colca says. 'Would your father have imagined his grandson marrying a Gael, no? It would have been unthinkable then, but who is to say my grandchild won't marry a horse while your generation is mocked and scorned for its cruelty in prohibiting all those beautiful unions that could have been?'

'Why are you this way, son?' she says 'Why? Is it my fault? Did my blood do this to you? Did I make you this way when I bore you?'

Raghnailt feels destroyed, empty. Colca, seeing her pain, grows distressed 'I don't know, but I did try to stop,' he protests. 'I never took any animal, but Emota; though I wanted it.'

She leans her head back against the dank, dripping wall, allowing her face to relax so it is blank.

'Stop,' she says. 'Stop talking.'

'You never saw me try because the battle was inside,' he protests. 'Every night for years I would sit by Moynagh lake and I would wash myself in its shallow parts until dawn, and many times there I dreamed of killing myself by taking a few steps more into the lake until the water was above my head.'

He runs his hands through his hair, and the chains rattle.

'But every morning,' he says, 'I emerged from the lake, ashamed at the blood that still coursed through my veins, and I would sit amidst the dew and let it dampen my brow, and within the morning light, which in the winter has such a strange and soft golden quality about it would kill a man with its softness, I would cry so many tears, praying to God to relieve me of my desires. Starlings, thrushes and robins must have made of me a holy thing, such a statue as I was when I prayed. They would land on me like I was Francis, but I was no saint, though I tried so hard to be good, but the whole living world was a snare made of lust set to trap me, no matter how I tried. Do you remember the Fitzsimmons woman three years ago?'

Raghnailt nods, tries to listen, but the fear is making it difficult to concentrate; she can feel it burning up her chest. It is as though my flesh were burning in flames, she thinks.

'She accused me of soliciting her goats,' Colca says, 'but it was not true; I was merely playing with their ears, making them wear little hats. Still I was chased out of Kells by the mob, and the shame was so great I went on a plank of wood on Moynagh lake and I drifted out to its middle, and tried to drown myself.'

'Son, please stop,' Raghnailt says. She can feel her heartbeat in her throat; puts her hands round her neck and feels the pulse battering against her fingers. 'My heart is sore,' she says. 'I think there is something wrong with me.'

'No,' he says. 'You must hear me. That night was so clear that stars reflected on the surface of the water, and that water was so still I felt I floated in a world made of the tinted glass of fine cathedrals, a looking glass world, and the lake lived with a thousand glowing minuscule things. It was alive, and the white sparks danced and danced and it was as though they were calling to me, and I was so in love with the world

I knew it was no easy thing to die, but I plunged into the water because my shame was so great and it was like I was diving into the stars. But in the darkness I remembered you, and I remembered you would not fare well without me, so I crawled along the floor of the lake, strange fish and under-water grasses caressing my ankles, until I was able to breathe once more, and soon after that I took the wife you told me to, though I could not desire her, just so as you would be proud of me.'

The vividness of this story has left Raghnailt confused as to what emotions she should feel amidst so much creeping anxiety; and still her neck pulses with fear.

'You tell stories just like your grandfather,' she says. 'And yet you have never told me any stories.'

Colca puts his hands together and shakes them at her, pleading. 'I can tell you more stories, Mother, but I was afraid to tell you; afraid you would hate me,' he says. 'Love me, Mother. I am alone in this world, and I am your boy.'

'I have always loved you,' she says, 'and I always will, but if you ever do touch an animal again I will die of heartbreak. I know it. All my dreams do say it.'

'I swear I won't; on my life,' Colca says.

She throws herself on him with the energy of a child. He wraps his arms around her and she feels the chains draping off her shoulders, cool against her back. The fear has moved upwards through her body, past her chest, and is now in her head.

I love him, she thinks, I love him so much. I must believe it, but fear does not allow love, and all I am now is fear.

Saint John wonders if he is confusing the woman's trembling, which has fed and nourished a trembling of his own, with the trembling that comes off de Flunkl, whose shivering is like a block of black energy that courses through him, infecting Saint John with its own fear. De Flunkl is just a blur in the boy's vision, but still he shines with a negative shine, like a deeper darkness that sucks at his own flesh, and then, a fox is darting behind a stone, somewhere, just beyond the street, and he knows that it is curling up for a nap, and Saint John knows the fox can smell him, though he cannot smell the fox.

De Flunkl waves his hands, affecting a casual stance, and says to Ambrosio, 'I have no fear of the sickness in this town. I do not get sick. I am too strong of limb.'

'Ah,' Ambrosio smiles, 'to be young and strong.'

'And you, you ragged bunch,' de Flunkl says, looking at his men, 'courage, if ye ever had any.'

'Come in and let us discuss business, since it is business you crave,' Ambrosio says. 'I can offer you some healing rosewater if you lot are more in fear of sickness than your master.'

Harold Tuite and William of Roscrea tie the horses to the post near the dwelling and water the trough with the deep pots slung off the post.

'You will leave a woman out in this heat, like a dog?' Harold shouts, as de Flunkl and Ambrosio begin to move into the house.

Ambrosio, still smiling, raises his hands, but says nothing.

'I will do no conversing or business while a young lady suffers,' Harold says. 'My morals do not allow it.'

De Flunkl pinches his eyes, and lowers his head, groaning. 'You do no business, and what matter are morals if the man is not a man of business? Does a goose need morals if it is a goose? Idiot serving man, please hold true on your pledge to converse no more,' he says. 'My dear Ambrosio of Kilkenny, kindly host, if this man has offended you by his unseemly prescriptions and his passing remarks on your own law-locked wife, I will rid myself of him with much promptitude. It would be a great joy to me to do such, if you deem it in any way even slightly pleasing.'

'Please, no,' Ambrosio replies. 'I find gallantry endearing, and besides it is too hot for any such playacting. Of course I do not want my darling burnt by this sun. Hark as I put my wife at her ease by calling a woman who shall shelter her while we discuss manly things. She is wont to disturb deliberations and chat, so it is, mayhaps, for the best.'

He raises his mouth to the sky, clears his throat once, and begins calling as though he were a cockerel. 'Alannah,' he shouts several times.

Saint John covers his ears, and shakes his head at this noise. The sound, to him, is grief-stricken, haunting, and somehow complementary to Mary's sobbing. It is a part of the dirty heat that weighs down the little town.

Once he has finished, de Flunkl strokes his chin thoughtfully.

'There is some purity in your voice, Ambrosio,' he observes. 'It was a constant and true note. You are larkish.'

Harold Tuite throws back his head and laughs.

'Why do you laugh?' de Flunkl says.

'You are a ridiculous, outlandish man,' Harold says, 'too full of performative elements to be godly or useful. Only one so young could accumulate so many affectations. Do not engage this man in business, de Flunkl. You are a child playing amongst men.'

De Flunkl steps forward, addressing himself to Ambrosio. 'My offer still stands regarding this heavily bearded dog, and I have cause enough from the slander he has directed at my manliness to disembowel him, but I await your wish. I am your guest, and you stand in lieu of the mayor here. Decide, good man.'

Ambrosio merely smiles at de Flunkl. 'Of course I would thank him not to refer to my wife again, but I would not wish any remonstrations against the fellow.'

He looks to the end of the street; and William follows his eyes. A little person is coming round the corner, small in the distance against the moss-infested stony mess that is all that remains of the disused monastery. William believes the person will get bigger as she approaches, but she does not; it is a woman so small that she must walk around the dead chestnut mare.

This little woman walks straight by William, barely approaching his chest, and stands before Ambrosio. 'You summoned me,' she says.

Her voice is strange, and, to William, she is perfectly proportioned, almost as thick in girth as she is in height. A swirling cosmos of light freckles adorns her face, and her mouth is chockful of teeth. Her hair is so plentiful and confused it reminds William of the thicket they trawled through earlier in the day. She wears a gown that has been made for a woman of normal height so it appears like a royal train, but though the gown is long the tiny woman is so thickly proportioned that it seems as though it has been tapered at the bosom. There is light down on the backs of her arms, like a shorn deer, and her breasts droop, heavy like bluebells.

If he were a superstitious man he would wonder if perhaps Ambrosio were a demon to have conjured up such a tiny and beautiful woman, but he is not superstitious, and Ambrosio appears to him to be nothing more than a freakish aberration of a man.

'Alannah, my friend,' Ambrosio says. 'How is Colca?'

'The same as he last was: dead to the world.'

Though her voice is strange, her snarling accent is familiar to William.

'Ah, the poor soul,' Ambrosio sighs. 'He will recover.'

'—But how?' William blurts out, addressing the woman.

He has been flummoxed by the knotted heat in his gut, and he did not realise he spoke the words aloud until he heard them himself.

'What?' Alannah says.

'How is your mouth so full of such teeth?' he says clumsily, unable to think of anything else to say.

'Are you feeling unwell, William?' Harold asks, concerned. 'You are coming at the world very strangely, I must remark.'

William, blushing at the stupidity of his own question, shuffles about on his feet. His head twists with dizziness and scintillas float around his vision. I am, he thinks, become a lusting boy again. Desire is controlling my thoughts, trapping me, and I have not known that particular passion for some years. The sickness, having grown so thick on the back of the last famine, confiscated all such yearnings.

'I do not snack on bread,' Alannah says. 'It is a dirty tradition, and is so full of little stones from the mill that pulp the teeth. I do prefer thistles, robins, roses and the scattered fawns who have lost their mothers; those clean, uncooked things are my sustenance.'

Having heard the woman speak at such length, William recognises her thick accent.

'You are a mountain Gael,' he says, the words sticky in his mouth. 'Have you come to this place by kidnap?'

Alannah stares at him; slightly suspicious, her lips rise over her teeth.

'My men insist on giving offence,' de Flunkl says, pulling at his cap in frustration. 'I expect this foolishness from Tuite, but, William, have you lost your mind? How dare you engage someone else's servant in conversation while they are engaged in receiving tasks?'

'I apologise, milord,' William says, blinking away fierce visions of Alannah's breasts, pendulous over his face as she sits her little body on his chest. 'It is the heat. My head is turning in on itself.'

Alannah goes over to where Mary is sitting. The young woman is still sobbing into her hands, her nose loosing strings of snot from each nostril. Alannah wipes the blood out of her eyes and then begins stroking the young woman's hair, whispering into her ear.

'Tell your husband that de Fonteroy is coming,' Ambrosio says to Alannah, 'and I will need help. This will happen very soon, so he must ready himself. Make sure you give him this news, promptly; and do not let him near my woman.'

She nods, and Ambrosio turns back to the retinue. 'Come now,' he says. 'Let the women soothe each other with their soft words while we escape this wretched heat.'

'I understand none of this,' Harold Tuite says to Ambrosio. 'It is easy to conclude that there is some mystery at play in this cursed town.'

Ambrosio, his robes trailing after him, dirty with dust, goes through the narrow low entrance of his abode, and says, 'You have not asked a question, so I need not frame an answer.'

'De Flunkl,' Harold says. 'I warn you that one does not step into a ravelling web if one can perceive it from a distance. You will become stuck. Leave this place. We will move on to Kells instead, or, if you would take mature counsel, to a church to purge our collective sin.'

De Flunkl gives him a look that is full of hate, and then goes inside. Harold grins tiredly, and William, looking at his companion's face, feels it is an insane smile, betraying a deep fatigue above frenzied jaws.

'Mark me that we are in some hell,' Harold says softly, gripping William's arms, 'and, for my part, curiosity at least powers my own descent into the furnace. There is a devil amongst us, but I do not know who it is yet, though I would lay my ill-gotten wages on it that this silver-tongued Ambrosio plays his part.'

'Will you leave?' William asks, trying to empty his mind of its ridiculous lust for the Gaelic woman.

'Are you scared?' Harold asks. 'There is no shame in it. It shows you value life. You said as much yourself earlier when I had become careless in my thoughts and my words.'

'I am not scared,' William says. 'I am shaken but not for the reason you suppose. I wish to ask you did you see that midget Gael glowing like some small sun?'

Harold, concern gleaming in his eyes, pats him on the shoulder. 'Has Saint John's sickness infected you? It must be a carrying sickness. You are seeing imaginary effects and are full of a quick-breathed panic. It is strange in one who is usually so calm. Is it the thing of crows we saw? It haunts me, too, still.'

William pulls away from Harold. 'I am fine. Pay me no heed. If madness wants me it can have me.'

'Do not worry, friend,' Harold says. 'I will not abandon you.'

'Yet I may you,' William says.

'Believe what you will, but I do not believe you are such a man as that. Let us go in now.'

William nods and they go down three wide steps into a squat room. Before closing the door after himself Harold looks outside once more. Saint John is still there, playing with dust, passing his fingers through it, on his knees; still blinded to the world.

Knocking interrupts reveries. Conn, the shepherd boy, glances towards the door; sees it rattling with an intense energy. His pleasurable longueur dissipated, he is brought back to himself; the crude noise dragging him into the lull of the present – and this, he feels, is surely a lonelier time, less compressed and emptier of incident than the one the woman opposite him has weaved around him with her words.

'Well, do I answer it?'

Widow Gertrude, sitting on a stool opposite him, her hands comfortably on her lap, has been recounting, at great leisure, her life to him, telling it with sighing embellishments; not passing over any minute details that could be improved by a greater feeling in the delivery, or by some enormous exaggeration. She pauses, cocks her head.

'Only the future knocks that hard,' she says.

'I do not understand,' he says.

'Not yet,' she says. 'Methinks they knock too violently to mean us well. Smaller and fewer knocks would suffice, and those that fall should be spread out more evenly. We are not animals being called from pasture.'

The knock, though growing slightly weaker in force, is persistent in its frequency. A woman outside the door begins screaming.

'This needs answering,' Conn says.

138

They have been here for six days, or has or has it been seven? He cannot remember. It is always dark and nothing marks the time but the story she tells, and their sleeps that interrupt it; but even still in her constant story she has not yet reached the birth of her mother. Her story gives the impression of being infinite and, to Conn, it would not matter when it is left off, because nestled within each part are hidden suggestions that lead on to the next part, but also a plethora of sufficient closures to make each part the finish, and the two are always tussling together in an uneasy truce.

'What?' Gertrude says.

'This knocking needs answering.'

From being outside so much in his life, he has imbued doors with melodramatic ideals. For him, they are romantic portals to the worlds within them. It would be a great pleasure, he imagines, to open a door with a sense of manly authority, to let someone in, or perhaps to keep them out; to have a little bit of ownership, a little internal place in a world that is so much made up of outsides.

'Give it a little time,' Gertrude says. 'Youth is rash, fomenting and stirs up trash that would, if left alone, sink to the bottom and disappear.'

'You would not have me answer it?' Conn asks.

'We are in a little happy coven here,' the widow says. 'A little woven cocoon of tranquillity nestled in the midst of an indiscriminate slaughterhouse. Why would we disturb it? One day, not far from now, we will have to answer what calls, but why now?'

The woman outside lays off screaming, and intensifies her knocking; now using both fists. Conn sits upright in his chair.

'You are like a hound that's caught a scent on the down-wind,' Gertrude says. 'But this urgency you feel, it is just youth. Something is coming, no doubt, and what will, will, yes; but we must nurture our peace while there is peace to be enjoyed. I am old enough, and have borne witness enough, to know that it is you and I, sitting across from one another in peace that is the rarest of events. Yes, to a young boy like you this vigil we share may seem eternal, but every now and again, eternity ends, and it is not always a good thing. These events are berries, ripening in their own time. We should await autumn's chill lest we pluck unripe fruits; otherwise children's bellies do ache, and perhaps little lives are lost.'

Full of volubility from the story she has been ceaselessly telling, her words are still excessively poetical. She is long drunk with their frisson, the words crackling against one another for days, breeding new, expressive images, and she is still somewhat dazed by the tapestry of her own narration, full of thick metaphor and rich meaning that she knows, without understanding it fully, Conn has, in some way, felt.

'I would never, of my own volition, open such a door in such a time,' she says, 'because in times like this, no matter how sick, men become very lecherous creatures.'

'I beg pardon,' Conn says, outraged, 'but I would not believe it.'

'You would not, because you are a gentle-hearted boy who is at this stage, as close to being a lamb as he is to being a man.' Here, the knocking intensifies, and Gertrude must raise the pitch of her voice, 'Still, you have a cock hanging under your navel and it will mature, and cocks, though very different in the nature of the diseases they harbour and the unborn children they disperse, still they all only want one very similar thing.'

'A wife?'

'Eventually, any type of hole suffices.'

Conn realises they are talking at cross-purposes, and he doesn't fully understand what she is saying.

'It is a woman at this door, not a man, no?' he shouts. 'I have not much experience in these matters, but I have seen a single ram attack whole flocks of ewes and make quick work of twenty or thirty in a morning, but I have never seen a ewe go at a ram in a similar manner.'

'Well,' Gertrude shouts, 'have you ever seen a ewe without a ram far behind her?'

Conn puts his hands on his cheeks and thinks. 'I have not.'

'Still,' she shouts, 'I do love men's company, as a whole, far more than I love women's, so there is no use complaining. I am a sociable sort and love being happy when there is opportunity for it, but you are here now, and you are my little man, so I need not welcome another one or anyone else into my home.'

She smiles at him.

'Boy,' she says, 'I would give all my knowledge if I had a jug that could pour it in your ear. I have forty-two years on me, now, and they are at me, and my hips are wrecked. I am no longer comely, and sometimes I think to myself if I have already experienced all I have to experience, but having a new, little friend like yourself gives me a great renewal in myself. I am very happy, and very fond of you.'

Conn opens his mouth, stares at the vibrating door and

falters. The knocking grows a mite louder and he must stopper his ears with his thumbs. He begins shouting in a stream of almost undistinguishable words, his voice seeming to come from a low, vibrating place within his skull, 'I just want to thank you for your hospitality, Widow Gertrude, and say that I would not let men hurt you if I was ever able to stop it with my own life, and I also would like to say that, no matter what you say about yourself, I find you very comely and convivial. You are remarkably undiseased and unmarked on your face for one your age, and you have plenty of teeth, and I have had a very pleasant time here, and I'd say these last few days have been the best days of my whole life, because I was often very lonely out on the plains, but not here, and I think you are very young in your spirit and your face, and you are excellent company, and I love your stories, especially the one you told me about how your great-grandmother stole that rich woman's comb, and how someone else was hanged for it.'

Gertrude blushes, and turns away from him, fanning her face rapidly with both her hands.

'What is wrong?' he shouts, his thumbs deep in his ears. 'I am sure I have said something wrong. I am often very awkward in my speech, because I am unused to talking to things that are not myself or the sheep I mind.'

'No, not at all,' she shouts back. 'You are very sweet. That story you mentioned is also my favourite story, as well, so I do thank you.'

'You are a very pleasant person,' Conn shouts, 'but I cannot stand the noise, and this knocking must stop.'

He stands up, shaking out his stiff limbs, and paces around.

Glancing at Gertrude, he sees that all the softness in her face is draining away. He has made a mistake, hurt her somehow.

'Open that door,' Gertrude shouts, 'a sword runs through your guts till they are spilling on the ground, and you are done, and then I am done. Would you have me done?'

'I would not have you done,' Conn shouts, kicking some straw about his feet in frustration.

And yet this noise is worse than hell, he feels. He has listened to thunderstorms of crows every morning; calves with twisted guts, screaming out their deaths near his ear, their lamenting mothers lowing their mourning for days on end, and he has not minded it, but certain human noises have an intrusive and sharp quality he cannot stand, one that is unmatched in nature.

'Why are you tapping your foot and walking in a circle?' Gertrude shouts at him. 'Is there something at you that wants to get out of here?'

Conn thinks of Gertrude's voice, her easy and fluent company, and how this past few days has been for him like some great carousing festival of sociability and laughter; a great joy to him.

'It is just the noise of the knocking,' Conn shouts back. 'It is driving me mad.'

'Have we not had a pleasant time of it here, no?' Gertrude says. 'Why flee? We have everything.'

Conn knows this is true, and he knows he is hurting Gertrude with his impatience. Why do I want to go? he thinks. The floor is covered in hay and straw; the room becomes pleasantly smoky whenever they light a fire, and even his coughing becomes warm then. There are plenty of bags of grain stacked up in the corner; a barrel of cider; clean wool to lie on, and she shares this all with him, like he was her son.

He has never known such luxury, and he never thought people could talk so much; get such easy and painless pleasure by it. He has been blessed, and in some ways, though he is guilty for it, he wishes this sickness would go on forever.

'I want to see Dervorgilla,' he mutters to himself, suddenly acknowledging this unexpected truth.

'What are you saying? I can't hear you,' Gertrude shouts. 'It will stop, this noise.'

'I have said nothing.'

'I do not believe you want to leave the house and go back to shepherding,' she shouts. 'You have spoken too ill of it at too great a length. Who is there to talk to you there, but the Gaels you do not understand? And yet youth's restlessness and anger is in you, and I must ask you what do you want that you cannot have here? Do not fool me with soft words. I am lifelong sick of lies, and afterwards being called names for my belief in them.'

Conn tries to think with the irritating noise penetrating even the padding of his thumbs. He does not want to go back to shepherding; the starvation is general now. If he was still out with his flock it is likely he would have already been murdered, so as to leave no witness to the flock's robbery. The chance curfew he fell under has, in all likelihood, saved his life.

The bishop's many sheep are probably scattered now, over the plains. He imagines them, greatly divided, easily preyed upon, and the happy thought comes to him that maybe all sheep will be destroyed in the sickness. Gertrude told him that nearly all the cattle were wiped out twenty years ago, so it is not so unthinkable it would happen again, but amongst sheep this time.

Perhaps there will be nothing left for me to do but wander from place to place, free of duty and care, he thinks. Perhaps the human population will soon be so greatly depleted that I am made a judge, or a sheriff, and must spend my life in great sociable acts of discussion, striking bargains, rarely alone. Perhaps Tedbalt will die with the sickness, and Dervorgilla will marry me.

I can't talk now, I must meet someone else. My wife, Dervorgilla, needs tending to, but mayhaps I will have time enough on the morrow?

He imagines himself saying these previously unimaginable words, and his chest puffs out with importance, and then the knocking stops for a moment, and the silence interrupts his reverie more than any noise ever could.

'Why are you so eager to leave?' Gertrude says. 'Tell me the truth.'

'There is no truth to the matter. The noise just annoys me. I have told you everything of my life, the little there has been of it. I have no secrets.'

'Perhaps, that is the problem: there has been too little of it,' Gertrude says, 'and you are too curious.'

There has not been much to his life, it is true. Nearly all his hours, previous to the sickness, had been spent waiting to see a person. He would come into town on Sundays, and he would always be disappointed by those he had made so big in his imagination, but still, once alone again, he would long for the society of others.

145

Such was the pattern of his life until by fortuitous accident he found himself restrained in town while curfew was declared, having spent too long eating Gertrude's supper, and now he has constant company for the first time since he was nine, and, for no reason he can fathom, it makes him feel guilty, restless. Once he grew insane with solitude, now he wonders if he is going insane with its opposite.

Yes, he thinks, the sickness is a great thing, for thrusting me so deep into human society and all its mysteries. Gertrude has been great company to me, and I am blessed, but still the world has given me an opportunity to become something different and new, if I survive this sickness.

Conn glances at the still door, its promise of light hidden behind it.

'Thank God,' he says. 'We can speak again as though we were not in a storm, which I suppose we are.'

But they do not speak. They sit in silence for a long time. Gertrude seems a little sad. Occasionally, he glances towards the door, almost hoping it will start knocking again. Eventually, she speaks, but in a slow manner, as though she has already been defeated by her own words:

'You are not suited to shepherding, I know it. Shepherding is the domain of murderous sorts, escaping some sentence or writ; it is too dangerous for you. You would not cut a man's throat to protect a sheep. You would not confront a fox, never mind a Gael who puts no store on your life. You are a quiet lad, and isolation is natural to you, yes, but you are too young to have had such great isolations as you have had.'

Conn, with his youthful pride, takes slight umbrage at her insinuations.

'I have fended my flock well against the Gaels,' he says. 'I did recount to you my exploits two days ago.'

'I think it was three days ago,' she says.

'I cannot tell.'

'That is not the matter I wished to speak of,' she says.

Her face has grown sullen, and her shoulders are sunken.

'What is it, kind Gertrude?'

'I am not sure if I should say.'

'You can tell me anything.'

She looks down, hunched awkwardly, as though she has a cramp in her stomach. 'I just wanted to take care of you,' she says, still looking away from him. 'It is not only you who have been lonely before this curfew. It is me, too. I find you pleasant and innocent, and you make me feel as though I still had some future left to me; just you being about the place affects me this way. Perhaps when this curfew ends you will let me mother you a little bit more, and then once the sickness ends – because everything does – you will let me continue in this fashion. I would hate for you to go back to the plains, spending the vital years of your life alone. You belong with others and I can teach you of how a man is to be manly and responsible, and I would ease your path into some other trade. It would be a great joy to me to help you along the path of your life. And I would demand nothing of you, but your presence. You are too young for any other talk, so it is not that that is my meaning. In brief, I would be your protector; I want to take care of you.'

Conn's chest grows excited. The depth of her passion seems so profound to him that it shocks him into a sudden cowardice.

'I will tell the others you are my lodger so it will not excite scandal,' Gertrude says, her voice growing hurried, 'but your only payment would be conversation with me, every now and again; not even every day. You wouldn't have to worry about anything. I promise. I would take care of you. I would.'

She looks into his face, and he tries to hold her gaze, but cannot. I am changed, he thinks, and I did not recognise it because there was too much flux around me.

A few months ago, he would have cried with joy at Gertrude's offer; he would have worked like a carthorse to make her comfortable, happy and proud of him. It has been so long since I had a mother, and now an uncommonly good woman wishes to make herself my mother. It is a blessing, he knows; but he feels like she is setting a trap for him.

'Well?' she says. 'You may at least answer me.'

Conn is confused, unsure of what to say. I don't know myself any more, he thinks, but he is no longer the lonely child he once was, the one who she sees when she looks at him.

Over the past two months his skin has become greasy, his arms ungainly. His voice whinnies when he speaks. Spots have swollen and spread across his face, and he has become ugly with puberty. Even the pure and sisterly affection he has always felt for Dervorgilla has become confusing, but, still he is young enough to not fully understand what he wants from that girl. He feels a violent revulsion towards the obligations Gertrude wishes to lay on him. How thin her skin is compared to Dervorgilla's; how small her face. How thick and full are Dervorgilla's breasts. Her small potbelly is thick like a hill, and her cheeks are fat, but this widow is thin, long, a weak sapling. Gertrude wants to keep him as her own, he feels.

I will not be used this way, he thinks. I refuse. I must see Dervorgilla again.

'Let me tell you the story again of how I struck a bargain with the Gaels,' he says.

Gertrude's expression does not change. After a while she crosses her legs and begins picking at the soles of her feet. The silence is painful to Conn, but he has too much pride to break it. Finally, she says, 'I see you have become a man.'

Her voice seems like it is coming from someone he has never met.

'You do not want me to tell it?' he says.

It confuses him that she is showing no emotion. She clears her throat and spits in the hay.

'Tell your story,' she says.

The knocking begins again, and the screaming follows after it. It seems like three women are screaming now, but perhaps this is a trick of the breeze. He is staring at the door, his heart racing, but Gertrude regards him absently, picking underneath a toenail.

'Tell your story, little boy,' she says.

The room the men have now come to is dank, low, narrow. It appears to have been, not so much built lower than the town, rather it is as though the town has grown up about the room, sinking it in punishment for its stillness and age. The middle of the room curves downwards and inwards, resembling some dug-out moat. There is a table scattered with many codices, scratched-out vellums, and on top of them, some newer parchments, half curled in on themselves, like dead moths. The back wall is a square mesh of half-full cubbyholes. To the left, as though waiting in a registrar's office, three sewn sacks of differing sizes sit upright, like a family, in a procession, on chairs, slightly slouching, heavy and brown. Three bodies in unceremonious sacks, waiting for something.

'Why are there three enshrouded dead bodies sitting in this room?' William asks, glancing round hurriedly, looking to see if there might be more dead people crawling out of the walls and dropping from the ceiling.

'Were they infected?' de Flunkl asks.

Ambrosio does not answer. He is shuffling along to the back of the room, humming to himself.

'This is some strain of madness and it bodes ill. Let us leave immediately,' William says to de Flunkl, who says nothing in reply.

'This room is a little too crowded with death for my liking,' Harold remarks.

'Heed not the bodies,' Ambrosio says, busy in the corner, swilling a mug in a barrel and drawing up some liquid, which he drains off in a gulp. 'They came upon a death more natural than the like you have been accustomed to while travelling through this diseased land, as your well-travelled boots and tired horses do tell me.'

'Demand the bodies' papers,' William says to de Flunkl, 'or I am gone from this place.'

Ambrosio looks at Harold, wipes his wet lips with his fingers. 'Regarding your earlier impertinence as to my willingness to let my wife fester in the Juneish midday heat,' he says, 'I have been thinking of my Mary, of my treatment of her, and perhaps I have been too generous for too long. You see, I, too, was once a gallant man, regarding love, learned even in its matters; but time is an unravelling. Time removes the traits and beliefs that you once believed made you what you are, so that you become, in the fullness of age, something a younger you would not recognise, would hate, even; a stranger to yourself, and full of disgust at the foreign person who occupies you in your last days. This is true of Mary, but also of myself.'

'The papers, by God,' William says. 'Why do you keep bodies in such close proximity to yourself? Are you mad?'

'I have sometimes thought,' Ambrosio muses, 'that my Mary is merely a purer distillation of what all women are. During times of upheaval, tumult and distress, women always return to their natural dissolution. That is why I thought that particular woman such a treasure. She insulates me from the shock of the world, because she constantly remembers me of the nonsense and sin of her sex. Nothing shocks me any more; nothing, that is, but the weakness of men.'

He takes another drink from his cup.

'No one has asked your opinion on the generality of woman-hood,' William says to him. 'We are asking for the bodies' papers.'

Ambrosio's eyes wander momentarily before they fix themselves on William of Roscrea.

'My little Mary,' Ambrosio continues, 'to whom I am quite addicted like I was some drunkard and she was some cider. You see, women – all yes, but especially Mary – are merely swine in different forms, alluring and sinnish, their fat paps sins, only existing to draw God-fearing men like myself into wishes to knead them, to play on lithesome nipples with my tongue, to clamp down on them with my teeth when I should be engaging in the bureaucratic procedures that ensure my body is fed, my soul saved. I would amass a fortune and retire, but instead my every waking hour is filled with either dread or lust. That is why when it began I was delighted at the disintegration of her alcoholic flesh; I thought my temptations would be slightly less. She smelled of rotting apples; her pores exuded it. Her failed flesh made me untrusting of humanity, but is it not the reason why I am alive? She reminded me of herself through all this summer. Others fell into women's traps, spread the disease whenever a bitch's smell took them, but not I; but then I fell in love with her fallen state as I had fallen in love with the woman she was before she fell. —Sirs, I have the great misfortune to love her; I even love the destruction of her flesh; even the slut in her, the lunatic, the child, the demons that course through her; they were always there even from her birth. —And I cannot stop it no matter how I try, and I cannot stop this love.'

'You have lost all control. Do not speak of women,' William says, waving his hands. 'I do not know them, nor do I care for them. You must return to the present matter.'

'Women are the present matter, my friend,' Ambrosio says. 'The present matter and the future matter. They are the matter that expelled us from the garden and put us on this fair island. Look around you and tell me is there something more pressing than the serpent snuck into our beds? Their bodies, fat, lascivious and soft, are the shape of our future. But like the serpent, opportunity must appear for the mask to slip. Look to Kilkenny, my birthplace, and see how a disintegrating society fares. I received news but six days ago, off my master, de Fonteroy – do not let his name fool you, he is a peasant who shall be visiting us shortly, by the by – that there is a woman, who amidst all this suffering, has been awarded a trading license in Kilkenny town. A woman with a trading licence.'

He pauses and looks at the ceiling and breathes a brief, private prayer before continuing.

'Muse on this a little while. This southern bitch saw a total destruction of humanity and used it to further her own interests. The serpent has arisen, and no mask is sticking enough to return its disguise now. And this is not the end: little whores, their husbands dead, will soon be trading openly, making monies gleefully while their partners rot in unflowered, unmarked graves. This breakdown is total, everlasting, and has enabled women to enter new spheres, even those most vital and manly spheres of industry and business. When I saw ye men approach on the horizon I thought I would get to speak to a man, at last, a sensible man, one who could read a little perhaps, one who loved God a little, and now ye are here and all I want is a kiss on the cheek from my woman. My woman, who chokes me like so much clawing ivy, and still I crave her; I crave her love, her approval, her caresses. I even crave the violence she brings to bear on me.'

William looks at the sacks of bodies. 'Let us leave now,' he says. 'This man is insane.'

And yet William does not move; he is frozen.

'Have I perhaps shocked you, man?' Ambrosio says to him. 'Were my words too true, like an arrow running through you? Do they hurt too much? Do you think I speak drunkenly? That I am merely a rambling fool? I did see the way you gazed at our little Alannah; I saw the stiffness in your gait; they enchant and soften the mind by hardening the body, do they not? You would do well not to trust Alannah, my good man, for she has lies and has deceit crossways in her, as she is both a Gael and a woman, a cantankerous concoction.'

'I do not heed women,' William says, 'but I would heed that breed more than I would ever heed you, you brazen lunatic.'

Ambrosio tuts, dismisses him with a wave of his hands. 'Go if you will go,' he says. 'The town is open and free to guests if you can find any hosts. The people are mightily suspicious at these times, though, and like to kill intruders if bothered. It is in their manner to do so; I've seen it with these eyes in my face. My only warning would be that you should go to from where you came, and in your wanderings do not meddle with my wife. Do not even speak with her.'

He then turns round, and holds forth his cup to de Flunkl; his tone suddenly shifted.

'A cup of rosewater, perhaps? I drink a good deal of the stuff now. It keeps me fresh and strong, sharp and healthy. My wont would be to eat fistfuls of rose petals, but I found it distracted guests, munching my fistfuls of pink summer roses, like some kind of savage Gael.'

He laughs again, high-pitched, his head thrown back, but his half-closed eyes still on the men.

'Oh, boohoo,' he sing-songs. 'Why so sad and mournful? I see you do glance with fret on your faces. Do I switch topics of conversation too easily? Papers, papers, papers; what difference would they make? Dead is dead. You think some papers will make the sickness go away, give it sense? It is just false comfort you seek. You may as well wrap these vellums round your head and set them alight. It is a fantasy to think if you record the death or the man they are more sensible than the unrecorded death and the unknown man. Besides, identifying papers only function if they refer to some higher authority, and where is your authority? Where is it? I do not see it?'

He begins searching through the parchments on the table, scanning them, discarding them. Then he looks up at them. 'I cannot find it,' he says. 'It is gone. We are alone.'

No one says anything, and he takes another drink.

'If it is the bodies that set you against me,' he says, 'do not worry. They shall be removed. At your ease; the gravedigger is coming.'

William finally moves towards the door. 'I am done with this,' he says. 'There is no normality here. This man is touched, and you are all mad if you stay here, as well.'

'You are clearly troubled, coming apart in the heat,' Ambrosio says to William. 'Leave and find your peace, but mind what I said to you of women. They are all liars and come together they could generate a flurry of lies that could open the earth with its weight, dragging you into hell, and, still, any man would rather their lies than their absence.'

'Where will you go?' de Flunkl asks William, his voice breaking. 'You have nowhere to go.'

William can see the boy is afraid. 'The world is completely foreign to me, now,' William says. 'It makes no difference to me where I situate myself within it.' He turns to Harold. 'I am sorry. I am abandoning you, but it is my weakness, not your own. You are a good man. Will you come?'

'You will not leave me for long,' Harold says.

He is so calm and certain, still; has seen many fluctuations and yet remains himself. William envies the security of his strength.

William shakes his head at him, and then leaves, ascending into light, emerging and disappearing into a storm of sunshine that he then confiscates by hurling the door closed after him.

Once William is gone Ambrosio's eyes search the room; he gets down on his knees, and looks under the sacks; and then in the cubbyholes and under the table.

'Why are there no flies here any more?' he says. 'There were so many you couldn't hear your breath; and now all is silent.'

Ambrosio continues this obscene searching for some time, shuffling about the room in confusion. De Flunkl turns to Harold.

'Why do you not leave, too?' he asks, his voice shaking.

'You want to. Men are talking here; it must be unpleasurable to you.'

Harold, his eyes still on the sacks of bodies in the corner, leans against the cool, damp wall. The big husk of a man scratches his beard, puts his hands behind his back, slouches. The tiredness that has so recently waylaid him seems to have gone off him.

'I want to bear witness to your descent into hell,' he replies.

The heaviness of the room is great, and its death is close, but Harold welcomes its death as he would welcome any summer's rain.

Outside the sun is even hotter after William's brief sojourn indoors, and he is dizzy like some new thing born into the world. His pupils, in a silent scream of pain, shrink to stifle the shine pouring into him. Turning twice, he is completely lost, his brain burning and his hand over his forehead, little lazy explosions of dust set off by his bootsteps on the dried earth. There is no one in sight but Saint John, who has taken off his tunic and is playing by the fountain in the dirt with the dead mare's intestines, wrapping them round his chest like chains.

All around William is the corpse of Nobber. Without exception, the small crooked doors are closed and the windows blocked. It is a slouched, small street, irregular and decomposing. Some houses have breath in them, surely, but these houses are closed oysters.

He did not notice the town before as he was immediately distracted by Mary, and then Alannah, but now looking at the houses he sees that they emit nothing. They are blank; they must be pried open. Happily would he bloody his fingernails wrenching open a door to see its inner life, but he knows inside there would only be grey death, or, at best, a huddled mass of the infectious. They, too, would resemble the single, grey beating muscle that is the stuck centre of an oyster, thoughtless, senseless, uncomprehending.

The sickness, he knows, is only what is not. The sickness is absence; it has no deeper manifestation than the nothing before him; though there is much fanfare at its passing through, once it leaves nothing remains in its wake.

This town wants to kill me, William realises, and it will have me. He is alone, trapped in a world that grows more unknowable to him with every passing moment. He feels death near; it is a reaching thing that will overcome him if he is not careful, and he is no longer a careful man. He knows that he may not be able to navigate around the orifice of death that wishes to engulf him, because the sane disinterest he has always fostered has come undone. Still, even through the depths of my fear, he thinks, I have my little lust. This lust is a beckoning thing, calling him, preparatory to death.

'Fool child,' William whispers to Saint John. 'We have come upon a weird place and you scuttle about the dirt like a wounded bitch, your senses knocked out of you. We must flee and be done with these insane ventures and Nobber's maddened peoples. They keep dead men indoors here, like playthings, ornaments to decorate the rooms they habitate. Their midgets glow, and they are too comely by half. Harold was right; the town is cursed. I can take it no more. It is infecting me with its madness.'

Saint John looks up at him, and William can see he is not recognised by the youth. Not even the boy knows his face any more.

'Why is there no one else in this devilish town but ourselves?' William cries, so loudly that the two horses turn their heads towards him. 'Are my only companions this brief assortment of degenerated freaks who do not value their own lives?'

Fear scuttles through him. A stranger is in my head, he thinks; a foreigner in my body.

'I am gone,' William declares, waving his hands. 'I will hide in clean monasteries if I am accepted, and if I am not I will become a hermit who lurks in the hardwood forests of the midlands, living off the sky-dizzied birds I poach, my only bedding the chainmail I will strap across my throat so it is no invitation to bandits. I have translated so much of other people's words, but now I must translate myself to myself. I must have solitude; I have forgotten who I am; been rubbed and worn into a strange, unthinking shape by the self-serving company I have kept. Too much socialising and drinking in taverns has undone this land and spread the sickness throughout it. I am a confused blur.'

'A fox who loves me,' Saint John replies, his voice thick and slow, 'awaits outside this town, looking to snack upon us, and I am become an old man.'

There are heavy rings under the boy's eyes. The bunched-up shadow he projects below him is like the concentrated essence of his blank unreceptivity. Saint John is no company to him.

And then a knocking sound begins, a sticky clamouring. It is a cold and unforgiving crunching, as different in mood from the forgiving noise of the woman who destroyed the crannóg as the warm jangling of thick church bells is to the timbre of the crow's shriek. William listens for a source, a hand cupped round his ear.

'This sounds like a cavalry coming,' William says, 'but it cannot be Trim's men of property who we so defiled. They are too depleted and frightened of their own peasantry to organise a search party to reclaim what they have lost to us. It is a strange sound of much gnashing, like many teeth grinding themselves against one another and into smallness.'

'It is the baby rat I stepped on come back to haunt me,' Saint John cries out, beating at his chest.

William looks down at Saint John, and shakes his head. 'I envy you,' he says, 'for your retardation is so total it is pleasurable, and I would not disturb it with any reasoning talk. Harold will mind you, for he is caring. Stay with him and you will be protected. If your death must come I hope it is as unknowable and unexpected to you as your own birth was, and for you, Saint John, as your own life is, which you misunderstand so happily. Perhaps death could not even strike one so stupid as you as a violation.'

Saint John, on his hands and knees, grunts, and then looks towards the sun again. He falls back in the pain of its glare as though it has struck him down with a quick, invisible hand.

As William goes round the corner, Saint John's ears are haunted by the cracking noises that sound like manifested hell, and on his hands and knees, he looks towards the tall man. He sees the remnants of Mary's wake, the glimmerings of blood and alcohol that have not yet evaporated reaching round the corner to where the dead mare lies, and then he sees William disappear and he shivers, believing that William has been devoured by jaws made of sunshine.

It is almost cool amidst the foliage, beneath this panoramic, shifting roof of treetops. Monsieur Hacquelebacq has grown calm now. Sparse light falls, latticed and intricate, through the foliage. He drags his fingers through some of it. These trees are thick, bustling and lively, waving at one another perpetually, in friendly greetings. Little light gets through the overlap of leaves, but that which does is like a sneaking thing, successful through many artful diversions and feints. He wants to applaud the spangles that illuminate his eyes, the flashing light that made it through these breathing woods.

He stole into the woods in a great fear, dropping his sack and leaving his animals behind. He had come across an unnatural thing; a moving, fleshy contraption, black and devilish in aspect. It was the most unnatural thing Monsieur Hacquelebacq had ever seen, but he is less hurried now. He has been here a little while.

The woods gurgle with insect life, and a tickle on his back reminds him he has long been infested with lice. He wishes he knew the names of all the insects he sees, but some creatures are so strange even names can't contain them, and those that are given don't even penetrate the outer limits of their most blatant essence. I am lost, he thinks, and, worse, I have left my little ark of animals behind me; perhaps they have fled.

There are occasional isolated pools of golden light in the

forest and when he makes his way to them, he looks up through the gap in the trees but the sun is directly above his head, so he cannot follow it. He wanders around, knowing he is making something of a circle with his steps, until he finally hears a knocking sound. At first, it is barely perceptible through the cacophony of birdsong above his head.

Perhaps I am near that deformed woman's tree, he thinks; the sound is familiar. He would prefer to avoid her, but if he could find where she was, he could follow the edge of the woods back to his animals, and from there go into Nobber. He walks towards the sound.

At the midpoint between two enormous oak trees, so old that some of their lower limbs have melded together, an elderly man with a long beard is digging in the earth. He stands in a hole so deep Hacquelebacq cannot see his knees. Next to him, a young green-eyed fox sits, its bushy tail held high, almost above his head. The man must have been digging since early morning to have accomplished a hole so deep and wide, but he is not sweating; his movements are slow, careful. His spade clashes against a rock and he leans over and plucks it out, leaving it on the pile of dirt that stretches up to his waist.

He steps out of the hole and leans his spade against one of the oak trees; and the fox stays still, undisturbed by any of his movements. Hacquelebacq watches the old man from behind a tree as he gets down on his knees and prays, his eyes closed and his joined hands stretched above his head; he notices the elderly man has very fine leather boots with thick laces running up their sides.

When the man is finished he lays himself down and rolls into the hole he has dug. His eyes opened up to the sky, he begins scooping dirt from the pile across his own body, covering his legs, and then his boots. Hacquelebacq winces at this and appears from behind the tree.

'Good man,' he calls, 'can you tell me which way is Nobber?'

The old man rises up, dirt pouring off his legs; when he stands in the hole he looks very short.

'I mean no harm,' Hacquelebacq says, 'but may I ask what you are doing?'

The man's breathing is frantic. There is dirt in his beard, and whenever he exhales small pieces of it fall off him.

'I am digging my grave,' he says.

Hacquelebacq clicks his tongue, as though this were the response he expected.

'I know it is silly,' Hacquelebacq says, 'but I saw a thing of crows and it set my mind askew. I became lost, though these woods are very small. Before you lay you down, could you direct me out of here?'

The old man turns round in his grave, earth shifting beneath him making a soft sound, and then looks back to Hacquelebacq.

'I wish I could help you, but I don't know,' he says. 'I came here at night, by accident. I wanted to bury myself by the lake; it was my daughter's favourite place, but I cannot find it any more. I am so lost.'

The old man's shoulders hunch up, and he begins sobbing.

'What ails you?' Hacquelebacq says.

'I gave her the sickness, you see,' he explains. 'I had it first; she was minding me; keeping me cool with wet cloth, dripping water into my mouth. I told her to stay away, but she said it was her duty, and then she spread it to her husband, and then her daughter, too.'

He moans, bashes his head with his fists, loosing more dirt from his beard. The birdsong above their heads grows louder; the little fox looks up at the trees.

'My arms were swollen, my crotch too, and I couldn't breathe,' the man continues. 'We were all there in the room, all of us sick, lying across from each other, all of us holding hands, praying together; and I closed my eyes, thinking that at least we were together, but I awoke and they were all dead. I could breathe and the swelling had gone down, and I wasn't sick any more. Then Colca came and he took them from me. He dragged them out by the heels, and locked me in my own house. He would not let me go with them.'

He raises his face to the sky.

'I killed my family.'

The old man closes his eyes, leans his head against his chest and whispers another prayer. His wrinkles are so profound that some of his tears have caught in them, cleared the dirt from them; one small drop below his eye almost glimmers. When he is finished he stares at Hacquelebacq. 'I thought I wasn't, but I was still sick,' he says.

He lays two fingers on his own forehead.

'The sickness is here, and it will never leave. I broke out last night, through the door with this very spade, and fled, but I got lost, and I thought as well here as any other place. This is a good place, no?'

'Of course,' Hacquelebacq says.

'You are a good man for saying so,' the old man says. 'Even if I go to hell do you think I will be let see my daughter every now and again?'

'I think so.'

'Thank you,' he says.

The man lies back down in the hole and begins piling dirt on himself, starting with his thighs. Hacquelebacq leans against a tree, watching him for a while.

'I hope you will say a prayer over me,' the old man says. 'My name is Séamus. Say it when you pray for me. My family won't need your prayers; I was the only sinner amongst them. They were good. I am very sorry I could not help you, but I am quite old and not much use for anything. My mind is all in fragments.'

Hacquelebacq walks over to the big pile of earth and sits on it, so that he is directly above the old man. A worm, cut by the spade, is now two worms, and they wriggle blindly as though dancing together across his chest. After a while, the old man grows tired and stops, lying down fully, his eyes facing upwards.

'The foliage is thick,' he says, 'but perhaps I will see a star or two tonight.'

'Would you like some help?' Hacquelebacq asks.

The man turns his eyes to him without moving his neck, and they widen as though seeing Hacquelebacq for the first time.

'Are you my nightmare?' he says.

'I am not the nightmare.'

'You are the nightmare of a child,' he says.

Hacquelebacq goes on his hands and knees beside the pile and begins scooping large mounds of earth onto the man's chest and legs. He does this until the man's whole body is covered with a thin layer of dirt, only his head left exposed.

The moist smells of the forest's undergrowth are so thick in Hacquelebacq's nose from the strength of his exertions that he must stop for a moment. He coughs at the strength of the scent. When he looks back at the old man's face, he sees a pink butterfly has landed on his cheek, its wings high and shivering, as though it is poised for something.

'It is so beautiful, isn't it?' the man whispers, trying not to disturb the butterfly.

The butterfly rises and falls with each gentle movement of his mouth.

'When my daughter was a child she could spend a whole morning chasing a butterfly,' he whispers. 'I would see her running about the furze for hours, but when she got close to it, she would never touch it; she would only kneel down and look at it.'

Hacquelebacq throws dirt on the old man's face, and the butterfly's wings flicker once and it falls to the side, and with the next scoop of dirt it is completely covered. He must work quickly now because the sight of the old man's breathing through the soil scares him. He can see the dirt rising and falling a little, crumbling away with every breath, and his outline is still clear. When the pile of earth next to the hole has gone down substantially, there is still a large depression in the ground, and the shape of the man remains, though it is less perceptible.

Hacquelebacq leans back on his knees, and rubs his eyes, getting dirt in them. He moans in pain at this, looks up at the foliage, feeling dizzy. Flies buzz around his head. Everything is a blur. Specks of dirt float across his vision, seeming huge to him, and he stays very still, blinking.

And then he notices the birdsong has gone silent, but he does not know when it stopped because of his own pain. The fox is focusing on some point behind him, its hackles raised, its tail bristled up. Faint voices are coming from the trees. Hacquelebacq cannot see anyone, but the voices are getting louder. He does not understand them; they are Gaelic words, and it seems like they are coming from above him. He lies down in the grave, peeking over its edge. This close to the earth the sound of insects crackles in his ears like fire. For a while, nothing appears, and then five people go by, going in and out of his vision as they pass beyond the trees; four of them are Gaels, their faces painted black, bows slung across their backs, carrying some few arrows in their hands. The deformed woman with the hole in her face is with them, still carrying her axe but fully clothed now; and she is shouting at them angrily in their own tongue. They answer back in a joking manner; the only word Hacquelebacq can understand is Nobber, and it is repeated several times amongst them.

When they are so close to him that he can hear them padding through the mulch, he breathes in some dirt through his nose. He pinches his nostrils to stop himself from sneezing, and this causes him to cry so much that his eyes are cleared of dirt. Insects are crawling over his hands, swarming him, decorating him in senseless patterns. His arms and hands are covered in ant bites, and he wants to scratch them but he is afraid the Gaels would hear even that.

Finally, the footsteps grow quieter; and Hacquelebacq realises he has been holding his breath. He gasps and then leaps up to follow them, brushing dirt off his front, but then he stops, runs his hands through his hair.

'I would forget my own head,' he says.

He kneels back down in the grave and digs up the man's legs; undoes the leather laces carefully and then shakes off the boots. The old man's feet look very white against the earth, almost like they are shining. Hacquelebacq does not cover them up again; instead he steps out of the grave, taps the boots against one of the oak trees to get the dirt out of them and puts them on; walks about in them for a moment. He sits on the pile of earth, much diminished now, crossing his legs and then uncrossing them, moving his head about so he can see the boots from different angles. They are very fine, he thinks; and then he notices, near his boots, a little clump of scallions.

The earth is very giving, he feels, and it would be a bad idea to go into Nobber so soon after the Gaels have gone there. He plucks a scallion, shakes it until the larger clumps of dirt have fallen off it, and then spits on it. They come up so easily, he thinks, as though nothing held them.

The fox wanders over, sits near Hacquelebacq, and together they stare into the trees.

William of Roscrea, from his new vantage point, sees, at some distance from him, a small hut, whose pillars are made of unshaven tree trunks. It frames a man in a leather apron amidst a cold forge hammering away at some small things on an anvil. Centred by the hut as he is, the man looks like the subject of a crooked portrait set amidst a larger warped landscape. Though the noise is disturbing, it has issued from a tradesman so it smacks to William of some forgotten regularity. Relieved to see him, William sets his hopes on this regularity in a town so strange.

He salutes the man, and the man halloos back, waving a mallet at him. Above the man's hut is a swirl of grey and green pigeons. They fly in one loose body, darkening the sky. And then all at once, without warning, like they were only one being gathering its parts about itself, they shrink and fold themselves into a single file, and, with a sound of fluttering, alight on the adjacent roof all at once, becoming silent.

As William approaches the man clears some small items from the anvil into a basket behind him, and then brushes down the anvil with the back of his hand.

'God bless you, be you farrier or blacksmith,' William says to him. 'I am William of Roscrea and I am but passing through this fine town of yours. I am glad to see a man who sets store by his work, and who does bring to bear on his labour an intensity befitting of a man. I was by yon fountain when I heard a noise that I thought was a thousand teeth clacking, and in my curiosity I came to visit the sound, and I am very happy to see it is but a blacksmith.'

At his close proximity William can see the man is a blackened wreck, entirely naked beneath his thick, leather apron. Behind this man are many horseshoes that hang on nails, and beside his bare feet is a large, closed basket made of willow and beside that again is a long, tall jug. There is a strange yellow dust about the anvil, too small and fine for the man to have cleared with the back of his hand.

'Well met, lithe and tall traveller,' the man says. 'My name is Colca, a farrier, and as you can see I am a very mighty man, blessed with arms like reams of saplings strung together in a supple catapult, ready to spring an injury on any man who does question me rudely.'

The man strikes a quick pose, tautening his sinewy arms, his crossed fists close to his ears. His face, hands and shoulders have been permanently blackened from the hot metals and fires he works with, but through the blackness streaking rivulets of sweat surge from the man's crown, leaving misshapen grey imprints in their wake.

'Now you have witnessed my finesse,' Colca continues, 'do you wish me to make you a horseshoe? Or perhaps even four, which is the habitual quantity, though I have oft met Meath men, a careful if salacious breed, who do like to take a fifth and keep it under their caps as they ride, lest accident befall them and a shoe, shoddily set, comes undone. But I assure you when I shoe a horse it has a certain sticking quality, a certain lasting impact as though it had verily become a part of the animal.'

170

'I do not doubt your power or your skill,' William says, 'but I need no horseshoes. I do not mean to be inopportune, sir, but why do you beat cold metals with so little vigour? They will surely fragment and blind you. Where is the fire in your forge?'

'Nobody has any use for my horseshoes any more since their wearers have become so edible, and it is far too hot for a fire,' Colca says, 'and it is likewise too sweltering for clothes. You may have remarked that I am naked beneath my apron. You should be wary any man wearing clothes in these times, as it is well known that the sickness is dispersed in an airborne manner through sweating.'

'But I have recently come from Trim,' William says, 'where lazy, unwashed people live in cold and damp structures and yet they die in their great swathes, giving the lie to your measure.'

The man harrumphs, gritting his squat teeth, which, brown as they are, seem unnaturally light against the glimmering blackness of his face. 'You are calling me a liar.'

William looks back over his shoulder to the dead mare on its side in the distance. 'You misunderstand me,' he says.

'You think me a liar because you passed through Kells,' Colca says, pointing his mallet at him, 'and spoke with that Fitzsimmons washerwoman slut. I cannot escape the slander and calumny they heap on me in that town, and I only an honest farrier looking to mind his family. Despite what they say of me I have never felt the need to engage in congress with swan, goat, mare, or any of the more beautiful and lascivious beasts that do stalk this land. You are a stranger to this town and do not know with whom you are trifling. I would do well to smash your skull in with this mallet.'

William realises, with a great and defeating disappointment, that he has met yet another insane person. 'Your head has been touched by the sun,' he says. 'There was no accusation in my words. I leave now.'

'If I were so full of perversions why would I have such a beautiful wife, then?' Colca says. He turns to the nearest house and yells, 'Goodly wife, come to.'

After a moment, the door to the adjacent house is pushed open and Alannah emerges.

'Is she not like some faerie come down from the mountains?' Colca says proudly.

'You are married to this man?' William says to her. 'You were surely kidnapped, then?'

Alannah looks up at her husband, playing with the feather between her fingers.

'Tell him how I make love to you every night,' Colca says, 'and how I harbour no perversions like they would say of me in Kells.'

The woman begins muttering in Gaelic to herself.

'Do you hear the noises she cannot help but make when her desire for me is this great?' Colca says to William. 'She does moan vociferously because I would nearly turn her inside out with the power of my thrusting. I am more a battering ram than I am a man. When I make love to her she does have to hold onto the edge of our marriage bed lest she is propelled into some neighbouring parish by my great strength; so you may cast far from your mind any supposition from Kells that I have made love with any goats belonging to the Fitzsimmons family or, indeed, any of the migrating swans of Moynagh lake.'

William ignores him, listening instead to the words the woman is speaking under her breath. He cannot catch all of it, but what he does gather is that she is reminiscing that once high-born Gaels would foam at the gob for her, men with balls the size of those of rams' before they are emptied into a flocks of wandering ewes; balls that dangle loosely between legs like the thickest Andalusian oranges in summer do hang in groves before they are plucked by young maidens' fingers; and that their cocks were set aloft like ancient ruins upon grassy mounds, soft and elegant, resembling nothing so much as the delicate curvature of a swan's neck. When she has finished her small soliloquy she says to her husband, 'Your mother wants you, she feels ill.'

Colca's face collapses in worry and he hurries inside the house. Once he is inside Alannah pushes the door closed after him.

'Does your horse need shoeing?' she asks William. 'I will have to do it if it wants doing. Let me find my crate to reach up to the forge. It will take some time to heat the fire, though.'

The forge is full of spent ash, long since gone cold. Thin streaks of blackened soot streak the chimney like reaching ghosts that were transfixed by a heat they could not escape, their shapes imprinted on the stone.

'Your forge has not been lit in some time,' William says. 'And yet I did hear your husband working on something.'

'He does work, but he has not worked as a farrier this last year,' she says. 'No one would trust him with an animal. Fortunately, de Fonteroy's residue is bountiful enough to keep us in scraps.'

William looks towards the anvil, the yellow dust upon it.

'You know that this Ambrosio, whose wife you offered succour to,' he says, 'and who is a lunatic, keeps three bodies in his quarters?'

'That is nothing,' Alannah says, waving her hand at him, 'barely worthy of remark. De Fonteroy will remove those bodies in a few hours.'

'He did not show us the bodies' papers, so I left.'

'I have never understood the Norman fascination with paper,' she says, 'as though it does not tell as many lies as tongues.'

William stares at her in silence for a moment, and then walks over to the anvil. He drags his finger across the horn and examines the specks thereon. They are so small and light that they have crept into the thin swirling lines of his finger-prints.

'If de Fonteroy is a gravedigger, what is his residue?' he asks. 'Is this it?'

He shows her his finger.

'Do you not recognise it?' she says, folding her arms. 'Taste it.'

He sticks his finger in his mouth, and sucks the substance. It is sharp and dusty, but the portion on his tongue is too small to clarify the taste or categorise it.

'I do not recognise it,' he says. 'Is it pollen?'

She laughs briefly. 'I would recognise the taste if they had pulled my tongue out with tongs,' Alannah says. 'It fertilises the earth, and it is so strong that if you put a sprinkle of it down in the Burren it would raise the liveliest flowers such as would not even grow on Tara. If a Gael has trouble conceiving, or if her womb is too small and tight for birthing without breaking the foetus's neck, she drinks this with spring water, and she will bear twins as easily as a cat. It had fallen out of use, but of late, my people trade well for it.'

He looks at the rolling pin, and then stands over the long jug below the anvil. It is half full of this strange powder. He points at it, and looks to her. 'This is de Fonteroy's residue?'

She nods, and it strikes William that he has always known the source of the noise; has always recognised the taste in his mouth.

'The sound was the cracking of human bones,' he says, 'the bones of those whose families could not afford the ha'penny for burial, for those without family or property.'

He kicks off the top of the wicker basket, exposing heaps of broken bones, cracked down to shards by Colca's mallet. Loose teeth, stripped down to the enamel, glimmer amongst the duller yellowing fragments of other bones. A lower jaw smiles out at him below half a skull that has been eaten away by grey syphilis. Inside this skull, as though hidden in a cocoon, a rotting, brown eye lies nestled, the eyelid still intact. There is a crooked femur shattered at the knee, its edge jagged, an array of small finger bones like trinkets and a large broken pelvis beneath it.

'You will be found out,' he says.

'And who is there left to find it out? That dead eye, perhaps? It sees nothing. I find that there are too many opinions in this world, and not enough food.'

William covers his mouth with the back of his hand, though there is no scent off the bones; his desire for her has made him accept even this. 'I understand.'

Alannah smiles. 'I must say you are as intelligent as any

Norman man I have ever met,' she says. 'You guessed the powder, and you are not overly repulsed by the practice. I expected to be rid of you by teasing you, making you eat it.'

'I am not surprised that some Gaels,' William says, 'their Christian inclinations quelled by this last string of popes' hatred towards them, have returned to their older practices, but I did not know this one still existed. I thought it a myth, though I have heard speak of it.'

'How is it that you know so much of us?'

'I am an interpreter of your languages.'

'And what,' she asks, 'is a person of any talent doing in the town of Nobber?'

'I take wages from a weak-hearted noble who would buy properties and lands in the towns more heavily struck by the sickness. He needed men, but I am done with him. He is a boy, a fool, and I smell death off him. But you, why is such a-one as you here?'

'I was traded away a few years ago for a few days of peace by my uncle,' she says, 'and found myself in this unfortunate place. I have been made Normanic under duress, and have spent the last three years living in servitude to this farrier, eating unclean foods and wearing ugly clothes like the kind you find me in now, with no one to talk to except my husband's mother, listening to ballads that drunken peasants compose. They have no ear for melody; they only care for its dancing.'

William uses the opportunity of her speaking to closer examine her face. Her mouth is moist, as though primped with beeswax. Her eyebrows, darker than her hair, are sharp and defined, giving her a stern look. He would give anything to have her on top of him, but he has always believed himself to be a gentleman.

'How would such a beauty as you belong to a farrier? I, myself, would only trade you for a high-born man.'

'That's gentle of you, but it was an advantageous marriage for some,' Alannah says. 'About three years ago there was much scandal around here given my husband's preferences. It was doing damage to the diocese, and its bishop who had wished to advance himself. He knew Colca could only either be tried, which would lead to infamy for the diocese, ending his own advancement, or be married off. He also knew it would be difficult to find a match for one so perverse; and he thought me to be suitable to Colca, given I, as a Gael, have many hidden practices to coax out love from sodomites and bestialists. Even then, I am more alluring again than most Gaels as my small stature has concentrated and purified my beauty, like an essence. If I couldn't shake Colca out of his proclivities, no woman could, least of all a Norman woman. But I could not, and have not.'

'It must be great grief to you to be married to such a man?' William says.

She shrugs. 'I was traded for fifteen male Gaelic hostages, which I believe to be roughly my worth, so I am not in shame. Besides, I have always caused such frenzies of lust I knew I would one day be traded away. In truth, I await old age with a lust equal to that which I inspire. All beautiful women who have sense wish to lose their looks. The attention leads to too much violence on their persons, unless they have strong relatives, and I do have them.'

William gets down on his knees before her.

177

'You deserve far more than this decaying town and this brute of a man,' he says. 'There is a horse by the fountain we can ride, and we can rid ourselves of this place. I will protect you until I have delivered you to your family, and I shall do so in exchange for nothing, not besmirching any of the womanly honour you accumulate around yourself.'

She cocks her head up at him like an owl. 'Do you feel I am a woman in need of a gallant man?' she says.

'I extended an offer,' he says. 'If it is refused, it is refused.'

With her free hand, Alannah places the crow's feather behind her ear. 'What is your name?' she asks.

'William of Roscrea,' he says, 'translator of Gaelic languages, no fixed abode, suffering no spouses and recipient of no rents.'

She considers for a moment. 'May as well you as any,' she says, eventually. 'Perhaps this is a better way. It could save some bloodshed. Rise up.'

William stands up awkwardly, and she presents her wrist to him.

'Take me from this Norman hell.'

William kisses the back of her hand, and a wave of desire cascades through his guts, overpowering him, and stars edge his vision. He imagines taking the small woman from behind on a mountaintop during a thunderstorm, and, in an effort to rid himself of this image, he tries to picture Colca grinding down his bones with the rolling pin, but his lust is too strong; he blushes.

She walks ahead of him.

'My uncle will feed you well,' she says. 'Two slaves will be sent to you, and they will milk you better than a suck calf, caress your feet and whisk away the insects of summer that would disturb your sleep. Honeyed mice and cows' tongues will be spread across your plate. A man of song will sing a long ballad that will last most of the night, but will replace every name in it with your own. For one night, you will live like a high-born Gael, and then you will leave.'

They have come round the corner, near the dead horse. Saint John is leaning against the fountain, his head slouched down into his chest. Though sitting on the ground, he is holding onto the fountain as though he were afraid of falling off some high place; and then a woman begins screaming from Colca's house, and William stops.

'That is a sound of murder,' he says.

'It is only Mary,' Alannah says.

'It is more than that.'

The pigeons, with the noise, have alighted from the roof. William is caught up again in their shade. They swirl close above his head; and then the pattern disintegrates. He can see at the end of the street, like an opening vista, the grand monotony of the countryside, the oceanic grass and shrubbery that beckon him to safety, the thing of crows standing watch over it all; and he remembers how Mary broke down in tears when he said he would listen to her story.

'I cannot abide this,' William says, clutching at his ears. 'I must intervene.'

Alannah shakes her head. 'Did you ever wonder why there is no one in this town?' she asks. 'It is midday, and not a soul is stirring. And yet there are more than a hundred habitants. Have you ever wondered why they keep to their rooms? Do you not think we all hear her? Be careful, you gallant and intervening man. De Fonteroy will remove your body if you do stick to this place too hard and uncover its secrets.'

'I will go with you soon,' he says, 'but I must ensure this woman is safe.'

Alannah turns away from him. 'You are too unreliable,' she says. 'I have known your type since I was a child; every new sound beckons you, and now it seems another woman has made herself available for this gallant man to save. Go, go to Mary. You are saving nothing, and either my husband will kill you, or you will kill him, and I care for neither of you, but don't you hurt the old woman in your brawl. I am fond of her.'

The house at the end of the street harbours so much noise that it seems to be rocking. The birds are everywhere above him in great confusion. Everything in him wants to run from this town, to be free of this place, but there is a frenzied vitality in Mary's keening that calls to him.

'I will return for you,' he says.

'I am done with you; you are as stupid as they all are,' she says. 'Do you think I ever needed a gallant man, or any Norman? Did you think I was not guileful enough to escape this place on my own?'

He walks towards the house.

'I do not think anything any more,' William says.

'Did you knock?' Concessa whispers.

'I do not remember knocking,' Ruth says. 'I have been in here with you, so it cannot have been me that knocked.'

The house is full of women, and they are making the room full with their talk. To Samthánn it feels as though they have been talking forever. Ruth is fat, small, and Samthánn wonders how she can be so fat when no one eats any more.

'The knock came from outside,' Neasa says, 'so it could not have been us. We are inside.'

'That child is trouble,' Concessa says. 'It could be her that knocked. We do not know her. She arrived with the sickness.'

'There are no marks or swellings on her,' Ruth says.

'I remember how she came to this place,' Neasa says. 'But I do not remember it now. Someone brought her here.'

Samthánn plays with the rock in her hands. Some of it is smooth, but one part of it is sharp, but it is sharp in the wrong place. This is like people, she feels.

'She is just an orphan,' Concessa says, 'from Kells, probably.'

'How is it that there are fewer people but orphans are more abundant?' Ruth asks. 'It is strange to me.'

'Faeries could be birthed by the faerie tree by the lake if the weather is right, but the weather is always wrong,' Neasa says. 'Are you from the tree, child?'

Samthánn has not spoken since the women took her in; they do not even know if she can.

'I remember once I did not believe in the power of trees at all,' Neasa says, 'but Cormac took me as a child to the lake. He said we must only visit at night, but when we went there I was very young, younger than this child is here before us. Perhaps I was six. Children are suspicious, but accepting. They are wondrous. A natural cavity is in that tree, a deep little hollow, and my father directed me to put my hand in the hollow. I do not know if hollows grow in trees, or if they are an absence of its growing.'

'Her skin is like Álmaith's skin was,' Concessa says. 'Do you remember Álmaith?'

She raises her chin and grimaces. Of all the women, Concessa is the most conceited. She seems older, but that could just be the way she speaks. Though she is blond, there is a black hair on her chin. It grows out of a beauty spot, and curls in on itself, seeming sharp.

'I don't like her eyes at all,' Ruth says. 'They are too empty and incurious and she is not polite to us.'

'When I put my hand in the hollow it grasped at a little wooden thing,' Neasa says.

She begins coughing, covering her mouth, and when she puts her hand down it is covered in blood.

'Álmaith was Segnat's daughter? Imagine having a hole in your face; your tongue would grow cold.'

The hen, whose feathers are always ruffled, as though it is in a perpetual state of shock, waddles near Samthánn's legs. On reaching her legs, it draws its head back quickly in an inverted stabbing motion, and pauses. The child's thin legs are an obstacle to it. It goes back to its corner, making a throaty protest with its clucks.

'I leant very close to the tree,' Neasa says. 'It was dark, but still I peered in with great concentration. It is not uncommon for other plants to grow on plants, but growing within this hawthorn tree was another tiny tree, the exact mimic of the tree in which it was placed. I did not find this uncommon, though, as most children look like their parents, even in utero, so why would a tree be any better? No, she was not her daughter. It was someone else's. I forget who. Or is a tree worse? I do not know.'

'That child's skin,' Concessa says, 'was too delicate, too fine. She used to sit out in the sun. A very quiet child too, like this one.'

'The next time I went to examine the hollow my father told me to close my eyes, and he had tied some coloured cloth round a low-hanging bough,' Neasa says. 'He always told me to put my hand in first lest it see your eyes too soon and give you back what you want to see instead of what is the truth. I still did not believe in any sorcery.'

'But you believe in trees?' Concessa asks. 'I do believe in them. It would be madness to not. They move so much, even without wind. Sometimes they are sad, sometimes lonely. I believe they talk to one another when we don't disturb them. I think they speak to one another with their roots. The way they twist around each other is the way that we hold hands when we are fond of one another.'

'I do as well,' Neasa says, 'but the next time I went there my Cormac said he would stand at a distance, and it was not fully dark. It was twilight and the birds were creating storms with the beatings of their wings and everything was orange and tinted as though seen through some warped glass, and I put out my hand and felt some soft and fleshy resistance, a slit that was opening. A frog was hopping about my feet. I am terrified of them. My mother was the same. If I said to my mother, "Imagine the texture of a frog," she would jump, yell, knock over her dinner, perhaps feel ill for days.'

'Álmaith was Segnat's favourite daughter,' Ruth says.

'I called my father and said I did not wish to proceed—'

'People will begin believing in trees again, the way it's going,' Concessa says. 'You must have a strong head about you in such times as these, or you will wander into ungodly pastures like the straying lambs now all the shepherds are dead of the sickness. Do you remember the pox when the Preston family began praying to bulls?'

'I do not remember the father's name it was so long ago,' Ruth says.

Samthánn stands up and pads along the walls, dragging her hand against them. Parts of the house are made of wood. One of the walls is wattle, but four portions of it are stone pillars; they hold up the roof. Samthánn runs her hand over a pillar and, finding it flat enough, taps her rock against it, and begins etching a picture with the sharp point.

'They tried getting back into Communion but were not let for a month of Sundays,' Concessa says, 'for Father Unction had said if you disbelieve when the animals are sick, how will you fare when the men are sick? And the sickness is coming, he said. It is riding towards us sinners, across the valley. It does not trip. Its steps are clean. It is so hasty it appears before its own shadow.'

184

'Proceed, my father said,' Neasa says. 'He shouted it at me. Keep your eyes closed, he said. I remember his voice, though I forget his face, and my hand went through the fleshy opening that was becoming more lubricated the more I went at it with my fingers. Its interior was soft, and tight, though loosening, and it gave off a smell so strong it made me giddy. A unique texture, and to me now, at least, unmistakable.'

A spark flies from the pillar, hisses out; an aborted shooting star. Samthánn has leant too heavily on the supporting beam with the rock. She looks to the straw at her feet, and sees it has not ignited. She gets to her drawing again, using less force now.

Only the hen is aware of her, out of the side of its head. It is warming two spotted eggs with the soft white down of its underside.

'One must remember the pain of children,' Concessa says. 'Perhaps we are too harsh on this child. She cannot have more than nine years on her. I wish I knew how she came to this room.'

'Are faeries evil, or just mischievous?' Ruth asks.

There are two brief knocks on the door, sharp and insistent, and then the sound of bare feet walking away. None of the women pay any mind to this noise, nor does Samthánn.

'Later when I was a mother, and had been much examined and played with in a matrimonial way by my beloved Tádhg,' Neasa says, 'I recognised the feel of it, that feel I had felt, and that knowledge that the tree was feeling it too, and I felt very dirty and wretched once I knew it. It was a woman's insides, her part of pleasure and birth, the hollow in the tree, though I blush to say it. What was strangest though was that even though the tree had a woman's parts, I felt it was a very mannish tree.'

'If you set Segnat's daughter out in the wind, her skin would crack and bleed in many places,' Concessa says. 'It was a very rare sickness she had. She lived till she was six, I think, and she was very quiet. Segnat never recovered her mind after that. She has been sad a long time; and she always says sadness means that when choosing between different things, you choose the least.'

'The tree is an ash, Neasa,' Ruth says. 'I do not know why you say it is a hawthorn unless you have gone mad with hunger.'

'I have gone mad with hunger,' Concessa agrees. 'But I do not know why you would say that when she was born with the disease. Her face did look like when mud is dried out and stepped upon. A mother's pain is eternal, but I think Segnat had prepared herself on seeing the child bleed from the face so much. You cannot completely love a child who is falling apart in front of your eyes. You cannot even touch it for fear even your touch is hurting it. To live without a mother's embrace is a terrible thing, but to live without a mother's love—'

'I could embrace this child, but I am afraid of her,' Ruth says. 'I am becoming dizzy.'

'I too want to carouse and make love, just one more time,' Neasa says. 'I always remember Segnat telling me that in cities there is more lovemaking because there are more hiding places, though I am sure there are more secluded places here near the woods, though they are uncomfortable and damp, bits of them getting inside you. I could hide anywhere.'

'I could hide in this room and you would not find me,'

Concessa says. 'Sometimes I feel I could make myself small as a mouse I am so ignored by others. I could hide myself in the middle of this room before all of you by making myself very still, so you would see right through me.'

'What happened next to the sick child?' Ruth asks Concessa.

Samthánn's arm is aching from her drawing. She cannot go very high because she is so small, so all her figures are near the ground. A translucent piglet beside her feet snores a little. It is asleep, almost dead. Its skin is new and has never seen the sun. She steps over it and moves to the wood. The impressions her rock makes there are less clear. It is more difficult to make straight lines, but her arms don't have to work as hard. Her fingers are cramping.

'Well, nothing really happened the next time I went to the tree,' Neasa answers, 'because my eyes were open, but I had Séamus with me that time, and he said the hollow had licked him with its tongue, and he played his fingers around the edge and said the rim was covered in teeth, and he pulled out a tooth and showed it to me. It was a big tooth, twice the length of a knuckle. What scared him though was that it was a perfect circle of teeth, he said. We have but a set of teeth at the top and the bottom of our jaws, but with this tree it was as though all around its lips were teeth, in a full circle. Children draw mouths that way sometimes, in the dirt.'

'Imagine losing such a child,' Ruth says, 'you would have to suppress the delight you felt at its death for you know it is wrong, and the emotion would be so mixed up with your natural love for what you made be born.'

'But he was at the age where his milk teeth were falling out anyway, so it could have been one of his own,' Neasa

187

says, 'but it was a big tooth, more like an ash tree's, I suppose, than the slender and crooked hawthorn's.'

'Do you feel Raghnailt would mourn Colca?' Concessa asks Neasa. 'I would not mourn him, and I know Raghnailt is good, though she has put up with much pains.'

'I teased Séamus a lot over his hiding his baby teeth like that,' Ruth says. 'And I pretended sometimes to be a tree and kiss him, and this would make him laugh, but he would get angry too, sometimes.'

'That is not your story to tell, nor your memory to have, Ruth,' Neasa says, growing angry. 'That happened to me, and not you, and I never told anyone so you could not know it, and it could not have happened to you for you have never been at the tree. Only I tie ribbons to it. Only me. My father is dead.'

'Segnat's teeth were so loose she could pluck them out of her mouth as one would pluck a flower,' Concessa says, 'but she was an old woman, then.'

Samthánn has covered a quarter of the house with her drawings now, moving her way towards the door. Her arms are sore and she feels lightheaded. The drawings come quick, pouring out of her. One tiny eye still follows her around the room. It is the hen, she feels its gaze. She feels she is surrounding them in her drawings, entrapping them in her visions.

'Why do you think this child resents us?' Concessa says. 'What is she daubing? My house is a wreck, and I would not have these dirty pictures along the wall. They are obscene.'

'It is too hot,' Neasa says.

She fans herself with the end of her skirts, blowing hay about her.

188

'The child does not resent us,' Ruth says. 'She is telling us things. They are quite beautiful, no?'

Ruth rises stiffly. Her knees crack as she shuffles towards the pillar. She kicks the sleeping piglet under some hay, hiding it. It squeals once, a sound of surrender.

'She is a Gael, no?' Concessa asks. 'I do not understand these markings. They are squiggles; nonsense, full of hate.'

'I go to the ash tree, still,' Neasa says, 'but sometimes I am too fat and lose my breath, and do not continue. Still, often I persist, but when I go back now, there's nothing. For years it has given nothing back to me. Its secrets are its own, or perhaps the faerie in it has died, while the tree in it has maintained its life, though it does not produce. I put my hand in and feel damp, rotting wood. It is no longer a place of magic. The world is dying, and when the world dies, its magic and its spirits evaporate before the fleshier parts of the world do desist. Still, everything is full of symbols, they multiply and persist about us, but even so they're all dead.'

'She is too blond to be a Gael, and her nose is too fine,' Concessa answers. 'I have never seen a more beautiful child. She does remind me of Álmaith.'

The knocking begins at the door again, and the women ignore it. Ruth, peering close at the lines etched into the pillar, doubled over almost, suddenly gasps, and turns towards Neasa. 'The child depicts all the sicknesses,' she says.

'They are but lines drawn by an idiot child,' Neasa says. 'They are childish, and I can make no sense from them. They are all tangled up, like rats' tails in a mischief.'

'Who is that widowed whore, that outsider, who thinks she is better than Nobber?' Concessa asks. 'The one who corrupted

189

that young shepherd boy and he barely a decade of years on him yet. She sucks his cock dry every night in his sleep and he does not know it yet, the bitch. Do you remember her? Is she alive still? I would like to beat the brains out of that slut's head until her skull was powder and her blood splattered across my cheeks, with her toothless mouth open all hours of the day, thirsty for semen. She sweats semen, the whore. On hot days like this, it pours out of her. The bitch; they're all bitches.'

'She was at every sickness, the child,' Ruth says. 'Here is an especially long one.'

Ruth drags her finger across a single curving line. The line loops, goes high, and then begins again, and it brings her over to the wooden part of the wall, near to where the child is sketching. Samthánn is almost at the door now, which is shuddering and straining with the knocking.

'This sickness will last forever,' Ruth says. 'This is a big sickness and it will go on for centuries, millennia perhaps, and it is this one. I see it. I can read her, like she whispers in my ear, but this part here is my death.'

She feels faint, and leans against the wall, trembling.

'I will not survive this drawing,' Ruth says to the child. 'Give me the rock.'

Samthánn turns, and regards Ruth, terror in her face, and clutches the rock close to her chest.

'Give it to me,' Ruth says.

'And then I went back there,' Neasa shouts. 'And the Gaels knew I trekked out there, and they taunted me. They had filled my tree with dead rats and crows, and my hand came into contact with them and I screamed. The tree could not have produced them, though, could not have stacked itself so thickly with rats.

It was the Gaels who did it, because they hate us, and they thought it was funny, but that tree was my father's favourite place in the world, and they desecrated it, and they were laughing at me. I could hear them behind the branches, hidden up in the trees, hunched up like shadows, laughing. I hate them.'

'Give it to me,' Ruth says, grabbing at the child.

The child takes a step back, almost tripping, glancing at her unfinished drawings. This close to the door, the noise of knocking is unbearable.

'Those drawings are not sicknesses, Neasa,' Concessa says. 'They are massacres. You are losing your mind, but then again, what was there to lose?'

Concessa laughs once, and begins coughing. Her lips are covered with blood.

'Is someone knocking at the door?' Neasa replies.

Samthánn scrambles to her feet, and, just before she throws the door open, the knocking stops.

'Do not open that door,' Concessa screams. 'You will let the sickness in.'

They all fall silent. The door creaks open, but no one has touched it. The child stands, illuminated in light. There is no one outside. Samthánn looks down, sees nothing. It is too hot for footprints. Whoever was knocking has vanished. A dead horse lies across the way, its throat cut, its intestines dragged all over the town. A boy is crying into a fountain. Inside the room, the silence encapsulates them; it is a prison. The child's feet move in a soft patter and she is outside, leaning against the walls, clacking her rock off them, drawing patterns.

'The sickness is in now,' Ruth says. 'It is with us.'

She closes the door, and they are within darkness once

more. Everything seems slightly closer now. It is harder to see than before. The hen stands up, ruffles its wings and sits back down again, protecting its eggs.

'I remember these things,' Neasa says. There is great meaning and threat in her voice. 'I remember everything.'

'What do you remember?' Ruth asks.

'Segnat brought that child to us; gave her to us as a gift. She told us we must keep her in the town as a protection against the sicknesses.'

'There is only one sickness,' Concessa says.

'Segnat said we had many ones on us,' Neasa says. 'Segnat said she could not help us, but that the child would; and now she is gone. I forgot all this, because my throat is so dry and I am so dizzy. The child, Segnat said, would help us make the right choice.'

'I remember, too,' Ruth says. 'We have done a bad thing.'

Neasa coughs, and looks at the drawings on the wall. 'They are depictions of work,' she says. 'Of peasants in the fields, cutting down the yield of the earth, but each blade of grain is individually rendered. Fields ripe with wheat, here; a summer's morning; peasants stooped over ditches, drinking water from cupped dock leaves. Their hands are brown with dirt. Women and children hold hands; it goes on forever.'

'I can feel the sickness in my bones,' Concessa says, shivering. 'It has grasping fingers.'

'I greet death every morning,' Neasa says. 'And it has never greeted me back. Why should we die? Why should anyone?'

'It is an ageless story,' Ruth says, 'but it is over, and it is a sickness, not a massacre. There is a difference.'

'Cartilage has a popping sound,' Concessa says. 'There are

many little holes in the child's flesh around the cheek, close together and bunched up like honeycomb, yellow ones, eating themselves with infection. Gaps in the flesh, pus pours like fountains, the life leaking out of you. Your life leaks out of me. It has always been a massacre. Someone is knocking hard at that door.'

'There is no knocking,' Ruth says, listening to the silence.

'Swelling begins behind the eyes and around the anus and then the pits of your arms burst open,' Neasa says, 'and I have never made love, I have only been made love to.'

'I'm thirsty,' Concessa says. 'Is the room growing dim?'

'I was loved once or twice,' Ruth says, looking at Neasa, 'but to what purpose?'

'It feels as though the thirst is only in the left side of my throat,' Concessa says, 'where I cannot swallow it away.'

They fall silent again, and look towards one another with guarded suspicion. A clacking sound comes from outside, a small tapping noise; the child is drawing on the house. Ruth taps at the piglet with her foot, pushing it deeper under the straw. It dies suddenly; the heat leaks out its body.

'Don't interrupt me,' Concessa shouts, though the room is silent.

'How much time has passed?' Neasa asks.

They look at one another again.

'I feel nothing,' Ruth says.

'Nothing?'

'Yes,' Ruth says. 'You know it is there, not inside you. It is what is not inside you.'

'Things disperse,' Concessa says. 'There is no magic, only God.'

'I remember these things,' Neasa continues, eyeing Concessa with hatred. There is great meaning and threat in her voice. 'I remember everything.'

Ruth sits back in her chair, and eyes Concessa. There is so much hatred in these looks, in these rooms. And then, all at once, the flood of talking begins again.

When Raghnailt was a child she thought she would be twice as good at living at twenty as she was at ten; twice that again at forty, but there is no growth, no progression. Nothing ever works. The same emotions strangle her. They are merciless, but shifting. No defence is mounted that cannot be destroyed by the liquid shapes they take, seeping through her skin like smoke, rising up again in her throat. And once they begin it feels constant, always total, as though it had never stopped; even now when she has a reprieve. She should be happy. She knows it, but she is only afraid. How is it that a place can be so empty of people, or event, but so full of emotion? Nothing happens in between, but the world has changed for her. Perhaps there is nothing behind these eyes that see, she thinks. The mind is a very thin thing, the soul even slighter; nothing seems to move within. Some other me just crashes about in the shards of my mind, but sees nothing clearly. I am so old, she thinks, but feel like I have just been born.

Her father used to say there was nothing real in feelings; the only reality was the prayers you offered to God; that emotion was the devil's work, a trap to trick you into moving away from God's light. He said that feeling always masqueraded as truth, and yet she has more emotions than anyone she has ever known.

I do not want them, though, she thinks.

Now, her son, whose love she has longed for, is close to her, wiping her forehead and checking her eyes; and it shows some sort of love. He is unused to contact and is too rough with her, but he is trying to be gentle. She has craved this, but now she wants nothing more than to be left alone to indulge her fear, let it loose and see if she can find its limit.

'Almost finished,' Colca says. 'You will remain in bed, Mother, and not go about just yet, will you?'

I was not made a mother, she thinks; I did not become one. I tried to learn, and was not enough for it.

'I am fine,' she says. 'I do not know why Alannah said I was ill.'

His face is almost sad. It is unrecognisable to her sometimes. I have not looked at him enough in our life together, she thinks, unable to read him.

'Do you remember my father?' she says.

'I remember nothing before he poisoned me.'

Raghnailt winces; tries to ignore the remark. 'He always said the world dragged on regardless of our feelings towards it,' she says 'Perhaps you are more an extension of me than I formerly believed, because I too have always felt apart and distant from the masses; and for this I want it to be true that we are living in the last days. I want the world to die around me, and I gave you this feeling through my blood when you grew in me. Your pain is my fault.'

'Stop this,' Colca says. 'You would wear a thing down to its very nub by talking over it so much. I am reformed and we are reconciled now; all will be well.'

It took the death of Raghnailt's husband for her to learn

that other people did not have her depths of feeling, that they did not imbue meaning into every social gathering they found themselves in; that little flowers and the noises of the wind meant nothing – or perhaps less – to them; that the offences she felt she accidentally gave often never struck their pride or even their notice; that they did not cry at nights thinking of relatives who had passed decades ago; that the loss of a loved one could be mourned and felt, but not destroy living forever thereafter.

She let her stillborn children destroy her life, imagined her own body to be only capable of producing mutilation and death; and could never reach the living child that was left her. Perhaps if I had spent more time playing with him, she thinks; less time trying to keep him safe, then we would have more memories to hold us together. I made so many mistakes that still haunt me. I never repeated them, but there were always more lying in wait for me. If I could somehow tell my boy that I have been in mourning for more than half my life; that he has never truly met his own mother, but no one could understand this, even I, who have done it to myself, can't understand it.

'Mother,' Colca says, his eyes widening. 'Someone is coming.'

The door bursts open for the second time this day, and a tall, sallow man enters. His bearing is refined, and though he is ugly it is in a pleasant, trustworthy sort of way.

'What is that noise of wretchedness?' the newly entered man says.

Raghnailt hadn't even noticed Mary's wailing and howling she was so lost in thought.

197

'You enter my mother's house?' Colca says, grasping about for a moment, searching for something. 'My mallet, I have forgotten it outside.'

William of Roscrea looks at his own empty hands; shakes his head.

'I, too, have left your mallet behind,' he says.

'Get out,' Colca yells.

'What torture do you inflict on women in this hovel?' William says. 'Unhand this girl, and deliver her to safety.'

Colca picks up one of the jugs, and hurls the residue into William's face, and William, coughing and blinded, stumbles about backwards, looking like some faded ghost.

'That was two months' eating you've made me put in your face,' Colca says.

He falls upon William, throwing jabs into his guts. Now that the two men are rolling on the ground, Raghnailt can see Alannah standing behind them, an incurious gaze on her face; Mary falls silent.

'Don't hurt him,' Raghnailt says to her son.

Colca, both his hands pressed on William's face, looks back at her.

'You wouldn't have me stick an intruder who violates our privacy?' he says, breathless from his exertions.

'No violence in the house,' Raghnailt says.

Colca leans close to the man's face.

'It was the Fitzsimmons woman, wasn't it?' he yells, shaking him.

'Leave him go,' Raghnailt says.

Colca slaps William once across the face.

'You are a brute,' Colca says.

He gets up off him, and William turns on his belly, coughing and red-faced behind the residue.

'What do you want, man?' Raghnailt asks.

William wipes some tears out of his eyes, rubs the residue off his face and spits out the sick taste of death from his mouth. The small house he finds himself in is disgusting, worse than any peasant's. He is shocked to find a tradesman's house in such disrepair.

'I heard a woman in great pain,' he says. 'I did what any man would.'

Alannah walks inside, stepping over William's legs, and sits next to Raghnailt.

'What have you done to this woman,' William asks, 'chained like this?'

'It is for her own safety, and ours,' Raghnailt says. 'You would not understand. Things are not as simple as we would like them to be.'

'There is no explaining this away. I've never seen its likes, the poor girl.'

'Watch your tongue when speaking to my mother,' Colca says.

He clenches a fist, and William crawls backwards away from him.

'No,' Raghnailt says.

Colca looks at her, takes a deep breath.

'You have come to listen to my story?' Mary says to William. 'Will you listen?'

'Of course I will, my lady,' he says, 'though currently I am somewhat compromised.'

Something is ending, Raghnailt can feel it; but endings

always last too long. She has felt her life has been on the verge of ending for a long time, and she knows that is the feeling that has ruined what life there was in her.

The violence is endless, she thinks. We are always on the edge of it, she thinks, falling into it, unbalanced by some gust of emotion, but no one should ever be in chains.

'You, man, take Mary away from here, if you want her,' Raghnailt says, and her voice is clear. 'That woman you want lies out under full moons, on lunar binges, never sated. You may have her if you are that way inclined. She is one too many in the house, setting us off against one another like she is flint and we are dried straw; and she is not my family. We are not able to keep such a girl. And you, Colca, my boy, no violence in the house.'

Alannah stands up and begins undoing Mary's chains.

'What are you doing?' Colca shouts at his wife. 'That is not your woman to give away.' He pauses. 'My God,' he says. 'It was you two undid her and let her loose on Emota? My own wife and mother.'

He clutches at his hair, falls silent.

'Have some decency in company, son,' Raghnailt says.

'I loved her, Mother,' Colca says.

'You are talking about the horse, no?' Alannah asks. 'Because you do not love your mother or me.'

'I am trying,' Colca says. 'You make it hard, though.'

William, still stupefied from the blows to the head he has taken, is already guiding Mary away. She throws her arms round his neck, whispers a story into his ears.

'I cannot let you go with her, interfering man,' Colca shouts after William.

'Let them go,' Raghnailt says. 'I am sick of her, and I am tired. I want to spend time alone with my family. If I am to ever sleep well I need a cleaner soul to sleep with. This lad seems like a good sort.'

They are gone out the door. Colca looks after them; he seems defeated, weak.

'The man will kill us, burn us out,' he says softly. 'He has ways about him that I do not understand. You are killing us with this. You have condemned us to death. I must get her back.'

'This is my family,' Raghnailt says, gazing out the open door. 'And no one else is crossing the threshold.'

It is just Alannah, herself and her son in the room. It seems like something that has been broken, but its parts are still there. Everything is quiet.

'Mother,' Colca says. 'He'll kill us, I tell thee.'

'But son,' she says, 'I do not care any more. I have my family now; that is enough.'

Another dark room, a different one, but I am grown sick of them. They are too much, and too many. We will go outside soon; I need the light; have always needed it. The light in winter is softer; it colours the world with more delicacy. It is more tender; easier to make memories in, but I will always love summer the best. Áoife soaks the cloth, and daubs Joseph's forehead. His throat rattles. There is nothing human in this sound; it is from some other place, from a creature they don't know of yet. She leans forward and sucks in his breath, thirsty for his disease.

'This is something, but it's not love,' Joseph whispers into her mouth. 'I don't know what it is. Selfishness, perhaps.'

'I will die with you,' she says.

She sucks his breath in again.

'Stop,' he says. 'It doesn't make it any better.'

He tries to shake his head, but his neck is too thick with swelling.

'Why can't I die?' she says.

She tilts her head back, puts the cloth over her mouth and squeezes it so his sweat drips down her throat.

'I don't care,' he says.

She daubs her own face with the cloth, and then falls to her knees, begins kissing his feet.

'You must forgive me,' she says. 'Forgiveness is gentle. You are like that; soft and kind. I need forgiveness.'

'I'm not ready.'

'But—' she says.

Joseph cannot turn his head, so he cannot look away from her, though he wants to. He can't bear the sight of her any more; for him, her beauty is too cruel now.

'But I'll be dead in a few hours,' he says, 'and you not forgiven. That is all you care for. Not me, or my hurt.'

'I will die too,' she says.

She puts her head on his legs, and he moans. She is hurting him. His groin is full of a pain like fire.

'You would have caught it already,' he says.

Every movement of his mouth is an effort to him, a tiredness leaching away his power; he is moving beyond words. Perhaps, he thinks, you are only given a certain number of words in your life, and once you've spoken them all you die.

'But I love only you,' she says.

There is a knocking on the door; her eyes widen in outrage.

'Leave us alone,' she yells. 'Have you no respect? My husband is dying. He dies, and you knock, you band of sluts.'

The knocking stops, but she is still in a rage. She upends a chair, stamps on it. She is strong, energetic. I am too healthy, she thinks; my punishment is that I will not die.

'Beggars, perhaps; give them food,' Joseph says, 'but they can't come in. You could spread it even if you can't take it, but maybe the food has the sickness. No, keep it closed.'

He thinks of his duty to his guests, but not his wife. He would ignore her tantrum, the physical expression of her guilt. Momentarily, she hates him.

'Oh,' she says, 'you think of everyone. A kind word for the

whole town, but not for your own wife. Everyone but me, and what I ask of you.'

She had sucked Eoin Preston's cock. He had played with her belly, run his fingers down it, like they were a little person walking. She had laughed, trembled. He tickled her, behind her knees, on her throat, circled her navel with his tongue. She had almost had a seizure she had had such pleasure from him. Her legs couldn't stop shaking, could barely walk for an hour. It was last autumn, and she had done it twice. It had made her feel loose and warm.

And she had lied to herself during every part of it. It is just a walk, she had thought; just my hand; a kiss on the cheek; my breasts; just a finger, and by then it was happening. She hadn't felt guilt at first. Afterwards she felt freer, more loving of Joseph, but then, day by day, seeing Joseph's little kindnesses, his gentle idiocies towards her that were so full of love, her guilt grew until it made her feel ill in the mornings.

'I will go to hell, and you will go to heaven,' she says. 'And then I will not be allowed to see you again.'

Without moving his head, Joseph turns his eyes up at her. He wants to vomit, but he cannot open his mouth; even his throat is too weak to push out whatever substance is growing inside him. Unmoveable things are stuck inside him. Already, his body is a carcass, but his mind moves. Fungus will grow on me, he thinks; it is so disgusting. She is almost invisible in this dark; he cannot see her any more.

'I need a confession,' she says. 'And there are no priests left. I cannot—'

Segnat had given her some dried leaves, ground down and mixed with goat's milk, and told her to take the third part of it; to hide by the Boyne, like a cat when it births. It was bitter, and left her teeth black, but she had drunk it all. She couldn't keep it. She could never be sure, and the guilt was already too big, making her blind; sometimes she couldn't breathe with it, would wake up crying, and Joseph would embrace her, hit her back until she was sucking air again; would ask her what was wrong, promising her everything would be fine.

'Forgive me,' she says. 'It is your duty.'

It bled out by the Boyne, a little rivulet from her leading to the greater water. A sheep had drowned downstream, snagged on an upended tree. It still floated and bobbed. Its wool had come away and its bare body was a deep blue. Crows were pecking on it. They looked like growths when they stayed still. The sheep's belly was swollen and taut, enormous.

'Someone must forgive me,' she says, turning round, 'somewhere.'

Hers was the size of a finger. It looked of nothing, all blue; so small it could not be too big a sin, but she had kept bleeding. She examined it for a while wondering who it belonged to, but it was too foreign. It looked like a worm, a promise of something, but no one had made any promise.

Segnat had been following her, and she couldn't believe Áoife had survived drinking as much as she had. She took her home, nursed her for two days.

'Once your body returns, your feelings will be enormous for at least a month, perhaps longer. They will seem bigger than the world, but they are only feelings,' Segnat had told her. 'After that, I don't know. Anything could happen, but you will live.'

Is this my life? Áoife thinks. This is all just shadows and hate.

She told Joseph the truth once she saw he was sick, thinking it would make smaller the length of time they would be in pain, but now he does not have the heart – no, the time – to forgive her. It is unbearable; she cannot stand it. She thought she would also be dead soon, but she cannot catch it. She eats corrupted food, poisoned leaves, and nothing. I will live forever with this pain.

'I am not trying hard enough,' she says.

She goes over to Joseph; kneels down before him and lays her arms on his lap. Joseph groans in pain.

'You love another,' she says. 'You love another, I see it in your eyes; that is why you will not forgive me. If I give you a child you are not allowed to die. You must stay and mind it. We are both so young, so you will get better. Twenty-six is far too young to die; we don't have time for it. We must live together yet, so you must forgive me.'

In her spiel her elbow brushes over a protuberance on his thigh, and his whole leg jumps, kicking her weakly in the side. Tears are running down his eyes, but his face is frozen, his mouth hanging open in a wide rictus. Every hour he looks less like her husband, and more like a shrunken corpse.

'Is this where the pain is, my love?' she says. 'Is this where the sickness is kept?'

She pulls down his leggings and he is screaming at the friction of the fabric against his own raw flesh. On the inside of his thigh, under his right testicle, she sees one white growth, like an overgrown wart. She holds his sex out of the way, and leans in closer; peers at it. The white swelling has a strange shape; it is like a small face trying to escape through his skin.

Is this a foreign growth, or our child that will never escape? she thinks. It is ugly. Around the swelling are light bruises, encircled in black; the outer limit of the infection.

He says something, but he is speaking so low, she must put her ear next to his mouth.

'Water—'

She gets him a mug of water, and, while she is out of his line of vision, takes a loose nail from his basket of tools. He cannot swallow, so she wrings the water into his mouth from a cloth, but even this makes him cough. He is drowning in his own fluids.

'I'm not ready to forgive you,' he says. 'I am too young, and selfish. I'm not wise enough. I will not be given enough years to become wise.'

But he cannot move his tongue any more; he is only making a humming sound. None of his words have been spoken. She doesn't understand.

'Don't worry,' she says. 'It will be fine.'

She drops to her knees, pierces the white swelling with the nail. No blood comes out, and he does not flinch in pain; there is no feeling in the growth. She pierces the blue skin around it, and a drop of blood emerges. She wipes the blood on her finger and then puts it in her mouth.

'If this does not kill me, nothing will,' she says, showing him the finger. 'See how much I love you? See?'

There is blood on one of her front teeth. Joseph is tired, but his eyes won't close. He dreams of hitting her, stabbing Eoin. He always hated the Prestons. You hate people for reasons that haven't happened yet, but you know they will. He dreams of loving Áoife more, of her loving him more, but none of it matters. He knows his gentleness towards her has always been her greatest punishment. He has always manipulated it; and now there is nothing left. There was no point to their life together. He is going someplace else, and he doesn't know where. I will miss her, though, he thinks.

'I can't die no matter what I do,' she says.

She is crying now, and the sight of her in pain hurts him. Her hopelessness has defeated the anger he thought would guide him into death.

'I love you,' he says.

She can't hear him, and he realises, again, he hasn't said anything. These words will be trapped in me forever, unspoken. My body has stopped, only the sweat moves. This is the last of me.

There is a knocking on the door, and it is open. Áoife is standing up, walking towards it. There is no one outside.

'He's dead,' Genevieve is saying to her at the threshold.

She has timber under her arms.

'No, he's still alive,' Áoife is saying.

'Not Joseph; the man with the fine horse, that one who incited the men. He is dead. We are alone, without masters.'

And then that woman is gone, vanished, and Joseph understands that he is drifting in and out of consciousness. His throat has closed and he can only breathe through his nose; but his breathing is something he cannot control any more, it is just something that happens to his chest. There are two doors in his vision, two wives standing before him. One of his eyes sags closed by itself, and he still sees two of her.

'I am leaving,' she says. 'You are too cruel. Your body terrifies me. It is disgusting. I can't watch it any more.'

So she is abandoning him. This feels too abrupt to be real; she was always abrupt, though; but perhaps he fell unconscious again, and is only given brief flickers of lucidity. Even with all his senses intact, though, nothing could ever have prepared him for the depth of this solitude. She feels no obligation to him, and he needs her company. The door is closed and she is gone. My wife is gone; he wants to shout it. Everything is dark, and I am alone.

Soon he goes blind. Nothing moves any more. Everything is paralysed, and it is too hard to breathe all the time. He imagines the children they would have had, what their faces would have looked like. You cannot have children with such a woman, though. It is for the best what has happened. Even still, he would have lived with her forever, just the two of them together. There is no shame in that; if he had had pride he would have given her up, and that would have been giving up his happiness. She was always his happiness; and she has left him as he was dying. This pain will never stop.

I want to walk in the fields, he thinks.

A sensation enflames his chest and everything in him is trembling. He is coming apart. A bitter liquid surges from his throat and leaks down his chin. This is what he will choke on. This is the stuff that will kill him, these few morsels. There is no pain, only joy. It is so good to have lived; to have spent so little time alone in a life so full of other people; to have been alive. Ecstasy runs through his blood, every part of him is full of light. He is glowing, and can see, coming out of nothingness, a pink shining like illuminated blood, and then something is wrapped round him. It is sore. The pain of her touch on his body is hot, terrible. His ecstasy disintegrates; only pain remains, but it has no centre; it is everything.

'I will never leave you,' she whispers in his ear. 'Never. I swear it.'

She squeezes him tight; her burning cheek presses against his. Her tears are poison on his skin, burning holes through him. If he could scream, he would.

'You belong to me,' she says. 'You are mine.'

She will miss him forever.

'Is this village empty?' Harold asks. 'There is much quietness and disrepair.'

'Not disrepair,' Ambrosio remarks, 'age. This place is old. The village, actually, is quite full, but the people will not stir forth from their residences for fear of disease, and the sun is heavy, as your rosy cheeks do bear witness to.'

'Such a quiet place, so evil in its quietness; quite the opposite of life, I find,' Harold says.

Ambrosio's jaw falls open, and he shakes his head. 'We are not in life's opposite, serving-man,' he says, 'we are in its very essence.'

'Excuse, once again, this fool I carry, this millstone round my neck,' de Flunkl says to Ambrosio. 'On witnesses, by the by, can you call forth some to any affairs we might share in this room?'

Ambrosio hands de Flunkl his own mug of rosewater, its edge caked with yellowish grime. Glancing into the mug, de Flunkl sees that amongst the petals, a fly swims within a wall of shade.

'We have several witnesses,' Ambrosio says. 'Your sallow-faced friend who we shall call back. The tempestuous skinny, tall one with the midlands accent, I forget his name. That bearish, shaken fellow in the corner' – he nods his head at Harold. 'My lubricated wife; the retarded child you left outside, and there is a good fellow called Colca; reliable and gentle, who will be joining me soon. I don't know what is happening that he is not here already. I should probably fetch him.'

'Quite a little crowd,' Harold says, 'especially given the room is already so crowded with corpses.'

'As I've mentioned,' Ambrosio says. 'The gravedigger, de Fonteroy, will be here shortly. He deposes the bodies, transports them; controls a fine mass grave on his allotment. Oh, it is fine. His grain didn't come forth this year so he hollowed out his earth and has been making much monies thanks to the church, which in its cowardly retreat says the graveyard is full, as though the earth has reached its outer limit on how much capacity her soily body can hold, and the remaining bodies are to be rejected like vomit into unhallowed ground.'

Ambrosio begins looking around himself, breathing heavily, his voice becoming more frenetic. 'Enough, the earth has said,' he continues. 'No more. Let the dead lie in the streets, dangle amongst mulberry bushes; let them lie in fields as so much fertilising dung, in offices of the law, in barracks. There is no honour for them any more. No religion for them any more. No succour or prayer for them any more, but de Fonteroy's graveyard thrives.'

'Fool child,' Harold whispers to de Flunkl. 'Have you been so much enchanted by the confused words of this man who does work beside three dead bodies that it has not occurred to you that this Ambrosio has asked none of us our names, and is yet willing to enter into transactions with us? He is a scoundrel, and some sticking judgement approaches us.'

Ambrosio waves a hand at the serving-man, having over-heard him. 'I have the air of a scoundrel because I have the soul of one,' he says, more calm now. 'Names are meaning-less. Show me your papers and seals when the time comes. Let us exchange pleasantries before formalities. More rose-water?'

At this de Flunkl remembers to sip the mug he has been holding and nearly spits out the liquid on tasting that it is diluted cider and that the rose petals in it are rotting, most of them sunken to the bottom and broken into sediment.

This man, Ambrosio, de Flunkl finally realises, is drunk, though he hides it better than his wife. He had not understood this earlier, because of youth's inexperience. I must be careful, he thinks.

'I am sated,' de Flunkl says. 'And I am ready for business.'

'Yes, my little de Fonteroy has business; what the Provençals call enterprise,' Ambrosio says, while going over to the barrel of cider and washing his face in it.

'That is a little French word I learned in Nantes before I took my vows,' he says, his thin beard dripping. 'It is a better word than business, because it implies courage and glory. I was a young man when I learned that word; back then I had more scholarly ambitions; but the word has stayed with me. I never did take them, though, my vows, that is, as I fell into the trap of a largely bosomed Wallonian named Hildegard, twenty years my senior. She had fat cheeks and a thick roll of flesh on her chin one could suckle at while lovemaking. I remember how her downy moustache tickled me when we made love. It sets me shivering when I think of it, even now. She taught me the word, and taught me how to employ it. Still, she was a devil, though a particularly foxy and licentious one; my first love, albeit not my greatest one.'

'Well, then,' de Flunkl says, feigning cheerfulness. 'Let us enter into this so-called enterprise with no more dallying.'

'So, state your venture,' Ambrosio says. 'No more luxuriant chat, I will become plainspoken.'

De Flunkl turns round and sees Harold of Tuite, still leant against the wall. 'The hour is upon us,' de Flunkl says. 'Give me my things, if you are still with me.'

'I will happily give you it. It is the deadweight that drags you down below.'

Harold lifts up the sack and hands it to him. De Flunkl roots through it, taking out a handful of scrunched parchments and some small items that jingle. He does this until he comes upon what he seeks.

He unfurls a map of Meath and stares at the little crosses he has marked on it.

'I am purchasing lands, and given the inopportune absence off your mayor, you are to oversee the transactions, it would appear. I wish to purchase the right of use, in perpetuity, of Cregg, Garmanagh, Leafin, Posseckstown, Muff, Rath and Seller.'

'Excellent proposition,' Ambrosio smiles. 'Let us exchange other people's property. What is your price?'

'Forty pounds, ratified, now, for the lands and attached peasants' dwellings and eight pounds for you if you carry it off.'

'Oh, you greasy little noble: that is twenty times less than what these lands transacted but five years ago,' Ambrosio laughs. 'I wish I myself had thought of such a scheme. You are a clever one.'

'Lands come cheap,' Harold says, 'when they are devalued

by multitudinous death and disturbances of the peace so great as this one.'

'You had no shame in Trim,' de Flunkl remarks.

'Shame is what you learn, what is impressed upon you once you have sinned. I, at least, recognise my portion of our shame,' Harold says.

'Most admirable,' Ambrosio says, rubbing his hands together. 'Undervalued land; most ingenious. The more I think of it, the better it becomes.'

'You will do it, so?' de Flunkl asks, putting the map away and then picking out two big, misshapen pounds from the pile of miscellaneous rubble in the bottom of the sack.

He stretches his back, rubs the pounds together, hearing them scrape, and flicks them, with forced casualness, onto the crowded desk where they scatter under the sheaves of half-folded parchments. Ambrosio finishes off his mug, leaning his neck back so far he seems like a stork tossing live fish down itself, and then throws his mug into the barrel where it splashes, jellyfishing to the bottom as the air is expelled out of it in downward thrusts.

Ambrosio picks up the pounds and scrapes them together.

'How many properties and acres have you bought so far on this innovative trek?' Ambrosio asks. 'I must ask for I am wholly in awe of you.'

'Too many,' Harold says, 'and we have only been travelling three days.'

'The specific number is immaterial,' de Flunkl says, his chest puffing up with pride, 'and does not regard the business at hand; but you may rest assured it is in the many thousands, more lands than could be ridden over in a day.'

Ambrosio licks his upper lip, removing a drop of liquid from beneath his nose. 'That such a little sack could contain so much of this country,' he says.

'And what do your sacks contain?' Harold says, pointing at the three shrouds slouched in the chairs.

'Will you oversee the transaction?' de Flunkl asks, ignoring Harold. 'We have checked the flurries of obituaries occurring in the townlands that will be transitioned back to the king unless there is a counterclaim.'

'The Bishop of Armagh still oversees Leafin,' Ambrosio says, 'and Muff, but you will still have your killing. I will transact it, but I would ask you another question first.'

He leans against the table, perhaps to hide his drunkenness; Harold has already noticed him discreetly stumbling once or twice.

'Ask away,' de Flunkl says.

'What are you afraid of?'

'What?' de Flunkl says. 'I am not afraid.'

'You are,' Ambrosio says. 'You twitch and tremble and your voice does crack. I thought at first it was your youth, which is always a turbulent experience, but now I regard that there does seems to be some greater turbulence within you? You seem unsure of your own genius. You are so in fear I can smell it off you. You are incomplete.'

De Flunkl shrugs, but when he begins to speak his voice grows clearer, as though he has been waiting some time to say what he says. 'I am young, ambitious and rich. The sickness is a gift to one as adroit as me, but still the clutching blindness of my peers does have its effects on the purity of my schemes. Even my servants are jealous of my spirit. But I must persevere now. Jesus was also sinned against, I always remember that. It is now I shall make my move upon the staggering world and the name of Sir Osprey de Flunkl will ring down throughout the ages. It shall flourish in posterity, and last longer than any honey would in the deepest bog. My line, and I, its founder, will be forever esteemed for my good management of stocks and my fairness and firmness with my requisite peasants and animals. But still I am unsure of myself because my victory can only be hallowed out at a later date, a posthumous one, and I must have faith in the trickling whoredom of destiny. But that is later. Now, I feel like the world is against me. I do feel it inside me; and what I fear most is posterity's silence, its possible disregard for my greatness. I feel, like an absence in my gut, the coming onslaught of the millennia forgetting me sometimes, and I would not have it. I am afraid of time emptying itself of me, becoming blank once more.'

'Liar,' Harold says, still looking at the shrouds in the corner. 'The world is only against unnaturalness, and you feel your sin to put you in another category above the common people, using the conflict you yourself have nurtured as proof of your superiority. It is what gives you pride, but it is imaginary. It is very easy to inherit wealth and sign deeds. If you are remembered, little boy, it will only be as one who merely took the trouble to be born.'

'You see what I must contend with?' de Flunkl says, appealing to Ambrosio, who only giggles.

'Please excuse me, sir,' he says, covering his mouth with his hand. 'I do not agree with this lowly man and I certainly don't wish to offend you, sir, but there is something you said that set me tittering. Yes, the world is against you. It is against us all, but, surely you know there is only one thing in this deathly room that will survive even twenty years and that is the two coins that warm my palm. No, sir,' Ambrosio continues, looking at the coins in his open hand. 'No offence given, but these are all that shall be carried through the ages. The property deeds that teem within your sack, all bunched up, flutter and fade into nothingness. Property is disputed, its borders coerced. Names are changed. Land becomes forest, or barren, or desert, or bog. But these few pounds, they will pass from hand to hand, fluctuating, devalued, reminted, but eternal in the value internalised within them, because as long as there are three men in a room' – he glances at Harold Tuite momentarily, then at de Flunkl – 'though the whole world is dead, and those three men all agree that it is worth cutting each other's throats for these, these coin shall last. And because they agree to it, there will be a power maintained in acquiescence to it that can harden and maintain its value.'

'This man is completely and utterly insane,' Harold says, 'and I have not yet understood a word he has spoken.'

'Oh, I'm no fool,' Ambrosio continues, looking up at Harold, 'don't mistake me. Money is the king's estate and the king's estate is almost broken, but it will remain because there is no vision beyond it. Not that the king has any vision. Forgive me, but he is injudicious and weak, and yet he is the recipient of a larger vision into which he falls accidentally. It is his birth right: this accidental, enormous inheritance. But his face is on these coins and they are the remnants of some older people's vision that cannot be abnegated with a mere word, or some fleeting desire.'

218

Ambrosio has become frenetic again. He slams the coins down on the table. Everything is silent for a moment. The coins shudder and spin on the wood until they come to rest in stillness.

'Whether we be with the king or against him,' he says, 'we are all for the face stamped on these pounds, which is his. Who else's could it be? What face could withstand such tumultuous exchange but his? All the legions of Babylonian whores could not withstand the wear and the friction of having been passed between men as much as his two faces on that table there.' He points at the pounds. 'What could replace it? The money is not the king, but the king is the money. They are intertwined forever. What can replace it?'

He looks at them for a moment, and then Harold shrugs. 'God,' he says.

'What?' Ambrosio says.

'God will replace us all; that is the authority you sought but could not find earlier, because you yourself are lost. We will go into God, or we will be pushed away from him. There are only two places. Within his love, or without it.'

'But the king is divinely appointed,' Ambrosio says, 'or at least his money is universally accepted, which is some kind of divinity. Leave God to God. I speak of the waking world, that glimmering, earthly space between two winks of an eye; his blessed plaything so briefly inhabited, which is this heavy world; a world so much fuller of things than his one. I speak of that, for nowadays when I pray that is all that speaks back to me.'

'God is all I will say,' Harold Tuite says. 'All I will say till I die.'

Ambrosio spits on the floor and crosses himself. 'You are taking my words into places I would not have them gone,' he says. 'I spoke of the world, which is the king's, and there are only two groupings that could decompose the king's estate; but they will not; the estate will not fall, it will flounder yet remain.'

De Flunkl puts his hands up in the air, as though calling for a truce. 'May we leave this discussion till luncheon?' he asks, sounding flustered. 'I feel like I have been in this stuffy room an age and I want my properties.'

'Tell me these two groupings,' Harold says.

Harold is holding for time, hoping something new will happen; but it is only instinct driving him now. He does not know why, but, somehow, he feels, this transaction must be delayed. I would not be the man, he thinks, who has overseen a formal transaction with dead bodies by his feet.

'You intrigue me,' Harold continues. 'Hell-bound lunatics have always done so, though it is a weakness I have only recently begun to permit myself, and you may look to my travelling master for the proof of it.'

He gestures towards de Flunkl, who sighs with the fatigue of this constant conflict he cannot remember which of them first broached.

'I will happily tell you,' Ambrosio says, his eyes widening. 'You know I have always wanted to write it down in a little treatise, my ideas on the overcoming of the king's estate; but I would be burnt for it as a treason-man or some Italianate heretic, though I think such a work would be surely in the service of the king; but I would not that I was burnt. If I had a protector I could perhaps venture – but I will never have a protector.'

Ambrosio's hand slips off the desk, and he stumbles slightly. Everything in Harold wants to help up this pathetic drunkard, but he restrains himself. There is something deeply obscene and despairing in this man; it is almost pitiable. The man flails about for a moment, and when he regains his balance, he looks up and grins, as though it were all a joke.

'I apologise,' he says. 'You see before you the other reason I could not write a sensible treatise. I was a good student once, but now my Latin is almost gone. I never finished my studies. You see, I loved too many whores; drank off too many flagons; fell in love with easy pleasures, gambled away all my books – I had a little collection once, it was my pride and joy; I was always falling out of grace, always losing a little more of what little I started with, but what most killed my ambition, ended it entirely, was—'

His face grows pale and he feels his own neck with both his hands. He was so full of words, Harold thinks, and now he is so tongue-tied.

'What would you have written if you had done so?' Harold says, his voice almost gentle.

'The properties,' de Flunkl says, shaking his head. 'What of the properties?'

'It would have had two parts,' Ambrosio says slowly, 'one for each group that could most endanger the estate; and its conclusion would have been how they could never undo it, even if they wanted it undone. If I had written it in some easy style it would have made a great accomplishment, been appraised and mulled over in more learned circles.'

'Tell me it,' Harold says.

'What is this?' de Flunkl hisses at Harold. 'What are you doing?'

'The first group is peasants,' Ambrosio says. 'The lands are emptied out now and there are too few peasants to till the earth, but still their only wish is that their wages be raised. They could, in this confusion, or any of the ones that have so often beset us, seize the country, reign it eternally, make it in their own lowly image, but even their dreams are limited by coin. Even they are trapped within its dreams, they who gain nothing from allegiance to it. Yes, they occasionally riot and come together in their little groupings to demand a few more half pennies, like they did in Cork last month, but they have lesser and fewer feelings than developed people like us, smaller emotions, and therefore less ambition outside what they can see. Ultimately, they're cattle that have learned language. Usually they are just speaking cattle, content with their lot of grass; but even now, when they do not have their lot of grass, there will still never be a peasants' reckoning. They have not the vision for it. And I will tell you another reason why, beyond the frequent deaths that overcome them. Peasants are flowing out of the country, fleeing to Calais and Liverpool to escape the pangs of hunger, because inside peasants are only two things: a brutish cowardice sanctified by God, which means they could never undertake a far-reaching venture like my lord's' – he nods to de Flunkl – 'and a certain wandersomeness that comes about from not holding property. They seem toe-tied, an imbedded part of their local earth, but then their stomachs set them on their traitorous feet and they pack up their whole families and go elsewhere, ensuring their bodies are saved, but giving up the greater gains that could be garnered from adventuresome risk.'

'This is most sensible arguing,' de Flunkl says. 'But, please, let us proceed on business; delay the conclusion somewhat to this fascinating discussion. I have already been tired out with the outlandish opinions of Gaels all morning and I have no wish to be receptive to more speechifying, although this is of a more sensical sort; and I mean no disrespect by it. I want to do my business; and so rid myself of ineffective servants by paying them off with my windfall. Nobber has become oppressive to me; and its heat does not sit well in me.'

'Who is the second group?' Harold Tuite asks.

'You know who,' Ambrosio giggles. 'In your heart, you know. Your master just spoke of them.'

'Ineffective servants?' Harold asks.

'Why Gaels, of course,' Ambrosio says. 'But they have no unity. Their rivalries are too many millennia old, older even than Christ. They can't leave them behind, and their culture doesn't allow them to realise there is anything beyond their clans. Even though they trade as far as Constantinople their value lies only in Meath's fat cattle and other such fleshy earthbound things. And fleshy things cannot grow as fast as our metals and loans, so they fall behind. They have been falling behind for centuries, and yet still they don't recognise it. Still, they wear those bright unwieldy clothes and speak that barbaric language. But if they ever did unite their warring factions, they would be a greater risk than the peasants, because their culture values glory and strength, whereas ours funnels vision through a flaccid aristocracy that interbreeds with a church that is wholly bent on outlawing courage, curiosity and its subsequent understanding. And I must say thank God for the Gael's constant internecine warring, because if you ever deigned to inspect such barbarity, Gaelic visions are deeply inhuman, animalistic and very, very far from God. They do not even care for money.'

'Animals,' de Flunkl says, 'but my properties—'

'De Fonteroy did tell me once how he did trade with a-one but last year,' Ambrosio says, 'and he gave this Gael a choice between a few moments with a buxom and frothy-lipped Galwegian whore he was transporting on his cart, or that money that would have bought the Gael five of them for an afternoon's pleasure, and the Gael chose the former, and said he knew that de Fonteroy believed him a fool, but who was the true fool that would take the expectation of joy over the joy itself?'

'I repeat, animals,' de Flunkl says, 'but prithee do stop this idle chat. Let us signature the documents. Presently, we must search witnesses.'

'Do you not think they are coming together now?' Harold asks. 'They are alighting on territories they have not known for some time; winning preferential treaties on the strength of their raids as they have never done before.'

'Individually, perhaps,' Ambrosio says. 'But do you ever see more than four of them working together in their—'

The door is flung open and William of Roscrea flies in, dragging Mary by the wrist behind him, his heavy boots clattering down the few stone steps as he descends in a pool of light unleashed by the open door. Mary is sobbing; de Flunkl steps back in shock, his hand over his heart.

'I knew you would return,' Harold says, feeling relieved, as though a weight has been taken off his soul.

William of Roscrea, his eyes narrow as pins from the sunshine he has just left, releases Mary and points a finger at Ambrosio, who leans back against the desk as though the finger had pushed him off balance.

'This scoundrel is no Ambrosio,' William says, 'and he would have been your very gravedigger had I not intervened.'

'I am leaving,' Alannah says.

'Pull us milk when you are out,' Raghnailt says, stooped over the hay she is clearing out. 'I'm sure no one will mind. The bucket is by the forge.'

'No, I am going home.'

Alannah is standing in the doorway, looking out at the street. A new life, for her, will begin. It is unexpected but welcome, like the second roses of the year. Though restless, she controls her excitement by concentrating on the stillness of her body and the small town that contains it, the listless green vista opening up before her.

Some end is approaching, but she does not mind. One place is very like another; she has left behind, and been left behind before. Even the pain of separation grows weaker with each new rent, becomes familiar. She wonders if she has grown foreign to her own family, if she is more like a Norman than she would have ever imagined.

'I am only telling you this because I am fond of you. You have been good company to me, kind.'

Raghnailt leans her broom against the wall. 'You cannot,' she says. 'You are married to him; that is a sticking vow. God has joined you two together.'

'I do not believe in that thing,' she says.

She does not look back at her mother-in-law.

'Do not say that,' Raghnailt says, sitting down on the bed. 'I was almost happy, but a few moments ago. Do not leave me.'

A butterfly flutters into the room, the colour of cream. It is so thin that Alannah can see the light shining through it. It does not take long for the butterfly to become entrapped by the webs. I would free it, Alannah thinks, but I am not tall enough. It is very beautiful.

'I once had a boy, a love, you know,' Alannah says. 'I was not fond of it, though: love. It was a smouldering tumour, big in the breast, a black carcass strapped across the back. He was sweet, sang songs for me, brought me little animals to play with. He would even pull their fangs before he gave them to me for fear they would damage my skin, which he loved. How do you take it when someone thinks so much of you; of your safety and your happiness? You are in a different part of the land and their thoughts are with you, a second being shadowing your body.'

'I do not remember,' Raghnailt says. 'I know, though, that our family will change its shape now, for the better.'

Raghnailt's hands feel the pillow, come into contact with a few strands of Alannah's hair that remain there, and the fear rises in her chest once more.

'He was from another mountain,' Alannah says. 'His soft voice, his hands, his veiny cock, balls on him like a sagging pouch of wine. Yes, I loved him, but very momentarily. He stuck too close to me, and I grew suffocated by his presence. He was so empty, even his breathing annoyed me. His voice was like crows to me, and my love for him faded. Still I am grateful to him for he did not reduce me. I was left without disease, without pregnancy.'

227

'Why are you telling me about this?' Raghnailt says.

'His voice began to drive me crazy,' she says. 'He was a weight on my throat, a restriction on my breathing. He followed me everywhere. I saw stars, my blood felt too hot. I was unable to sleep he vexed me so much. Do you think two people can live together? Perhaps four, or eight or twenty, yes, but not two?'

'You're not making any sense,' Raghnailt says.

'I left the most part of myself behind when I came here,' she says. 'I gave up my past and myself, but what is that to a cousin, a sister, an uncle, a clan? They asked me, and I came; now they ask, and I return.'

'You are ours now,' Raghnailt says. 'You are my daughter.'

Alannah turns, and goes back to Raghnailt. She holds her hands. 'I have been called back,' she answers.

'I need you.'

'You would not understand,' she says. 'I am as different from you as a wolf. You are but a foreigner here, and this land you dally on is not yours to keep.'

Raghnailt pushes her hands away. 'I am sick of your veiled words,' she says. 'You make yourself distant on purpose, more unknowable than you really are. It is an act of obfuscation to justify yourselves, to make yourselves seem different from us because you do not like us. You Gaels just love yourselves too much; I cannot stand it. It is fake, I know it. You spend your days discussing your little differences from us, as though they were real, and they are not. You are not magic, you are not mysterious, and you are not different. You have made yourselves up. It's all lies, and it is so conceited. There is nothing that could not be understood if you spoke openly and plainly.'

Alannah brushes Raghnailt's cheek, and embraces her. 'You are so sweet, so good,' Alannah says. 'Just like a woman, believing words are tools that can shape people, that if there are enough of them in the right place you could pile them on top of one another and build something good. You are so good it makes my heart burst with it. I love you for it.'

Raghnailt pushes her away again. 'Get away from me,' she says. 'I am not some silly old woman you can coddle. You are my daughter, and you should respect me.'

'I am your daughter, and I am gone. There are no words that could keep me, and you are not the violent sort to restrain me – that is your son, and he would not mind to see me go.'

'He will love you now,' Raghnailt says. 'He has been too violent with you, and neglectful of you where he shouldn't be, but that will stop. Things will get better. He has sworn it. Mary has been taken away by the sallow man, and we are pure family once more. He will spend more time around the house with us; we will soften him with our company until he is made good again. We must build him anew, together, for you are my daughter and his wife, but we are more like sisters, the fun we have together, no?'

Alannah kisses her hand, growing even more enamoured with this woman now she is leaving her. 'You believe that?'

Raghnailt nods.

'You fill me with pity, but you must be strong,' Alannah says. 'Go to the door and see a long man succumbing to sunstroke and lust.'

Raghnailt shakes her head.

'You already know?' Alannah asks.

'I know nothing, and I want to know nothing.'

'It is important to not be weak.'

'I am but an old woman who needs her daughter and her son to protect her,' she says. 'Allow me to be weak regarding my own family, my last joy.'

Alannah grabs her shoulders. 'No, you are not that old. You are strong, but you want to be loved, and you think weakness provokes love? Norman women are shocking creations, snivelling bitches to a soul. How do you survive a day?'

'Why are you being so mean to me?'

'Because I love you. Go to the door now.'

Raghnailt shakes her head. 'I will not.'

'People are easy to leave behind,' she says. 'Our feminine natures breed sympathy in us like mushrooms that grow in the hollows of trees. The tree feels no harm is being done, but their life is sucked away without notice. Leave me behind, as I do you.'

Raghnailt's eyes widen; she clutches at the bed. 'You have gone mad,' she says. 'We have not loved you enough; it is our fault.'

'Of course I have gone mad. The world is at war, no?' Alannah says. 'But we each have our own little apocalypse; everyone has their own one. Mine will come someday, and I would not be attached to someone like Colca while the Gaels grow stronger. He is a brute, and if anything is left in the world after this sickness it will be the Gaels. It does not touch us, because we are so free, so much ourselves.'

'What nonsense,' Raghnailt says. 'What lies you say.'

Alannah does a turn around the room until she has calmed herself. She kicks at the hay. 'I am sorry,' she says. 'I am so excited I am raving. Go look out in the street.'

'Will you stay here if I do?' Raghnailt asks.

Alannah shakes her head. 'Not a single moment more.'

'I don't understand,' Raghnailt says.

'You do.'

Raghnailt rises and goes out to the door. Down the street, she sees a young man lying on his back, moaning near the fountain; two new horses tied to a post; a small blond girl, bleached white in the light, presses against the walls of Toqville's house. Her son also is there in the street, with the dead horse. She sees it and falls against the door, as though struck by a great force.

Colca turns his head towards her, his eyes shocked amidst the blackness of his face, and withdraws from the horse, lowering himself down so he is hidden, thinking himself unseen.

'You would not keep me with your son, would you?' Alannah says. 'You are too good for that.'

She helps her mother-in-law back to the bed. There is no more emotion left in Raghnailt; her mind is empty; she will not clean the house today.

'No.'

'I love you,' Alannah says.

Raghnailt nods.

'I would ask you to not go outside today,' Alannah says. 'Stay indoors till nightfall. There will be some confusion released soon. You must stay inside.'

'I will.'

'Say farewell to me,' Alannah asks, standing over her.

Raghnailt gazes at the webs on the ceiling. 'I have just remembered it is Sunday,' she says. 'Do you think the sickness will end soon?'

Alannah doesn't answer.

'No matter how close to the end,' Raghnailt says, 'people still do their duty as much as they're able, if they're let. That is the proper way to live.'

'If no one else knows how good you are, I will always know,' Alannah says. 'Kiss me farewell.'

'My love for my boy has accumulated since the day he was born,' she says, 'it has only grown bigger. I want it to stop. Will it?'

'I don't know. How could I know?'

Alannah sits down next to her, brushes her mother-in-law's hair back from her eyes.

'Go, get out of this town,' Raghnailt says. 'You are young enough to begin once more. Leave me now.'

Alannah takes her hand and presses it to her lips. 'I will wait with you a little while, Mother,' she says. 'I do not have to go just yet.'

'That man is an imposter of the grossest proportions,' William of Roscrea says, 'and he has killed many men, and even women. He has used the confusion of the sickness to remake himself as some official of the estate, but he is nothing but a vagabond pretender. The mayor is dead, and this rogue has driven the villagers into hiding by threatening to reveal their truth, which is that they, the villagers themselves, killed him, his wife and his son, in a mobbish fit after the outbreak of the sickness.

'This vagrant, who stumbled upon the scene, promised he could bureaucratise away the murders so they accepted his shenanigans and lodged him in the position he now pretends to, and out of which he makes his monies. But once the towns-people repented, the liberalness of his blade and their own actions meant that they could have no recourse to any justice, they being so guilty themselves.'

Harold gasps and they all look at the man, even Mary, whose teary face is pale beneath the blood and who is shaking with either delirium tremens or fear. The man who was Ambrosio looks appealingly at de Flunkl.

'My liege,' he says. 'I beseech you. Will you stand by and watch a good man slandered by the report of a woman? Let me call forth Colca and he will make sensible plea for me.'

Mary releases a wail that fills the room like another living body. 'That devil,' she screams, 'forced me into strangeness with him out of wedlock. He said I would be torn at the roadside by bandit Gaels unless he protected me, and I humoured him as a wife for fear. He said either he took me, or every man in the town would. I only did so for my daughter, but even she he has stolen from me in gross and unspeakable violations. But I swear to you, I never saw him before last month, and furthermore . . .'

She points at the largest shroud.

'. . . that sack is full of the mayor. Next to him lie his wife and his only son in their littler sacks. And if they do leave these properties there shall be no proofs against him, or this accursed town.'

She finishes, fainting back into William's arms. The nameless man lunges forward as though to catch her, but is stopped by Harold, who steps in front of him. Harold is almost retching, overwhelmed, and then, almost immediately, he draws a breath and his face goes blank.

'You speak of business with a wanted murderer who brings the estate of the king into disrepute,' Harold says to de Flunkl.

Harold, silent and emotionless for the first time all day, walks slowly over to the sack, wrenches it firmly out of de Flunkl's hand, leans over and begins searching within it.

'Produce the paperwork for those corpses or you will hang by the law's noose,' Harold says, kneeling over the sack, peering into it, rooting around.

A mote of light crosses the room from the door, and the nameless man is perspiring so much he must blink his eyes. He raises his palms up.

'Consider this one thing, sir,' he says, directing himself to de Flunkl. 'I have carried off several properties, their surrounding lands included, successfully in the newfound role that I have been blessed with, and come to much more naturally, I add, than has been proposed here. Ye are not the first to stumble upon this town with this venture; that is all I ask you to consider, before you make any rash judgements.'

'Produce the papers of these corpses,' Harold says.

'We will remove the shrouds and match the documentation with the rotting facial features contained within,' William concurs. 'That is all that will be considered.'

De Flunkl is thoughtful. He bites his nails, looking down.

'No,' de Flunkl says, his voice fluttering like a pigeon's wings. 'Show me also the papers for the properties you have carried off.'

The man's face relaxes in relief. 'Of course, my lord.'

He moves behind the desk and starts searching in the packed cubbyholes, his hands trembling, glancing towards the shrouds occasionally. Harold Tuite raises himself off his knees, draws his hand from the sack and there, in his right hand, is a hunting knife.

'You would do business with a pretender,' William says to de Flunkl. 'I do not serve you.'

'I will only respect the paperwork relating to the dead,' Harold says, his voice booming in the low-ceilinged room, and then he points the knife at de Flunkl. 'I also no longer serve this man, and I never respected him.'

'So, de Flunkl,' William says. 'I suspected you wouldn't mind bartering with a scoundrel; that the implementation of your venture preceded your morals, of which you have none. Such unnatural schemes I have already gone along with, for the cost of my damnation, and I am little better than you for going along with it so far as I have done. You would usurp anything, all natural law, for your glory and the swelling of your properties, but there is one thing this suffering damsel reported to me that I did not tell you.'

De Flunkl looks at him, defiant, though still trembling.

'This man changes monikers more frequently than cuckoos change nests. What his real name is no one knows, but all the previous ones he has adopted have been wanted by many sheriffs. He is acclaimed and much wanted all over Cavan and Louth since the spring – when the recrudescence appeared, most fortuitously for him – for surprising, killing and collecting bodies. His infamy sprang up from the fact that after his liberal slaughtering he would have the gall to charge the very town in which he engaged in slaughter for the removal of the very corpses he himself produced – and he would be charging this damned town presently for our corpses if I had not warned you. He has lured many men into commerce with him with his easy, headlong manner; and then murdered them once they signed some poorly dated contract. Afterwards, he buries them with anonymity on his own lot. He robs the corpses he manufactures of their papers, their very clothes, and masquerades as all the men whose names he has confiscated. At every stage of the nefarious process he is well compensated. That is truth he spoke; we are not the first to Nobber to buy it up; but, with God's blessing, we may be the first to leave it with breath still in our bodies.

'He is the devil, as Harold's premonitions so remarkably foresaw, and I am sure Ambrosio is only his latest incarnation. It is a name I am sure that has been stolen from a worthy and real Ambrosio that was slaughtered for the colour of his eyes and the fatness of his purse. There are no transactions you could carry out here that would bear out any legality in any court. There is only looting and banditry; the tears of maidens and the squalling of widows, and I have saved your worthless life by this intervention, even though you, de Flunkl yourself, are another form of scum, and to my greatest misfortune, you are the particular scum that has settled at the bottom of my soul.'

'Colca,' the man who was called Ambrosio yells. 'Colca, come hither.'

'What is the devil to do when his demons abandon him?' William says. 'This town is too strange even for one as evil and erratic as you to tame. You chose badly, man, when you came here and you chose badly when you took up with that farrier.'

'You would take the word of a drunken slut over me?' the man yells, his face bright red. 'De Fonteroy, my partner, will be here soon. He will vouch for me.'

'Another moniker, no doubt,' Harold says. 'Or perhaps, just another scoundrel. The land swells with them.'

'You want the papers, serving man,' the man says to Harold. 'Here are the papers, look to them.'

He holds forth a roll of parchment wrapped strangely round his fist.

'You are my men,' de Flunkl says. 'There will be no slander of my name and there will be no mutiny at this crucial hour.'

'Do not look at anyone else,' Harold says, wagging his fingers at the nameless man. 'There is no need. It is only you and I in this room. Give me the papers.'

The man continues looking at de Flunkl.

'It is my voice you will respect and heed,' Harold Tuite says calmly. 'I am the only one who your life respects. Hanging is quick, at least.'

De Flunkl looks to his men, and then looks away. His shoulders collapse; his superiority broken.

'Give him the papers,' he says.

The man nods, giving a weak grimace, and walks towards Harold. Harold holds his hands out, but the man ignores his hands and pushes the parchments into Harold Tuite's chest, who steps back, breathless, the ruddy colour draining out of his face. The roll of parchment falls away to the ground, revealing the hilt of a small dagger protruding from his heart.

Everything is silent for a moment. Harold releases a loose sneeze of blood from his nose and looks down at his front.

'I am killed,' he says, 'by a nameless scoundrel.'

Then, slowly, he falls sideways heavily, and the man is knocked down and trapped under the weight of the dying Harold.

Harold Tuite breathes and shudders with big wracks and the man tries to wriggle out from under his weight. William and de Flunkl look at each other, frozen, and Mary comes to and screams at them.

'You are useless excuses of men. I shall do this most necessary work.'

She runs over to where the man is trapped under Harold Tuite.

'What have you done to us?' the man wheezes. 'Do you not reme—'

She stamps on his head once with the flat of her foot. His skull cracks back on the flagstone underneath him and he groans and goes unconscious, his eyes upturned in his head.

Harold Tuite is still gasping air loudly, his eyes wide in panic, and she sits astride his back.

'For leverage,' she explains to the men who watch her.

Harold Tuite tries to turn his neck to see why there is a young blood-covered woman on top of him, but he doesn't have the strength.

'You are not my family,' he says, choking, a teardrop of blood leaking out of his right eye.

Mary leans down, and places her hands round the neck of the man and starts throttling him.

De Flunkl and William watch for a long moment and then Mary turns her head up towards them, while still engaged in throttling the man.

'Don't look at me like that,' she screams, spittle loosing itself from her lips.

William and de Flunkl are speechless. They watch on as the man's face goes purple. Then, when his face is so dark that the features are rendered almost invisible, his tongue pokes out of his lips and lolls loosely out the side of his mouth.

William blinks once; decides to leave. He turns and walks up the stairs and de Flunkl follows after him.

Outside, the light is big, multifaceted, throwing all colours in strong relief. The world is too loose and too big to grasp in one set of eyes. It cannot be held in anyone's hands, in any one person's senses, and the two men are blinded by the sun, and too many things are happening at once.

There is a Gael with his face painted black sitting sideways on one of their horses, like a lady, picking at the calluses on his feet with incredibly long fingernails. Another Gael is untying de Flunkl's horses' reins from the post to which they have been secured.

'Our horses,' William of Roscrea yells, running towards them, and an arrow slides through him from behind. He looks down and sees the tipped head has come out through his bellybutton. Silence breaks through him; it flows like a river. Gaelic words come out of the sky and he looks at the big curving blue expanse above him, listless in its lazy, ever-present power, and he hears the mutilated sky, in Gaelic, apologising for killing him, and he thinks of how it makes sense, that, of course, God is both a Gael and mischievous.

And then it occurs to William that he is dying.

The voice is coming from the sky, but it is behind him. It is saying that it is sorry for killing someone with such a remarkable faculty for the earth's native language, and that in kinder times it would have had him visit the clan, and have fed him well, and have given him the head of the table as the choice, honoured story-teller.

William tries to turn towards the voice and the muscles in his stomach blossom in a pain that explodes through his system. Blood is leaking inside him in the wrong places. He feels a hole has gone through him the size of a fist, but he knows it is not true and the cause of his pain has narrow dimensions.

Finally managing to turn, he sees Saint John has taken off his tunic and is still playing in the dirt with the dead mare's warm intestines, draped over his shoulders. Then he sees two Gaels, holding bows and fistfuls of arrows with crows' feathers for fletching, crouched on the roof of the dwelling from which he so recently emerged. The crazy, carved women jingle around their necks and they look sad now even though their faces are still grinning. These Gaels' faces are painted black, too, and it is as though they have painted their faces black in mourning for him.

The whole world mourns him. He is the centre of this moment and he feels wonder at this appreciation.

'I enjoyed our discussion this morning,' William says to them, waving at them a little. He stumbles, feels himself fainting.

His gaze lowers involuntarily and he sees de Flunkl is pressed against the wall, hiding in the shade of the doorway. There de Flunkl's eyes gleam a little too strongly, and it occurs to William in a rush of insight that de Flunkl himself was the devil Harold predicted they would meet in Nobber.

He was always the devil, and William knows he will grow more into his mischievous role, that he will deepen himself into it, and that all his trembling was the pangs of growth, the outward manifestation of an ungodly energy that will expand until it has conquered the whole earth.

'I am gut shot,' William says to him. 'I would like to go to that peaceful crannóg we came upon earlier. Poor Harold was fond of it. At least I was killed by better men. May God save his dead children. But,' he says, in an afterthought, 'I do want life, though.'

He turns again, confusions searing his brain, making him blind, and then when he can see again he is sitting on the edge of the fountain and the Gaels have lowered themselves down from the roof.

Saint John is sitting next to him now, holding something to give to him. The intestines are still hanging loosely around the young man. His shoulders and ears are tipped red with sunburn. Soft and gentle, that tingling feeling from the sun; William imagines it. I will never see the sun's light again.

He sways, worried that he might fall backwards into the fountain and drown; sees Saint John is holding a baby rat out to him, cupped in his hands. The little rat's nose is pink and searching, sniffing at him. It is young to the world and curious.

'The Gaels gave it to me. Feel its warmth, its beating heart. Life is like nothing else. It is beautiful,' Saint John says.

The pain is everywhere now. There is nothing outside it. Tears roll down William's cheeks. He leans forward, his gut spasming.

'Stupid child,' he whispers.

There are now two Gaels astride each horse. The oldest gives a yell and a sack is dropped. A legion of rats stream out of it, dispersing like smoke, flooding the town. There were perhaps fifty rats, and now, already, they are gone to ground. Terrified of the light, they will live beneath this town forever. William looks up once more and sees Alannah, in a blur, jumping up cleanly into the lap of one of the younger Gaels. Three Gaels on a single horse; they are a many-headed monster; a busy people. She has cut the hem of her dress to above her knees, he notices. The oldest Gael yells again and the Gaels start riding hard and the clatter of hooves is thunder inside William's torn belly. He feels the earth's trembling through his boots sending hot sparks up through his bones.

The most beautiful creature in the world is riding away, the woman he should have gone with, but he is not jealous. He wants for nothing; perhaps a sip of water. Happiness is flooding through him, and he smiles. He loves the air, loves it in his mouth, but now leave William with his small death, growing bigger inside him. He keels forward.

De Flunkl, on seeing the Gaels leave on his horses, slides back into the house and he is shocked to find that he can barely see the far wall of the little room for all the flies swarming about, can barely hear through the buzzing Mary crying over the nameless man, hugging him in her arms. The man's neck is all angular and limp; a slim bone peeks sharply through the skin, jagged and red, a blue vein wrapped round it like creeping ivy, and de Flunkl averts his gaze from it. It is an intrusion into death too far, that sneaking bone, he feels.

'Big Cat,' she sobs. 'Come back to me; I will be good this time.'

Harold Tuite is dead underneath her, too, his eyes blank and upturned. The three sacks of bodies above them look as though they are spectators at some gladiatorial sport. De Flunkl feels himself perfectly aligned with the scene, and he realises that if there is a victor it is him and only him, and this sets his heart beating fast.

'I am the master of all this,' he whispers.

He tiptoes to his sack, swatting flies from his cheeks and eyes as he moves. He slings the sack over his shoulder and then goes over to the table and pushes all the loose papers on it into his sack, pushing them down and compressing them so they fit. Then he goes and empties the cubbyholes, putting in all the items that will fit until his sack is heavy and brimming. Finally, he picks up the two pounds that are all that is left on the bare table and lodges them in the lining of his cap, which he straightens on his head.

He sneezes, and Mary notices him, leans back and looks up at him from where she kneels on Harold's corpse, breathing deeply, the sweat on her forehead breaking in patterns through the horse blood that still marks her. Four or five flies are feeding on her face, but she does not remove them.

'Are you leaving?' she asks, each word etched out between a sob.

De Flunkl slings the sack over his shoulder, and his knees almost give at its newfound weight.

'You have your sack full of dreams now,' she says. 'Though I don't know how you came by it. My husband was a-one like you, always picking up pieces of paper with his hands that were full of dreams. Sometimes, I swear it, men feel to me like something they make up as they go along, as though the constant inventions of their madness are all they have to prove they exist; and your sack full of papers appears to be such an invention as this. Excuse my ramblings, sir. I am fatigued and distraught. My Big Cat is dead, consumed in the fires of hell, and he is alone, without me there by him to soothe his burns, blow on his blisters and whisper my love into his ears. Do you think this fair?'

De Flunkl looks at her, edging towards the door.

'You are leaving now, I take it. May I go with you, sir? I have no one left to love and take care of, now my Big Cat is gone. I will be faithful to you.'

He begins climbing the steps.

'Do not leave me in this mad town, unguarded,' she yells, panic overtaking her. 'Take me with you or I'll be killed by these rogues. I beg it of you.'

De Flunkl runs out, leaving the hacking noise of flies and frenzied wailing behind him. He looks to his right and sees William of Roscrea is far away down the street, crawling on his hands and knees out of town. Saint John is following him at a respectful distance, the intestines no longer slung round him, but their blood streaked across his back like whiplashes.

'I will survive and prevail,' de Flunkl shouts at them. 'And you will die and rot in the unmarked graves that spot country places that will bear my name, and will bear it down the years, and the generations and all the lusty millennia that rush to greet us.'

And with that, he sprints the other way and is gone.

Saint John, dazed by the onslaught of the sun and the mushrooms he ate, does not hear the last words of the master he was born into, and William's senses are becoming closed off one by one; he does not hear them either.

Underneath the crawling William, as he leaves the village, the dry dirt of the worn street transforms to thick, long grass that it is difficult to crawl through. He has gone blind, but he pushes forward, the tail of the arrow occasionally bumping off the ground, moving in his guts, but he no longer knows any pain, only numbness, mainly felt around his tongue and lips. He moves slowly to what he believes must be the lake, but he is moving in a slow arc, doubling in on himself, turning back towards Nobber. Then his hands fail before him and he leans down on his side and curls up into a ball, nestled amongst the grass, moaning slightly, wheezing until the moaning stops and darkness swallows him up.

Saint John tucks the little rat in a fold in his clothes, pulls the arrow with crows' feathers for fletching out of William and drags him by the legs to the edge of Moynagh lake, and there he props William under a blazing red maple tree. Saint John brushes the leaves and twigs out of William's hair and sits down next to him. He is exhausted; he has been dragging William for a long time.

'Did you see my drawing rock?' someone says. 'I need it.'

Saint John opens his mouth to yell in fear, but no sound comes from his mouth.

'No?'

A half-naked woman with a hole in her face and an axe over her shoulder is walking by.

'Is that body from Nobber?' she asks. 'You must take nothing from that place.'

Saint John shakes his head.

'No, I see he is not of that town,' she says, 'that he is your own; and that though you were there, too, you were not truly there. You cannot go back to it; it is dying.'

The woman is sunburnt; her axe drips with blood. Her face is broken, warped; a single tooth grows out of her flattened nose. To Saint John, she is glorious, beautiful.

'They rejected the child,' she says, 'made the wrong offering. Worse than that, I fear there may have been no right one to make; that this has all been meaningless, and I have wasted the last days of the earth tripping up on mere confusions. Nothing will be born, not today or any day; the madness will spread. You must not go back there. Will you return?'

'Never,' Saint John whispers.

'I will be by the stump if you see my rock,' she says, pointing behind herself with her axe. 'I must wait there and watch, because there is always someone coming into Nobber. I am very sorry for your friend.'

She disappears behind the trees, and soon a tapping sound comes from the crannóg on the lake. Saint John listens to it; to the lapping of the wavelets, the turning of the earth, the steady rumble of the foliage, and falls asleep.

'Is that all?' Gertrude asks. 'Is it finished now?'

Conn flinches, whipped out of his story by the coldness in her voice. She will never allow him to forget his cowardly rejection of her.

'Do you not understand?' he says. 'This is the very first Sunday that there has been no lamb left waiting for them. Every fourth Sunday before this, for years, there was a-one; but now is the curfew, and I am trapped, my duty undone.'

'I understand,' Gertrude says, 'but I do not care.'

'Did you not like it, the story?'

'Have you no other stories?' she says. 'Is that your only one?'

'You wish to wound me because I have hurt you,' Conn says.

'Hurt me?' Gertrude says. 'Why would I be hurt?'

The knocking begins again. Somewhere during his story it had stopped, but he was so caught up in the telling he did not hear it.

'Don't primp yourself up in significance,' Gertrude says, affecting nonchalance. 'I took pity on you because you were exposed to the elements for so long. Living outdoors so much has made your skin ancient and dusty. It does not produce the oils necessary to your age. Your face is falling apart. I thought I would do you a kindness; that is all. I am sorry for it now.'

And then the door swings outwards. The room's shade grows paler. Through the door, Conn can see a few people trudging out of their homes, their faces blank, and soft, like they have just awoken from sleep. One woman in the middle of the street stretches, yawns. The murmuring of indistinct sounds comes through this open door; there is the flicker of a fomenting crowd. Conn, outside of Dervorgilla's marriage, and some other religious festivals, has never seen one.

'The curfew is ended,' he says. 'We are free.'

Gertrude stands and goes to the wall where her broom is hung. She examines its brush, plucking some broken birch twigs from it. 'I have light enough to clean by now,' she says.

'Is this not good news?' Conn says.

He rises and goes to the door, puts his hand into the light. It is hot against his fingers, unfamiliar. His skin shines white; this is some new kind of heat.

'The curfew is not over,' she says, beginning to sweep. 'Sickness rages; and you would do well to stay indoors. Curfews do not end themselves. There are great declarations, formal rites, not unseen meddlers casting doors open, exposing the decent people inside them to gossip and the violence of the street.'

'I must go,' he says. 'I must see Dervorgilla.'

Straight away, he knows he has made a mistake. Gertrude crumples against the wall as though she has been punched, dropping the broom. Quickly regaining her composure, she stoops and picks up the broom, and this all in one fluid movement.

'What ails you?' Conn asks.

A true man, she feels, would ignore this weakness; would

be sensitive enough to leave me at least my pride, but here I am dealing with a half-boy; not one thing or the other.

'I am not used to the fresh air,' she explains. 'Living in this coop, I have grown clumsy. Perhaps I am getting old.'

'Yes, perhaps,' Conn says.

He is not even listening to her. What is left, she thinks, of this boy I adored?

'So, it is her,' Gertrude says. 'She is married; and has a child. Yet youth seeks youth. It could be true that I have been blessed to not have had too much company throughout these last few years. It is bothersome, no matter how I have craved it.'

She begins to sweep again.

'I don't know any more. I speak too much. I'm ranting,' she says. 'Go. I do not want to see you any more. I have had too much company this last few days. I'm tired of speaking; tired of it. My heart is too sore from idle talk.'

'I will come back,' Conn says.

He has already become a coward, she thinks, the type that does not even have the decency to look you in the eye when they lie to you. I was too enamoured to recognise that somewhere along the way his loveable qualities were aborted by the ruthless passing of time.

'I lived before with a man, my husband,' she says, 'who I could not please, though I tried to. I thought my love was enough to make him tarry a while, but my love only made him hate me more. Hate is a strange thing, another presence; it presses close to you in small quarters like these, a third person in a room made for two. I will not welcome it back again, and I will not welcome you again. My pride won't allow it.'

'But I do not hate you,' Conn says. 'You are my friend.'

'You are both too old and too young to be friends with,' she says, shaking her head. 'In any case, our friendship provokes. They already call me a slut in town, because that was what my husband said about me when he was drinking to justify his own absence from my bed. After twenty years in this town, they still haven't accepted me.'

'Let me return,' Conn pleads, inflecting his voice with a tinge of desperation that Gertrude finds disgusting.

He is like a half-trained dog that has seen a pigeon, she thinks; straining at the heel, frothing at the gob. She is disgusted. He wants to get out, but is hedging his bets, because he knows propriety will not allow Dervorgilla to receive him.

'I must clean my house,' Gertrude says. 'You're in the way.'

She turns upwards the broom and beats the cobwebs off the wooden ceiling. Strands of filaments glide down, strewing themselves across her head.

'Goodbye.'

Though she had protested, her vanity is still greatly wounded by Conn not looking back as he races out the door.

Once her ceiling is clean, she recognises in this wounded vanity a hopeful sign. Perhaps there is enough of her left to remain strong. She plucks away the cobwebs all tangled on the edge of her broom. They are a flowing swirl of silver; gossamer thin, stirred by the faintest breath, invisible in the shade. She puts the broom in the light of the doorway. The filaments sparkle, move like hair underwater; and as she is watching them someone tosses a dead crow into her house.

It barely misses her, landing in front of her feet with a soft thump, and she screams. The crow has landed on its back; its wings are broken, twisted upwards. Its tail feathers are awry, covered in clumps of dirt; a long, rusted nail runs through its neck. Young boys are laughing down the street, and she looks towards them for a moment. She quickly sweeps the crow out and closes the door after it.

Outside, Conn, who has already forgotten her, is running. It seems like only a moment since the curfew commenced. I am a butterfly, he thinks; my cocoon split. I am in the world, in the beating heart of life. Anything will happen.

He imagines a great romantic meeting with Dervorgilla, a scene in which he is some kind of hero, but his reverie stumbles on the surroundings. Everything is disjointed, but only slightly. No one is moving in a normal manner. The people out on the street are not going anywhere, but they are walking. There are too many of them around him; too much noise, but no sociability. Men and women speak across one another, not listening to the answers they have just requested. Something shivers through the townspeople, a jovial carousing that must spill into violence. There is too much edge on these tired faces. Someone waves at him. He is blind with the sun, does not turn his head. His name is called. Goosebumps blast across his flesh; it is too hot. He is at her house already. The flowers he left her are still there, diminished now, sunken into themselves like yellowing corpses. They will turn into dirt, trodden underfoot. Perhaps, he thinks, she is dead. She has always taken the flowers I have given her.

'You are alive,' someone says. 'That is good. How goes the flock? Are you just arrived?'

Eoin Preston is sauntering by; hammer, nails, timber under his arms.

'What is the matter?'

He stops; grabs Conn by the shoulder. It is a friendly gesture, but too rough.

'What are you doing?' Conn asks.

'I am going to run two long nails through Colca's skull,' Eoin says, 'one through each eye.'

He places his middle finger and his forefinger on his own closed eyelids.

'What has he done?'

'What has he not done?' Eoin says. 'He interloped with an outsider. He disgraced us, and we are done with him. I am not one to be confined. This lot of timber is to break his back over, for he has a long spine. Gabriel wants to secure him to it while we drag him through the town, but we can find no horses. Glynis will do it, drag him along; he is strong. Perhaps Joseph, too; he is strong, as well. Will you come with me?'

Gabriel Preston runs up behind his brother, his face pale with sweat. He tugs at Eoin's sleeve.

'Concessa is dead,' he says.

'Many are.'

More people are coming up behind Gabriel. Two men stagger, as though drunk. There are moans of grief, coughing sobs. A child laughs.

'I must see Dervorgilla,' Conn says, beginning to knock on her door.

'Was it you knocking?' Gabriel asks.

Conn is anxious to be inside Dervorgilla's house. This chat has a jagged edge to it; they are tripping into a mob.

Though he knocks hard, she will not answer.

'Stop,' Eoin says. 'This is too much. You already know.'

252

Conn looks around. Through the bodies, he can see the houses. Their walls are covered in scratches, loose scrawls, but they have no meaning he can discern. Beyond the town, there is some black slouched shape in the distance. Nearly all the doors of the town are open, but not Dervorgilla's. People are moving in and out of each other's rooms like they are common property. Faces are full of listlessness and fatigue. Every eye blinks. There is no organisation to this. This is not a gathering, Conn feels. Something bad is coming, but we couldn't see it before; and we still don't know what is coming towards us.

'I must see her,' he says.

He pulls opens the door, ignoring the crowd forming around him, and finds himself in a dark room.

'Dervorgilla?' he says, and begins to choke.

The stench of the house hits him like some physical force; tearing his eyes up, setting his nose running.

And then he sees her, shimmering and pale in the dark, her gown thrown low over her shoulders, exposing her breasts to him. She is giving herself to me, Conn thinks, for all the flowers I gave her over the years. At last, this is a naked woman, he thinks, but naked bodies better frame the beauty of the face. It is her face that is most beautiful. He has never seen anything so perfect.

'Conn, my brother,' she says, her hands stretched out to him. 'What is happening?'

He is inflamed, growing dizzy and swollen; his cock raw against his leggings, but the stench confuses his senses; he feels as though he will faint. She takes a step towards him, and his ecstasy mingles with asphyxiation. Confusion makes him stumble; a momentary fit of blindness eclipses him, and he does not know what to feel any more.

'The babe will not feed,' she yells. 'They will make fun of me. Do I not love enough? I am giving no milk. Give me some milk, Conn.'

She is pointing down at a heap on the bed. Amidst grey cloth, he sees a small, swaddled baby stretched out on its front, blue in death. Its head is enormous, and its body withered down. Dead for days its tiny lips are already black, and it lies between the legs of Tedbalt, whose putrid carcass is decomposing, sunken beneath his work clothes. Steam rises off him, blending the little light above him into a wavy mirage, and his face is covered in a blanket of sleeping flies.

'Why amn't I making milk?' she asks. 'Am I worse mother than them? Do I not love enough? What will they say?'

Tedbalt's eyes are open. His face, cast in shadows, is waxen, inhuman. It is like he is made out of melting candles. One of his incisors is caught on his lip, giving him a stupid, evil air.

'I can't put my arms down, brother,' she moans. 'It hurts to put my arms down. My back is sore.'

Dervorgilla's arms, held above her head, are shivering with such force that they are almost a blur. Amidst the matted hair of her armpits are swollen protuberances with smooth surfaces. The swellings are hairless, yellow and thick, one under each armpit, like hidden apples growing out of her. One of them is covered in stale pus that has erupted at some former point. Around each buboe is a purple circular bruise, perfect as the concentric ripple of water.

'Help me, brother,' she says.

Conn swallows but his mouth is dry, full of the nauseous

death in the room. His fingers tremble as he feels his way across the wall towards the door.

'I am going to get you some milk, sister,' he says.

'You won't tell anyone I am not making it myself,' she pleads. 'I would be so ashamed.'

'Of course not,' he says. 'I will return shortly.'

'You are so good,' she says. 'You always bring flowers to me.'

'I will bring more to you; I'll fetch them now.'

'I missed you,' she says. 'We will not go so long again without speaking together?'

Her arms are still high above her head, almost touching the ceiling.

'No, we won't,' he says. 'I'll return.'

He slips outside, slams the door after him, breathing the fresh air in gulps.

The crowd around the house has dispersed somewhat, but Eoin Preston, his head cocked to the side, remains. Conn motions for the hammer and nails. Eoin opens his mouth about to speak, and then pauses; instead placing a strip of timber against the door so its ends are overlaid across the doorframe.

'We must get used to it,' Eoin says.

Conn hammers in a nail. His hands are shaking so much that he drops the second one. Then later, he hits his thumb with the flat of the hammer. It must be broken, he thinks, but he does not feel anything. The crowd around him grows once again, looking on at the sealing of the house.

'Who is it?' Dervorgilla calls from inside, her voice slightly muffled. 'Conn, is that you? I'll be there in a moment. My clothes, I must fix them.'

Someone laughs at this.

'Conn, is that you?'

It is a cruel voice, mimicking hers, somewhere behind him, and then the crowd falls silent again. Conn's hands are shaking so much that now he drops the hammer. Eoin picks it up, and finishes off the work for him. Another Preston appears beside him, hammering more timber onto the doorframe.

'Let's go,' Eoin says. 'We will find the man who is to blame for this.'

A shadow falls over Conn, and he looks up and flinches in the light. Three geese are flying, ragged and disordered, across the town. They are low in the sky, almost touching the roofs. They disappear, and then his eyes go back to the sealed door.

'There is no one to blame for this,' he says.

'You are mad to say that,' Eoin says.

Inside her house, Dervorgilla, her hands growing stiff over her head, can hear many people moving outside her door. It is like the sound of the lake in the evenings. She sits down on the bed, her leg accidentally touching Tedbalt's arm.

'Sorry.'

There is no pain now, just a certain breathlessness. Her eyes dilate, becoming small and then big again. My body, she thinks, is toxic, swollen with foreign pus. It is unknowable now, has been misshaped, invaded. I am disintegrating, grotesque. There is nothing of me left in this body. It disgusts me, and my mind is a stranger in it. There is no future; the world is ending.

'I may as well have not been born,' she says, aloud. 'There will be nothing left of what we were.'

Nobody mourns us, she thinks. All the past will be

destroyed, and the present is too tumultuous and erratic to mimic its precedent. Erased, she thinks, our bodies will rot in mass graves. We will melt into one another, grow indistinct. Nothing remains, not dust, not regret. Your self drips away like blood from a gash, forgotten; it is not a kept thing. It becomes earth, swallowed up.

'Oh, well,' she says.

Dervorgilla knows her family is dead; has known it for a long time. You are given things you do not ask for, and then once familiar they are taken away. That is what happens, but she will continue to pretend, because the truth serves no purpose.

'Who is it?' she calls.

There is a knocking on the door, and then a boisterous guffaw. Someone is laughing at her, taunting her. They are cruel, but she doesn't mind. It is just people, the way they are, and Conn will be back soon.

The great sleep is being shaken off, but it is a false awakening. Doors are left open, property become communal. Madness, like a veined river, runs through the town, and in her youth Raghnailt would have loved it, but I am not young any more, she thinks, and always thought I was old when I was young.

There are perhaps sixty people out in the street, mostly women. The close town has been halved, rent in two. There should be more than a hundred here, but there is not. The only category that remains is the living, and they are, in the last, unified; the dead are another thing. Inside shaded doorways are forty or so corpses. She can see a few drawn faces, like secrets, poking out. There is a smell of frenzy. The corpses are hidden, but they seep into the living, the false shades amongst them. There are not enough hands to bury them any more. There is no more society, no more family. Society is slack, full of hypocrisy. It is gone. There is only this mob, burgeoning, becoming one.

They are dragging her son down the street.

'Stop,' she yells.

She leaves the shade of the doorway and the world is shining. She has lost her daughter; I cannot lose my son.

'Stop this instant.'

Collectivity is a shimmering apex, an emergent property,

always poised on the edge of existence, always ready to storm and enclose some new centre, always ready to become it; and yet at the very moment of its appearance it is already beginning to disperse, the pieces hurtling apart.

'Your womb is poison and gives poisoned fruits, and you are a bitch,' a woman says.

She is pushed. Her elbows shudder with the impact of breaking the fall. She looks up and sees Áoife above her wearing a face contorted in hate.

When collectivity exists you question why it doesn't always. The mob is neutral and there is little solace in it. Individuals, surely, are not real things, Raghnailt knows, just the part you are locked into, the most self-sufficient part of an accidental whole. Yet there are brief moments when collectivity tumbles into wholeness, and it is never lacking. It never needs more than itself; it can always be added onto or reduced, its perfection unaltered. It is short, though, consuming itself in heat, but, for a brief moment, it will dazzle like a second sun.

'I have my dignity, my years, my family and their name and you will respect it, Áoife,' Raghnailt says. 'We are as one. No matter what sickness individually undoes each of us; we are all of God. We are his children.'

'God hates this town,' Áoife shouts.

Colca is on his back, his arms held above his head. He has been dragged backwards down half the street. Blood pours from his destroyed shoulders; his back is flayed.

'Your son is dead,' Genevieve, a second cousin says. 'My daughter was in the next house from me. He kept me from her. I cannot hold her to my breast any more. She is dead. My Gestalt is dead. I cannot touch her.'

The words are spoken plainly, without emotion.

Colca is looking at his mother, but there is no recognition, no fear, just a sullen acceptance; it is something weaker than anger, yet akin to it. There is no love in his face. She averts her gaze, cannot look at him; he is too cold. Their life together has been a failure.

'We have no choice,' Genevieve says. 'I just want it to be already done. I am so tired.'

Raghnailt, below them, still on her knees, wishes she did not recognise all their faces, know them so intimately, but she has known them all since birth. They are also, though more distant to her, her family. I can see their genealogies in their mouths, their eyes, their noses; can trace their likenesses in their stances. I can remember the stories my father told me of their grandparents. This town is too small; the world is too small. I know everyone in it.

'He is my son,' Raghnailt says. 'You will not kill him. He is mine.'

Áoife steps forward and kicks her in the gut. The crowd stirs, closes about her. Raghnailt collapses down, breathless. She is under a communal act of suffocation, but what irks her most is the burning sensation on her neck, the clamminess of her clothes. It has been a long time since heat this great has come upon her.

Eoin Preston is breaking through the crowd. He helps her up. His face is dusty, beautiful in its plainness. He could do anything, Raghnailt thinks, if he had been tamed properly, but he is too trapped in his emotions. Nothing restrains him long enough to mature him. He, also, she thinks, was the great disappointment of his mother's life.

'No one touch this fine woman,' Eoin says. 'Her father and herself did us many years of service; she suckled my aunt. She has not brought this on us, only her son.'

Albus, a winded peasant, steps forward, his face covered in his hands, yet he is still distinct; still plump like all the Feagans have always been.

'How can we respect any tragedy?' Albus shouts. 'My two sons are dead, my mother also; my wife. The sun blazes through the heavens and yet I freeze. No one hears my cries any more. I am alone in a house stuffed full of corpses, and you say a life can be respected?'

Eoin draws himself up to his full height. 'My mother is dead, too,' he says, whipped into a quick outrage. 'And you will respect her in death as you will respect her former life.'

Albus retreats, diminishes himself amongst the other bodies that press close. His uncle once courted her; Raghnailt remembers him. Still fat as a fool, he died in the midst of the last famine, thirty or so years hence. She had been twenty-two then, and shy.

A woman, unseen, behind him is crying, buried in some other shoulder. The crowd is momentarily still. Raghnailt stumbles a little, and Eoin balances her by the elbows. She is dizzy, but her vision becomes sharper. There is no pain in her gut, only a kind of hollowness; something crucial is visible in the animosity of the faces that confront her.

I must make some supreme effort, she thinks, and if I do not do it now it will forever burden me, and yet speaking has never felt so difficult. She wants to sleep, but is afraid; knowing if she sleeps now she will always wake up alone.

'What are you accusing my son of?' she says. 'Justify your violence.'

'He parcelled us up like lambs,' Eoin says gently to her. 'He colluded with the nameless beast, the great evil. Stole from us our freedoms; menaced us.'

She is still leaning on his arm, glances up at him. 'You all did that,' Raghnailt says. 'You all slew the mayor with that devil. Colluders, every last one. You all did that, not just my boy.'

Little Pádraig collapses to his knees and groans. Two women keen, find one another through their moaning and embrace.

'I have no priest,' little Pádraig cries, raising a fist to the sky. 'I have no king, no sheriff. No bread to eat, no wheat to make it with. I will be overrun by Gaels. My family is gone.'

In the midst of his speech, Raghnailt grows distracted; her attention is caught by a small girl she does not recognise; a small blond child near the end of the street, doing something to a house with both hands.

'I will pay no tithes if I have no priest to show me my God,' Pádraig says. 'Why will he not answer me? Will anyone answer me when I cry?'

He rises slowly to his feet.

'Segnat told me he ground up our bodies for money,' Glynis says. 'That he whittled away at our bones till they were slivers, sold them to the Gaels.'

'I am going home,' Pádraig says. 'I am going drinking. I cannot mete out justice. For what? To who? I will be alone with my family of corpses. I will bless them with alcohol, make little crosses on their heads with it.'

He pushes through the crowd. They watch him go. He does not close the door after himself, and Raghnailt notices he has gone into the wrong house.

'I await your accusation of my boy,' she says.

The mob presses in slightly. Many eyes examine her; the sound of many frantic breaths. Eoin wraps his arm round her shoulder.

'I say,' Raghnailt ventures, 'that he has protected you. The sickness came, and he put you away in your houses to separate you. He isolated you from yourselves, halted the spreading nature of the sickness. He has saved all your lives.'

'He brought solitude on us,' Áoife says, 'so as to better slaughter us individually, to rule us easier. He brought that man into town; who is the root of all our badness.'

'Colca did not bring the man here,' Raghnailt says. 'That is a lie; and you only wish that the man was the root of all you have done.'

'No, you lie, Raghnailt,' Glynis says. 'Isolation stopped nothing. Concessa was a saint, who kept to her rooms, never seeing anyone this four years, and sickness has killed her.'

Áoife hits her own chest at this, and a few others take up her cheer. When people's bodies are pressed close they become darker, Raghnailt thinks. At the end of the street, she sees the child is etching figures onto a house with a small rock.

'So, then, good Raghnailt how come Gertrude,' Glynis continues, 'who is a slut, lives? How come? She loves gangrenous men for their last given money, has their sicknesses discharged into her gap, mixes salivas with them. Why is she alive? There is no rhyme to this sickness. Your son has deprived our pleasures and our movements, our last moments of tenderness with our families. He is guilty.'

They are cheering at this; even Eoin nods.

'Guilty of what?' Raghnailt says. 'I don't understand.'

Someone spits at her, but it falls short, darkening a little spot of ground at her feet. Her son has been obscured behind the movement of legs. The crowd is swaying.

'You will not hurt her,' Eoin shouts, covering her with his arms. 'You are cowards. You hurt a good woman, do you?'

'He fucks horses,' Genevieve says. 'He fucks them, and is always naked. Angela Fitzsimmons said she saw him officiating a mass over two goats in the woods. He had put little hats on them, and then married them, one to the other.'

There are yells of outrage at this; deep groaning sounds from a woman.

'That is another lie,' Raghnailt says, 'and it is not the question. He confined you to your houses for your health; and now you dance together as one. You will all be dead by nightfall. You are killing yourselves with this.'

'My daughter is dead,' Glynis shouts. He pushes forward, swinging wildly. Three men start fighting, and the violence spreads. Eoin relinquishes his grip on Raghnailt and begins subduing Glynis, who is the tallest man remaining in town after Joseph and Tedbalt. Gabriel Preston jumps on Glynis's back and is stoving his head in with his elbow. Glynis goes to ground, and once he is down, the circle around Raghnailt widens.

'You are done,' Eoin says.

He is breathless, his hands on his hips, standing over Glynis. The Prestons are so young; their vigour overpowers their elders, to a man. Everyone is silent, and still again.

'He would grind my daughter's bone into meal,' Glynis says from the ground, his hand pinching his boxed ear. 'He would take her when I am not guarding her body. You know this is true, Raghnailt, and you know what we do is right.'

'We are taking this burden off your hands,' Eoin says. 'We must break his back.'

'He is done, he is,' Genevieve says.

'You will not be alone,' Eoin says, looking at her. 'We all love you.'

Gabriel nods beside him, only coming up to his shoulder. 'We do, Raghnailt,' Gabriel says. 'We love you.'

'You can come visit us every day,' Eoin says. 'Our mother is dead, our uncle missing, perhaps fled the country. A feminine presence, soothing in the corner, would be very welcome to us lonely boys.'

Raghnailt is shaking her head. There is an emptiness in her chest like her body is someone else's. I am losing my son, she thinks. I cannot stop it. I cannot save him, and I will be in pain forever.

'It can't happen,' she says. 'It won't happen. It's impossible. You can't.'

'We love you, Raghnailt,' Áoife says. 'I am sorry I hurt you. Give me your hand, and let me kiss your cheek. Let us be friends. Forgive me.'

'You are a good kin,' Genevieve says.

'You were always good to us,' Albus says. 'Always kind.'

Raghnailt wheels round, but the mob is behind her as well. She is enclosed within them, but now they are covering her in their love. Her breath is sharp; panic overcomes her again. She is the centre now. I have wanted love my whole life, she thinks, and this is how it is given to me.

'You are all mad,' she yells. 'This is a false reprieve. The sickness is still here. Just because you have come together in

265

the sunlight you think it is over, but it is here, creeping through you now. Give me my son back. Go to your homes this instant.'

'But we can't,' Genevieve says. 'There's no one left.'

'There is no choice,' Áoife says. 'It is already done.'

'I could get no peace in my house,' Glynis says, on his knees now. 'There's always someone knocking, a friend or an unknown, and what am I to do? Embrace a dead wife? Will she keep me warm? She used to hum in her sleep, even musical then. She lies there, now, blue, before the hearth, forever quiet and cold. I cannot sleep next to her any more. You would condemn me to that loneliness?'

There is nothing hidden in these people, Raghnailt realises. She sees through them, sees everything. They are nothing now; they have been broken, and they are killing her son so they don't have to face themselves; so they don't have to be alone; so that they can delay their own interiority a little longer. They would rather death than loneliness, but the loneliness, she knows now, can never be stopped. And still, she knows that someone will have to die for all this pain that has no centre and no source; all these effects that come from nowhere. Her son will perish so they do not succumb to disintegration, but it will not work; will only be temporary. It is coming. They will kill her boy, and I will remember every word of this forever, and still she can think of nothing other to say than:

'I ask you one more time what he is guilty of.'

Then she sees, down the street, Mary dragging the small girl away by the hair. The child is protesting, swinging her drawing rock against her, but Mary is too strong, and they are moving towards the dark sentry who guards the edge of the town.

Raghnailt tugs at Gabriel's sleeve. 'Run, get that child and bring her back to me,' she says. 'It is not safe; and Mary is not sound of mind. Gaels roam free; the paths are compromised. Bring her back.'

Gabriel turns his head briefly to her, but he has not heard her; he is looking down at Colca.

'Get the child, Gabriel,' she says.

Glynis is shouting again, flailing madly; Gabriel holds him back, not heeding her or Glynis, still gazing at Colca. Raghnailt notices a thin, interrupted trail of blood running out of town. Intestines draped over the fountain; drying in the sun. The child is gone; it is too late.

'All these opinions,' Colca says.

A wide circle forms around him. A new silence is produced. The centre is a fluid thing, and it has shifted to her son. Four men are holding his arms. He shakes his head. He is tired, too, like some saint's relic, a thing of wonder, a living thing already consigned to the past.

'Be quiet,' Raghnailt says. 'Do not say anything.'

'All these opinions, I'd rather be dead,' he says. 'My whole life, all your stupid opinions have rained down on me, more intrusive than any sickness. Break me in half, but do not weigh me down with your opinions any more. You will have my corpse; rail against it.'

'Do not provoke them,' Raghnailt says.

'Whatever I did,' Colca says, 'I would again.'

'No,' Raghnailt says. 'He did it to isolate the sickness. Do not listen to him.'

'Every last one of you,' Colca says, 'will be dead by the end of summer.'

He is looking everywhere but at his mother; avoiding her gaze.

'What have you done?' Raghnailt whispers.

Eoin has let go her shoulder; he is moving.

'Why do you wear no clothes?' Áoife shouts.

She leaps on Colca, bites his ear. They are all falling upon him now, a squabble of birds over a sliver of food. Punching him in the chest, transforming his face into blood.

'No,' Raghnailt screams. 'No. Take me; I am the guilty one. He's my child. It was my fault. He's mine.'

Someone knocks Raghnailt on the back of the head, jarring her vision. She falls; tries to get up, but there is a knee in her back, pressing her down. Her son is screaming like he has just been born. Then, slowly, the crowd is moving away, she can see its edge, legs above her move like flickers of candle-light. It is leaving her outside of it.

The child was drawing perfect circles on the walls with her rock. Raghnailt can see them now; little enmeshed whale's eyes on the walls of the houses, planted one inside the other.

'Give me my son,' she says. 'Give him back.'

Her son is crying for her, like the child he once was. His pain has made him an infant again; his voice is young; she would recognise it anywhere. She wants to stroke his hair, sit him on her lap; her breasts are heavy with milk for him. She wants to be young again; to rear him once more; make him perfect, make him tender with love for his wife and his mother. He will speak with his mother gently in the evenings, make his wife laugh. She will make him perfect this time.

Someone is shaking her, but she can't see who it is.

'He is not yours any more,' a woman is saying to her. 'We cannot even give you his body back.'

She draws her head back. The sun, white, burns her skull. It is an eye, she sees. Concentric rings that are eyes flood her vision. The eyes are full of rainbows. Colca is always calling, but never for her. His mouth is full of blood, his lower jaw hangs open, broken; she can still hear him. They are dragging him out of town.

'My baby,' she yells. 'Give me my baby.'

The woman is stroking her hair. 'It will be fine,' the woman above her says, and Raghnailt recognises Áoife's voice.

'You will all be dead soon,' Raghnailt says. 'All of you will be eaten by the sickness, every last one. This is the last summer.'

She is succumbing to dispersal. Blood trickles down her left ear. She sees everything in double. I am broken, my vision impaired. It has been hot for a long time, and I have lived too long.

'I hope you are right,' Áoife says to her, 'but whatever happens know that none of this is your fault. It never was.'

The enormity of Raghnailt's shame and failure agitates her chest like a second heartbeat. The voices and screams are more distant now, but she still sees the eyes, visible to her even with her own eyes closed. There is no meaning to the visions that choke her and tear her apart, and there never has been; but still she will see the eyes forever, in everything. She will want to die, but will not.

'A child could have been saved,' she says.

She could not have loved him more.

Hacquelebacq drops to his knees and sticks his little finger through the earth. On bringing it up, he sees his finger has pierced layers of musty foliage, sodden stacked leaves from autumnal pasts. The leaves closer to the fingernail are older, and those nearer the knuckle are fresher. The past is a layered thing and what is closer to the surface is always newer, he thinks, feeling somewhere hidden in this a profound observation.

It is a great shame, he feels, that bodies are buried so deep; it unnaturally cheats the proper order of the world, which stacks itself sensibly in its unhurried chronology. Bodies should lie atop the earth and sink at a natural pace, as befits their rate of decomposition, so that if future generations are of a meddlesome sort they can, on digging them up, be able to layer time more accurately. Perhaps, he thinks, the earth is growing each year with its accumulations of dead leaves, and all the bodies we bestow on it, thickening and swelling it up, and after several thousand years it is not unforeseeable that the earth will be twice what it is now.

After the roof of his mouth had grown sore from his fill of scallions, he had hurled a rock at the little fox and watched it disappear beneath a bed of ferns that swayed in its wake. He had wandered around, feeling secure in his new boots, until he came across an ocean of swarming ants that seemed to grow out of the base of an oak tree like an enormous tumour. Millions of them, looking like one enormous, writhing ghost. The ants never stopped moving, piled on top of one another in a layered stampede, scurrying in some private panic that would never end; but taken altogether they seemed to move slowly, in clipped waves that rose and fell and then rose again; and every now and again their shifting shapes seemed to form a screaming face. Out of their centre protruded a wind vane, which some few ants crawled up and down in an orderly line.

Moving closer, Hacquelebacq saw the ocean of ants covered some fat man whose heart had been skewered by the wind vane poking out of him. His face was invisible under the thick clusters of ants, and by his side was a sack of wind vanes, and some few broken jars, dripping unguents, which, exposed, had hardened into a thick slime. Hacquelebacq examined the sack, and, seeing nothing could be salvaged, left quickly, wondering if the woods were functioning as some kind of graveyard, but now, on his knees, he realises the whole earth is a graveyard.

He takes the bed of leaves off his little finger, discards it, rises and urinates plentifully against a tree, watching the bark darken as his steaming fluids slap off it. It is very damp, and his hair has taken on a life of its own. A bleating comes from behind him, and he is no longer lost. He follows the sound, touching off the trees he passes with the flat of his hand.

The trees become thinner, and he comes into paler shade. Through the lattice of trunks he sees the two lambs, the waddling goose with its broken wing and the two calves, all their heads surrounded by little halos of incessant flies. He

271

had abandoned them in his great hurry, and he sees that, through sheer luck, in their movements their ropes got caught underneath some stone and they were left stranded, waiting for him.

The badger has slipped its noose and vanished. To add to this, his goose is dying, swishing its arced neck back and forth in a trance. His ark continues to diminish rather than grow. Still, his sack of ropes is near. His livelihood remains to him; and he has his new boots.

A small distance from him a young woman is conversing loudly with the structure that impeded his entry to Nobber. She is waving her hands in the air, but the sun is too bright for him to maintain his gaze. He cannot make out her figure, or even the figure of that demonic structure behind her.

If a little woman is not afraid of that thing, he thinks, then neither am I, taking the ropes from under the stone, and twining them together into one large knot. He leads the animals towards her, and they follow, nodding their heads back and forward in time to their steps.

As he gets closer, he realises the young woman is gabbling insensibly and with great emotion at this structure. Perhaps, he thinks, she is in grief.

'Ahoy,' he cries.

The young woman spins round, and drops to her haunches. Hacquelebacq halts. The ropes slacken, and one of the calves walks gently into his back, nuzzles the cloth of his tunic.

'What are you?' the woman says.

She is blond, quite young. He sees her face is covered in a thin layer of dried blood, broken into cracks by the rivulets of sweat that course down her forehead.

'I sell hanging ropes, my fine lady,' he says. 'I was coming to this good town of Nobber to see if there are any tradesmen who would like a calf, or some rope. My name is Monsieur Hacquelebacq, and it is a great honour to meet such a comely sparrow, and so unexpectedly.'

'My name is Emota,' the young woman says, pointing at her own chest, 'and I slew the beast. You are free.'

'I am free, Emota, you say?'

The light behind her is an outlined halo, defining her shape, and then her face becomes nervous.

'They say it was me knocking Monster Hack Back,' she says, 'but it was not. I am not sick, though they say I am. It's just sometimes I remember who I am.'

One of the calves, the bawling orphan who is lonely for its mother, lows behind Hacquelebacq, and the noise is so close that he rubs his ear. He looks up at the structure behind the young woman, feeling slightly embarrassed that he was ever afraid of it. It is but a slanted wooden cruciform. A few crows are tied to it with sprigs and shorn ivy; many are nailed on, their wings at unnatural, contorted angles they have been pressed so closely together. They are mostly dead. Clearly, a warning of sorts. He imagines it belongs to a Gael or a peasant; or possibly a child has done it, it is so crude.

'Did you make this?' Hacquelebacq says, pointing at the thing of crows, which, vaguely, resembles a man.

She looks behind herself. 'No, I did not make her,' she says.

The girl, Hacquelebacq thinks, is completely mad.

'Emota,' he says softly, 'you sound very put upon, and I would like to be of service to you.'

'You could take care of me,' the young woman says. 'My

man is dead, and I cannot remain married to a corpse. He was a blot on the landscape; a dark, sick thing. He used me terribly, but he took care of me and I miss him. His name was Big Cat, but I tried to forget it was sometimes.'

'So you are alone.'

Hacquelebacq secures the animals under a nearby rock, plucks a dock leaf from the ground and approaches her slowly, his hands raised in front of him.

'Your face, Emota,' he says, 'is slightly besmirched, and it is obscuring the expressivity of your features, which I perceive as beautiful, though clouded behind blood. Mayhaps you will allow me to remove it? Present your chin to me.'

She does not reply, but goes on her knees before him. He spits on the dock leaf, gently rubs it off her cheek. Docile, her head moves gently with the suggestion of his fingers. When half of her face is cleaned, he too drops to his knees, taking great care to let his free hand brush across her breasts.

'Whose blood is this?' he asks.

'The dark horse's,' she says.

'And how old are you?' he says.

Very delicately, he daubs a stain from under her eyes. Dried blood falls away in small sheaves.

'Turn over the dock leaf,' she says, 'it is dark.'

'How old, my dear?'

'Thirty-three.'

'You cannot be more than nineteen,' he says. 'I'm sure of it.'

'Well, if I am not thirty-three then I am sixteen,' she says.

A crow squawks on the structure behind them. Hacquelebacq looks at it, but he is no longer afraid of the monstrosity.

'Sixteen is a wonderful age,' he nods, 'the last great age of woman. It is all decline thereafter. Freshness evaporates, sagging commences. Folds, thick, sprout on the chin and chest like tumours. Bosoms become too large. The skin around the eyes splits like splintered wood. Strange, river-like marks appear on the thighs. It is all rather imperfect. That which should not be loose becomes loose; that which should be firm becomes soft, and that which should be soft becomes too soft. The body's beauty disperses. Nothing remains, but husk. Woman was not made for all the years she bears. Man is a little better, but not by much.'

She closes her eyes, and he runs his thumb across her closed eyelid.

'I was wont to visit Nobber,' he says, 'but if it is such an infectious and frightening place, as it seems to be, I shall skip over it. Other towns would serve me just as well. They are all the same, towns. They smell of corruption, and they have no proper drainage. Do you find me handsome, Emota?'

'Slightly handsomer than a very ugly man,' she answers. 'Your hair is shockingly orange, which is loveable. You are not a Gael, though?'

'No, I am no Gael. I am something else.'

He finishes with her face. She arches her neck to the side and her face is shining in the sun, white and reflective, but the rest of her is dusty, still salted with sweat, and splatterings of blood. He is slightly disappointed with the face staring up at him. The blood obscured several blemishes and an unhealthy pallor.

'Still,' he says.

'Still what, my liege?'

'Will you come with me?'

He lowers his face to her, and the scent of fermented cider on her breath is strong. Gagging momentarily, he holds his breath. It is not a bad smell, but it is thick and penetrative; his nostrils flare.

'Where?'

'To Trim, where life is easy,' he whispers. 'And will you kiss me?'

He discards the dock leaf he is holding and presents his cheek to her. After a few moments, he looks at her.

'You will not?'

'I would not leave the town in its sickness,' she explains. 'It has been good to me.'

'It is too hot here,' he says. 'Let me lead you by the hand into the woods. They are cool.'

'But the sickness still grows; I hear it breathing,' she says.

'Where is the sickness?'

The girl's eyes scan around her and then she points at Hacquelebacq's goose. 'That fluffy, white thing with the brilliant beak.'

He shows her his hands, pushing them close to her face. 'I'll break its neck with these hands and then we shall flee together,' he says, jokingly.

The girl draws back in horror. 'It must go on trial first.'

He thought he could remain abreast with this girl, but she is perhaps too haphazard for his needs, he fears.

'Trials are a sport for nobles,' he says. 'There is no justice in them; it is but meaningless ritual.'

'I want a trial,' she says.

She sits down, and crosses her legs, exposing the inner part of her thighs to him. Hacquelebacq looks at them for a moment, and then points his finger at the little, dying goose.

'You stand accused, goose,' he says, 'of bearing the sickness with you on your flights around this country, dropping it below you on the people you have crossed over.'

One of the lambs, he sees, is asleep, its legs tucked under itself.

'You fly over things don't you?' he asks. 'You consolidate the sickness in your wake? I must stop myself from clutching you by the beak and giving you a good shake I am so angry at you.'

Everything is very still. The heat is making it difficult for him to think, to continue inventing in this obscene manner.

'Goose,' he says, 'it is a lucky thing your wing was broken, stopping you in your path so I could restrain you and bring you under the rule of law. If found guilty of being the sickness you will suffer death, dismemberment, cooking, eating, be vomited out, or passed through the intestines, turned to excrement. It will not be a good way to die.'

The goose is on its side before him, its fluffy front rising and falling slowly. Its long neck lies, unfurled like a rope. It will not, he thinks, live long.

'You have engaged in usurious practices,' he says slowly, struggling to continue playacting, 'stolen children from their mothers; blasphemed; eaten your own kind; engaged in sodomy.'

One of the calves is straining on its rope, arching its thick neck to the side, unsettling the anchoring rock.

'Tell us, had you accessories? Did any other geese, or any creatures, ease your path into sin? Perhaps a lamb whispered in your ear while you slept, told you that you should do these things? Your offence is great and I warn you that your silence will lead to a verdict against you.'

The girl stands up and begins walking away. 'Emota,' he says. 'Where are you going?'

'To find witnesses from the town,' she says. 'We cannot have a trial without one. This will not do at all. You, who are so just, will wait.'

'You are the witness,' he says.

The girl laughs at this. 'I am the judge,' she says.

She continues walking away towards the town, and he pulls at his hair in anger, loosing a few orange strands. He wonders if he should follow her. She is not attractive enough to merit my troubles, he thinks, and she is far too volatile to control, but, really, he has nothing else to do.

He looks at the woods, and wonders again if he should wander away. His hands move across the grass. It is made of moss, clover, buttercups, all knotted together. He notices someone has left some kind of banner behind them. It lies in the grass, at some distance from him, but he does not want it at all; it is a very ugly thing. A frog leaps across his lap, startling him a little. It gives an impression of wetness, an oily little creature. The frog then hops away, an uneven trajectory. When it breathes its head doubles in size. Hacquelebacq knows he could not catch it for himself, no matter how much he wants to.

Time, a little of it, does pass. He does not particularly want to see the girl again, she is not worth his efforts, and the thing of crows has once more begun to unsettle him. He tries to remember what the deformed woman with the axe said to him earlier; that certain boundaries could not be passed. Or did she say surpassed? he thinks. The thing of crows is surely some sort of outer limit of something, but it is just another empty ritual, like this disgusting trial of animals he oversees. And then, over a small ridge, he sees the young woman is coming back, with another, smaller girl. He lies back and watches their approach, feigning disinterest, though his breathing grows hurried.

By the time the girls arrive, the goose is dead, and all Hacquelebacq's doubts have fled.

'Already, Emota?' he calls to her when she is within hearing distance.

She waves at him. 'I found her on the edge of town,' she calls.

The little girl is blond, too, but much younger. She holds a rock to her chest, raw and whitened from use.

'What is her name?'

'She is mute.'

'Mute?'

'Yes,' the older girl says, 'so she will make a very good witness because she can tell no lies.'

'Of course.'

The younger girl's face is passive. Hacquelebacq smiles at her; notices she has not even glanced at the thing of crows

'Let us recommence the trial,' the older girl says.

Hacquelebacq shakes his head. 'You must go back to town,' he says. 'We have no lawyer of the defence, and it is not proper. Someone must intercede on the goose's behalf, or this trial will soon become a farce.'

The older girl's face drops. 'I will return promptly.'

'Hurry,' he says. 'We are awaiting you.'

Once she has disappeared from view Hacquelebacq rises and stretches out his limbs.

'It is too hot here,' he says to the little girl. 'I have a head-ache. We should rest in the woods until she returns.'

He goes over to the animals and picks up the empty noose from which the badger escaped; brings it over to the girl and drops it over her neck.

'Do not be afraid,' he says. 'This is just so you don't get lost. I was lost in the woods earlier myself today, and it is a very scary thing. It is so dark in there.'

The child looks up at him, without curiosity even when he pulls the noose tight. A crow begins to caw, and he jumps at the sudden sound. One of the crows is moving its beak, but the rest of it is still. A long nail runs through its neck, and still it lives.

Monsieur Hacquelebacq shivers, and waves his hand at it. 'Evil thing, no?' he says. 'I do not like it.'

He wraps the rope round his wrist, leads them all towards the woods. The rope is slack, there is no resistance. The animals and the child follow without protest. Hacquelebacq looks back to the girl. She is unblemished; her breasts have not yet blossomed. Though small, she is long of limb. I will grow very fond of her, he feels.

They are near enough the trees to be in their shade. The dead goose trails behind them, coming last in the procession, still dragged along by its twisted neck in the sixth noose, but Monsieur Hacquelebacq has forgotten all about it.

When Saint John awakes it is early evening and a slight, spherical swarm of midges is hovering around him. William of Roscrea has gone hard and cold behind him, his face waxy and sunken, his chin and cheekbones grown even more prominent. The maple's shadow is long, and a young rat is crawling across his legs. The birds are in cacophonic evening song above him. He feels hunger and rubs his eyes. A jingling comes out from beyond the depth of the trees.

Saint John brushes the rat off him and it scuttles into the undergrowth. He stands up, accidentally entering the swarm, and two midges get caught in his eyelashes. He blinks them away, and one gets mushed in his eye, its legs falling apart, disintegrating in his vision, and he blinks several times until he can no longer feel its tiny body on the white of his eyeball. His vision is slightly blurred and he looks to the lake.

Above its shimmering body, well reflected, are high clouds that bunch up to the south and move towards him. They are so thick that they look like another, higher world, one with its own intricacies and mysteries, one that is softer and more caring, and for a moment the vast consciousness of the world is something Saint John can feel shake through him. A warm breeze runs through his clothes, pleasant against the sweat that has crystallised into sparkling salt on his chest. The grass shivers; the lake is unsettled slightly, and then a stench destroys his calm; a sick smell that floats over everything, making him gag and retch with its power.

Behind him, the loose jingling of rocking bells gets louder. He hears the clipping of hooves and the crack of a whip. He turns round and sees a dwarfish man, bald, with hawkish eyes, sitting on a trap drawn by two horses. Garish red bells hang from their manes. The man is well dressed, though he wears comically large pointed boots. He is covered in dust and yellow pollen from his travels and the trap he draws is piled high with dead, splayed bodies. There must be thirty behind him, spanning the height of two men.

The trap draws to a halt and the old man motions him over. 'Boy,' the man says, 'were you in Nobber earlier today?'

Saint John looks at the trap and sees, somewhere amongst the bodies piled on, Harold Tuite lying facedown, his bushy beard noticeable amongst the more nondescript shrouds that are stacked in untidy heaps beneath him. Near a decaying woman, there is a man who Saint John has a vague recollection of. He remembers seeing his dismembered head floating somewhere, though the memory is like a dream and the face is now very different, horribly transfigured. It is a monkish blond man in capuchin robes whose whole face is now purple, and he bares bloody teeth, snarling angrily at the world with hungry, open eyes.

'No, sir. I am just come upon this place.'

'There have been marauders passing through here,' the man says. 'I came from Trim this morning for a collecting of the dead and found several nobles much distressed and regretful for transferring lands at extortionately low prices, lands their populace will need in the coming harvesting seasons and life-times. I followed hot on their heels, hearing they were passing north, and have just come upon a scene of much carnage. A naked man, black as darkness, was hung off a machine of crows the townsmen had in their madness made, as an offering to something that I dare not name, and below this hanged man was an enormous and deep pool of blood in which living crows swam; there was another dead man, a holy and good one. They would not tell me his name, but I know him; he was a friend of mine, a good man; we had done much good business together, and, finally, a childish lunatic woman who drowned herself in a fountain. I knew they had other bodies, but they would not give them up. I did not collect the woman as there is amongst the town people some dispute on if she was a suicide, and I do not collect them.'

The trap rocks on its wheels slightly, creaking. Saint John looks up and can see that, under the dust on his face, the man has cold, bloodshot eyes. He looks a little more awake than anyone Saint John has ever seen before.

'A woman cannot suicide in five hands of water,' Saint John says.

The man shows his teeth in what could be a smile. 'You said you had not passed through Nobber,' he says.

'Do you have such deep fountains in that parish?' Saint John says.

'I don't like your lips or what comes out of them.'

'Who are you to talk to me thusly?' Saint John says. 'I am a liveried man.'

'I am Charles de Fonteroy and I collect the bodies of the neighbouring parishes, and I speak what I will. If it was you who oversaw this carnage in Nobber, I am leaving. I am old, unable for any struggles, and, if he is not still in hiding, I will inform the sheriff of this encounter and you will be hanged, even if it is just on the suspicion I will bring to bear on you. And, mark me, I will bring it to bear on you.'

'It was not me,' Saint John says. 'I came in from the port of Dundalk this afternoon.'

'Whoever you are,' the man says, leaning over and spitting onto the ground, 'do not pass through Trim. The people hate you.'

'The people do not hate me,' Saint John says. 'There are no townspeople who hate me. There are no townspeople. They are silent during these times, hiding amongst their own dead families, separate and alone amongst them. They are no longer of any town. They have been dissolved and individualised by the strife that you profit from.'

'I say it again, the people hate you.'

'Nobody hates me,' Saint John says. 'I have never done a hurt on anyone.'

'You speak a lot for a young man. Too much,' de Fonteroy says, and then he points the handle of his whip behind Saint John.

'Is that for me? Produce the pennies for his removal, for that man who has had some ill hurt.'

Saint John turns round and looks at the slouched form of William of Roscrea, shaded under the dark red leaves of the maple tree. Horrified, he sees a slug is travelling across William's cheek, leaving a glistening shine of slime that travels up his neck and across his chin. Saint John looks back at the trap stacked high with foul-smelling bodies.

'No, he will not go with you. You will get no coins off me. I will bury him properly.'

284

Saint John listens to the birdsong, which has become louder and more frenzied since this odious slew of tangled, mobile death arrived in their midst.

'If he was infected I must take him,' de Fonteroy says, and it is like a question.

'He was not infected. A Gael killed him.'

'Gaels have never come through here, not for a hundred years,' de Fonteroy says. 'You are lying. Your eyes are unnaturally wide and I fear you, though you pretend to be some gentle lamb. You have either been touched by infection yourself or are drunk beyond proportion; or possibly this is the lunacy of fresh murder that can be glimpsed in your visage.'

'Liar. You are a liar, and everything you say is lies,' Saint John shouts. 'I have been touched by a mystical vision beyond your schemes and it has shown me that you are a self-serving rogue. The scent of death that assaults me presently does not come from the bodies you carry, but from your own tainted flesh and the business you make with it.'

'Like I said, I am old, though I was young this morning,' the man says, stretching his hands to the sky and cricking his neck. 'And if I was still young I would throw you on the top of this trap and pour lime in your eyes till it burnt your brain out. But I am old now, and your youthfulness and energy shine out of your roving, lunatic eyes that scatter their gaze everywhere. But I swear this, if that thin man under that tree was not infected, then you are a murderer and that poor lad was murdered at your hand. So, I am leaving.'

The man whips at the two horses and the trap begins to clatter away.

'You will be caught and hanged,' the man calls out.

'And the Gaels will get you,' Saint John shouts. 'They own these lands and they are the better for it. I saw it in the visions that the earth created in me so I could escape the likes of you who crowd the world with so much death; who profit so greatly from the unnatural pains our people bear.'

'There are no Gaels in these parts,' the man shouts back, not turning his head. 'These are the delusions of a murderer.'

'You will find there are,' Saint John shouts out. 'But I hope they don't get you because I have a last blessing for you before you go: I hope the sickness takes every last man, woman and child, and leaves you alive, alone on this island, and then you may pick up the dead's bodies for always, and always bury them for always, and you may collect your coin off their corpses but have no one to exchange it with, and you may claim all their property but have no one to guard it from, and after much monies and bodies were accrued and you had had your fill I would let you live forever so you could drown in the suicidal silence of yourself.'

The man does not reply, does not even look round, and Saint John watches the mound of bodies sway with the rollicking of the trap until they turn round the bend of the thicket and are gone, but the smell they brought still lingers.

The world is natural and green again, though the sky is turning a dark pink, and Saint John feels a panic rise over him, and some strange tightness in his forehead. His loneliness and sobriety rise up within him. The grass, he feels, is too long about him, the birdsong is too tumultuous and fearful and the lake is too big. He drops to his knees and begins crawling around the bases of trees, searching for mushrooms of the kind he had eaten earlier, digging into the ground with his nails, like a piglet searching for roots.

He scrambles around for hours in a listless blank. At one point he comes across a sharp stone, worn down and whitened by recent use. It is sticky in his hands. Peering closer at it, he sees it is covered in fresh blood and tangled in some few strands of brilliant, orange hair. He hurls it into the lake, and continues scuttling back and forth, zigzagging through the undergrowth. He is frenetic. There is an enormous energy and a hunger in him, but he does not find that which he craves so much.

A noise of crashing comes over the lake and it brings him back to himself. The evening is fully grey; the colour of the sky has drained away into an oppressive world of shade. He recollects himself and finds that he is amidst a thick patch of nettles that grows higher than his head. His hands are bleeding and numb with nettle stings and the bites of ants, his finger-nails torn and raw; his face is swollen and raw from multitudes of thistles. He can only half-open his eyes because of the swelling of his cheeks, and he wonders where the day has gone.

He stumbles back to the lake to find where the noise has come from and sees bright flames are licking the end of a broken bridge that once connected a crannóg to the mainland; parts of it falling off into the water with foamy hisses.

Staring at the flames for a long time, he hears faint bells jingling again and wonders if the noise is only in his mind; and then he goes back to the maple tree under which William of Roscrea lies.

It has become so dark that for a moment Saint John cannot

see what is happening. The corpse has fallen over on its side and the little fox that has been following them for three days is eating at the fingers on William's left hand, shaking its head violently to rip them asunder and free the bones from their sockets.

Saint John sits under a beech tree opposite the scene, resting his sore head gently against the rough bark, and watches the fox jumping around, kicking up with its back legs, its jaws nibbling the fingers with an inhuman speed.

His head is clear, and he is sober. His eyes adjust to the darkness and now he perceives a faint orange glow from the flaming bridge that disrupts the darkness. Everything in the night is visible to him.

The stars appear like sores in the sky, one by one, accusing the infected land they mirror. The moon ripples its light towards him over the gentle, broken crescents of the lapping water that sends its white shine towards him in a straight line. The moon has chosen him for something, but he knows this feeling is a lie. There is no choosing; there is only becoming.

Throughout the night, he thinks of the future. He wants to swim out to the crannóg, to feel the cold water about him, to find shelter in some new isolation, though he knows there is no isolation but that which you choose to inflict on yourself. He wants to continue searching the undergrowth for the mushrooms he needs to release him, but he is too tired, and he knows the mushrooms will not release him, because there is nothing to be released from.

I will die without having understood what happened this morning, he thinks. He remembers being beside, but not within, some struggle, some war, though even this doesn't matter any more. Everything is at war, but the war is impersonal and there is no war inside himself. He knows he is nothing to the world, and that to be one person is a meaningless, useless thing, and it is in this that there is strength. Some awareness stretches beyond all this. He can feel it observing everything now, but he does not recognise it; does not know if it loves, hates or is indifferent. All that he knows is that it is beyond him; that it is there.

Saint John raises his knees up to his chest, welcoming these realisations. The birds are asleep; their forms little dark blocks of deeper night above his head, trapped in the myriad knotting of branches. The only sound is the water soothing him with its lapping, and the fox's low and throbbing growl. The fox's eyes shine in the darkness, and still it ignores Saint John; it will ignore him forever.

There is only the night. He looks at it, unable to sleep. He wants to always be able to recall the starry sky before the rain is loosed from it; the sky that hangs over these dark rustling trees; that hangs over this shimmering lake; that hangs over these resting birds; that hangs over him, who has become so alone and so full of wonder at everything. He wants this to be all he can see in this big world that is so much to be loved, so much to be desired, so much to be wondered at, and in whom I have always found such frenetic, sensual rhapsody, such glory, such indifferent splendour and such great disappointment.

Saint John feels the chill of the night against his cheeks. A breeze rustles the tree above him; this beauty belongs to no one. He is ready.

It begins to rain.

In his first year of shepherding, when he was nine, Conn lived in fear that the bishop would have him hanged for the false belief that it was Conn himself who was responsible for the continual exodus of lambs from his flock. Then, one blustery afternoon, as a troupe of brazen Gaels were flying off with seven lambs under their arms – as they did nearly every other day – he had burst into loud, wailing tears. The eldest Gael in the troupe had turned on hearing this. He pulled his donkey's ears to direct it back, and trotted towards the child. This elder Gael, who was naked from the waist up and who wore seven wooden necklaces that were obscured by a red beard that reached down to his navel, spoke to him for a great length of time. Conn shook his head repeatedly, understanding nothing, but the Gael persisted in speaking at him in mountain Gaelic, waving his hands about demonstratively.

'Sir, I do not know what you are saying,' Conn said several times. 'I do not take your meanings. They are all beyond me.'

After almost an hour of this one of his sons, or perhaps a nephew, finally came over, with a defeated air, and translated for the elder Gael.

This young Gael held a bleating lamb under each arm. Occasionally the lambs would kick and waggle their tails, trying to escape, and then would go catatonic in fear, and slump in his arms.

'Why will you not chase us, you tearful boy?' the young boy translated in a drawling monotone. 'You have not much spirit, and give little joy to your neighbour. By your age I had already killed two slaves, one of them in righteous combat; I had won three tournaments of hurling amongst eight far better-equipped clans, pucked one ball over the Boyne where it danced on the water sixteen times though it was not even wooden – it was like a swan dancing before it passed to the other side. And on that same day I won a flock of swirling starlings for my troubles that do haunt me when I sleep, for I cannot make good on my claim to have them as they are always away and out of the country, and when they do come home they always mither me in the summers, following me about the place in a great and swarming murmuration and making their nests close above my head, but just out of my reach to taunt me; and by your age I had also given great pleasure to six distinct daughters, two of whom were not only comely, but, also for their ages, wonderfully hairy, and that I have done with only with this edge of my tongue.'

The young Gael then said a few words to the elder, after which the elder Gael stuck out his tongue, and pointed at its underside. This Gael had dyed his teeth blue with berries, giving him a fearsome aspect.

'I did not even need to penetrate these maidens with my tongue to bring forth their internal sweats,' the younger Gael said, with a nod that referred to the man who was his uncle or his father, 'for my tongue work was so rapid, playing on the edges of them, that they had already fainted in a foamy joy, and were quite buoyant and eclipsed with a rosy colour on the cheeks of their arses that remained for three whole nights. From then on, they gave me the name of Very Delicious Harp, for how well I plucked women to make sweet, luscious and dulcet sounds shiver out of their throats.'

The young Gael paused, and looked at the elder, then continued, still in an uninterested monotone, 'Here, there is some laughter, which I will not translate. I objected to the name for I thought my tongue work more similar to the skilled rapid double time clicking of a player on a bodhrán, playing on the surface of things as I did with my tongue, rather than plucking at them or their interiors. But names are earned and then given, but they are not, misfortunately, sensible.'

The young translator finished his spiel, and there was some silence; Conn was very confused.

'Well?' the younger Gael said.

'You did all that when you were nine?' Conn ventured.

The boy translated, and Very Delicious Harp became visibly shocked, taking a step back and letting out a long, shouting tirade, which woke up the lambs under the younger Gael's arms.

'You are nine?' the younger said, in an unhurried manner quite distinct in tone from that which Very Delicious Harp had used. 'This is said with great shock that I shall not conduit in my translation. You Normans age terribly, like bacon cracked over fires. I thought you twelve. No, you are too young to protect a little flock such as this from mighty men such as me, and the us that me entails, but us Gaels are fond of children because they often turn into adults, though most of your kind turn into Norman adults, which is disagreeable and troublesome, but still though you are too young to protect flocks, you are at a reasonable enough age to strike bargains, so let us do so. The proposition is thus: offer me a delicate lamb, of the greatest succulence and gaminess every feast day, and I will hunt more worthy prey from a different flock, one of greater risk, for my joy will be greater with that; for we are a hurdy-gurdy sort, who far prefer banditry and chasing to easy meat.'

'When do Gaels feast?' Conn asked.

'Every day, of course,' the younger answered without consultation, 'for we only have every day. You Norman children would do well to mimic us in feasting every day; already many young Norman children do mimic our beautiful clothes and ravenous hairstyles and manly bearing; follow us a little more closely and it would make men out of peasants, and women out of prudes, for they should always be sluttish and happy, like bubbling wine over a fire.'

Seeing the younger Gael speak at such great length without interpreting, Very Delicious Harp clipped him on the back of the head, setting him staggering slightly, and setting the lambs under his arms bleating again in shock. Conn, meanwhile, did a few quick calculations in his head, and said, 'It would be better if you carried on in this robbing way, I would lose fewer sheep than if I offered you one every day.'

Once this was translated, the elder Gael grew very animated again, pointing at Conn a great deal and yelling at him.

'Do you know what I am giving up, you white weed bleached in the sun?' the younger translated. 'Do you even consider it? Of all of these mighty feats I have accomplished, tell me is there a greater joy than to be astride a donkey, to hug your legs round it and slide till you are nearly downside-upwards? Is there a greater joy than a race, where a Norman, all sad for he has lost his little sheep, chases us through woods, crying like a child, and shooting arrows at us? You are confiscating from us the privilege of hunting and the enjoyment of catching lambs by the tail and tossing them in the air and catching them again by their fluffy tails, all in the hot moment of riding; all this we are giving up for your tears moved me very slightly, for I am a feeling man. You are not only a small boy, but a little one, as well.'

'A great joy for me, sir,' Conn answered, 'would be to not be hanged at the behest of the Bishop of Armagh.'

The Gaels discussed this amongst themselves, and then the younger turned back to Conn:

'We would accept a death by arrows or drowning or cruci-fixion, or perhaps being eaten by dogs for you; for that is worthy and natural,' the younger said, 'but hanging is a bad way to go, so you only have to remember a lamb to us once every fourth Sunday, and we will hunt other flocks with mightier men. I, and the us that entails, hate the bishop, for he is hateful. Now, this is a most generous offer, no?'

Conn nodded, and Very Delicious Harp spoke some more.

'You are of Nobber, we presume?' the younger Gael asked.

Conn nodded again.

'Well,' the younger Gael said, 'if you do deal cruelly with us and do fail to deliver our little lambs to us we will rattle that town with such vengeances and undo all hitherto existing deals as have ever been taken between our two clans until your little place is subdued. We will set up such confusions that you will be undone in your minds, for your minds are so weak they notice many frivolous things all at once, so it does take very little to undo them, and we would have the undoing of you done by midday, I feel. See, even in this is our native generosity, for a Norman would rather punish the child who broke the agreement, but we are not cruel to children, so we will merely visit ourselves upon those who raised, or rather did not raise, the liar, as a corrective to their rearing. We will be the manly fathers to you that your own unmanly fathers were not ever.'

'Just the one lamb?' Conn asked.

'Just a-one,' the younger Gael said.

Conn was becoming very happy, and then he remembered what his recently deceased mother had told him; how Gaels were inherently deceptive, paying no respect to deals or transactions unless they were made with other Gaels, and even then they would only keep true to a deal if it was with a Gael from their own tiny clan.

'How do I know this is the truth?' Conn said. 'What guarantees have I?'

The younger translated this, and the elder nodded understandingly. Very Delicious Harp then cleared his throat, took a step back, pointed his mouth at the sky and began singing.

The song was plaintive, most of it made up of moaning, wordless sounds, but at times it became lively, at which points all the Gaels would stamp their feet. Conn was at first fascinated by this strange, throaty display, but the song continued until he was almost asleep on his feet. Even the lambs, who until that point had been frozen in fear, fell asleep under the younger Gael's arms.

The song eventually ended near sunset, and Conn estimated, though he had no means by which to guess the time, that the song had lasted at least a quarter of the day.

'Very good, but . . .' Conn said, once the elder finished the song.

The younger was crying free tears, and Very Delicious Harp was bent over, wheezing and sucking in air like he had been winded.

'But what?' said the younger Gael.

'It doesn't answer my question,' Conn said. 'How do I know you will keep your word?'

The younger sighed, tutted and turned his eyes upwards. 'That is how you know.'

They got up on their donkeys and rode away; and after that Conn always left them out a little cut-throated lamb on a flat rock that was marked in their runic language every fourth Saturday evening, so it would be only slightly eaten by crows when they took it away at dawn on the Sunday.